ROGUE TARGET

(A TROY STARK THRILLER—BOOK 3)

JACK MARS

Jack Mars

Jack Mars is the USA Today bestselling author of the LUKE STONE thriller series, which includes seven books. He is also the author of the new FORGING OF LUKE STONE prequel series, comprising six books; of the AGENT ZERO spy thriller series, comprising twelve books; of the TROY STARK thriller series, comprising five books; and of the SPY GAME thriller series, comprising six books.

Jack loves to hear from you, so please feel free to visit www.Jackmarsauthor.com to join the email list, receive a free book, receive free giveaways, connect on Facebook and Twitter, and stay in touch!

BOOKS BY JACK MARS

THE SPY GAME
TARGET ONE (Book #1)
TARGET TWO (Book #2)
TARGET THREE (Book #3)
TARGET FOUR (Book #4)
TARGET FIVE (Book #5)
TARGET SIX (Book #6)

TROY STARK THRILLER SERIES
ROGUE FORCE (Book #1)
ROGUE COMMAND (Book #2)
ROGUE TARGET (Book #3)
ROGUE MISSION (Book #4)
ROGUE SHOT (Book #5)

LUKE STONE THRILLER SERIES
ANY MEANS NECESSARY (Book #1)
OATH OF OFFICE (Book #2)
SITUATION ROOM (Book #3)
OPPOSE ANY FOE (Book #4)
PRESIDENT ELECT (Book #5)
OUR SACRED HONOR (Book #6)
HOUSE DIVIDED (Book #7)

FORGING OF LUKE STONE PREQUEL SERIES
PRIMARY TARGET (Book #1)
PRIMARY COMMAND (Book #2)
PRIMARY THREAT (Book #3)
PRIMARY GLORY (Book #4)
PRIMARY VALOR (Book #5)
PRIMARY DUTY (Book #6)

AN AGENT ZERO SPY THRILLER SERIES
AGENT ZERO (Book #1)
TARGET ZERO (Book #2)
HUNTING ZERO (Book #3)
TRAPPING ZERO (Book #4)

CHAPTER ONE

December 11
5:55 pm Greenwich Mean Time (12:55 pm Eastern Standard Time)
Aboard the *Royal Highlander*
Approaching Glenfinnan Viaduct
Scottish Highlands, Scotland

"She's not slowing," Paul Ringo said, his voice cracking just a tiny bit. "If anything, she's going faster."

"Aye," Billy Lowman said, using the fake Edinburgh accent he had learned to perfect years ago. He had to shout to be heard over the wind. His strong hand gripped a cold iron rung near the open train door. The train lurched, hard to the right. Billy held himself steady, staring out at the shadowy, racing landscape.

"I can see that. It's a bit of a *kinch*."

Kinch was Scottish slang for problem. Even in this situation, Billy would not break his cover. It was a point of pride with him. He went into character, and he kept it until the end of the job, no matter what happened. Something bad was happening here, but he was still Billy Lowman, and he was going to stay that way.

He had all sorts of accents he could do. The posh accent of upper-class British aristocrats. The cockney of the London working class.

Irish? He could do an easy Cork accent, and an almost undecipherable Donegal. American? He could do Brooklyn, New York. He could put on a passable version of the ridiculous nostalgic twang the Nashville country musicians were trying to do.

Of course, he could do an exceptional (and very funny) Canadian Canuck accent, and a good Cape Breton Scots. He could even do a Quebecois speaking English, although he had mostly forgotten his high school French a long time ago.

Doing accents came with the territory. He often pretended to be someone he was not. But it had occurred to him many times that his skill had mostly gone to waste. He should have his own TV show, or at least a stand-up comedy routine.

"We'll go off the rails," Ringo said.

1

Billy and Ringo stood in a foyer between train cars, the doors to the outside wide open, cold air rushing in with the howling wind. The train was going very fast, and in a moment, it would begin the long looping turn that would bring it across the old stone Glenfinnan Viaduct. It seemed to be moving much too fast to take the curve.

Right now, the speed was almost sickening. It had passed frightening a while back. In another moment, if this kept up, it was going to become terrifying.

Billy nodded. "Aye. That we will."

He called himself Billy Lowman, but it wasn't his name. Paul Ringo wasn't the other man's name, either. None of the five men on this job gave their real names. They didn't know each other at all, and that in itself was a minor miracle given the small world they inhabited.

They'd been recruited separately by an unknown person or persons and given a simple task. The group of strangers was to hijack and rob a luxury sleeper train on a three-night journey through the scenic Scottish Highlands. Once the job was over, they would part and hopefully not run into each other again.

It was the start of the Christmas season, and Billy supposed rich people were nostalgic for the rugged beauty of western Scotland. *Mull of Kintyre*, and all of that nonsense. Billy never liked that song. He didn't like sappy sentimentality in general. People who did, people who fell for that kind of thing, deserved whatever happened to them, including being robbed on a train.

The job had gone exactly as promised, until just a few moments ago. 50,000 pounds sterling had appeared in Billy's offshore account, a princely sum for three days of work. It was an overpayment. If all five men got the same amount, then the sponsors of this job had paid out 250,000 pounds for a job that might bring in half that.

And that didn't even include the cost of the tickets for the cover story that the men were actual passengers. That was 11,000 pounds each, adding another 55,000 pounds to the total. A terrible waste if you asked Billy Lowman.

In fact, at this moment, in the hand that was not gripping the metal rung, Billy was holding a satchel with perhaps 45,000 pounds in it. Not nearly enough to justify this robbery. There were only thirty-one real passengers on the train, and they were barely carrying any currency. They had paid for their tickets before boarding. The food and alcohol on board was included in the price. Shopping at the fancy whistle stops along the way could be done with bank cards.

This heist had brought in what amounted to tip money the passengers had brought with them. Tip the food server. Tip the wine captain. Tip the man who turned down your bed. Tip the driver who picked you up at the end of it all.

The diamond earrings, necklaces, rings, and watches these people had been wearing would bring something, but a person would have to sell it and at a discount. That stuff could be hard to get rid of. It wasn't worthless, but it also wasn't cash.

"We have to get off this train!" Ringo shouted, his voice rising toward panic.

The train jerked hard as it entered the long curve. They were about to cross the viaduct. It was a famous bridge perhaps two stories above a wild fen, just before the approach to a sleepy and isolated town. But they should be going much slower than this to safely cross. The train was supposed to start slowing before now.

Someone, somewhere, had hacked into a computer and taken command of the train and the railway signals. That was the point, wasn't it? This was a test run. The sponsors had learned to control passenger trains, and perhaps freight trains, or boats, or who knew what else, from afar. And now they were testing the skill with a quick train robbery.

But why? Why reveal what you could do with a small-time score like this?

At the far side of the bridge, the train was supposed to slow to five miles an hour, just long enough for the stickup crew to jump off and disappear into the woods. It was late afternoon, but at this time of year, it was already black as midnight out. Once they were off, the train would speed up again. It would blow through the next station before slowing to a final stop miles down the tracks, away from any town.

Meanwhile, the crew would walk through the darkness to the boat launch at Loch Shiel. There was a motorboat waiting for them there. They would drive the boat perhaps fifteen miles down to a caravan park in Acharacle, where a delivery van would then drive them into Glasgow. From there, they would go their separate ways.

Everything on this job had gone exactly as described, and nothing had given Billy any reason to doubt the plan.

Until now.

"Steady!" he shouted. "It'll slow."

He was speaking more from hope now than certainty. The train was lurching madly. His heart was racing, though he'd long ago taught himself to remain calm in all situations. Outside the door, a low stone wall appeared. They had reached the beginning of the bridge. It was no longer a question of getting off. It was too late for that. The train would never stop on time. It was a question of the train staying on the tracks and navigating this sharp loop ahead.

He glanced through the door to the first dining car. The tables were covered in white tablecloths. There was a stainless-steel bowl as a centerpiece in each. A small menu was on a stand by each place setting. Everything had been arranged just perfectly by the train workers. Those table settings were surviving the sudden wrenching lurches of the train just fine. None seemed to have fallen to the floor yet. And everything in that car was still going exactly to plan.

The wealthy diners hadn't moved. No one was eating anything. They were all seated at their tables, hands zip-tied behind their backs, ankles zip-tied to the table legs, blindfolds covering their eyes. Billy could hear their little moans and exhalations and shouts of fear through the door. He understood it completely. He might even have felt a pang of sympathy for them. They were helpless, and the train was going too fast.

They had been lucky duckies their entire lives, and now this *bad thing* had happened. A terrible thing, really, and getting worse all the time. It was remarkable how passive most of them had been in the face of it.

Billy and the others had all come aboard disguised as passengers. They each carried tickets for a single sleeper and entered at different stations. Billy had treated himself to a new three-piece suit for the occasion and wore his best Italian leather wing tip shoes. He'd felt like James Bond boarding this train.

The man in charge of the stickup crew was an old boy with salt-and-pepper hair, a face bloated from decades of heavy drinking, and a pronounced paunch, who called himself Jackson Mack, "Jack for short."

Jack was currently up at the front of the train with the driver. He had smuggled five hard plastic, one-shot guns aboard, one for each man. They were what Billy had once called zip guns. Nowadays, people called them "ghost" guns. They were homemade, untraceable, invisible to metal detectors, powerful, and almost completely unreliable—just as likely to blow up in your hand as shoot your target.

"The instructions are to not hurt anyone," Jack had said. Jack had affected a Midwestern United States accent, generic American. Maybe that's where he was really from. "But also, to make an example of anyone who tests us."

Billy had done just that earlier today. The example was a muscle-bound action hero with a perfectly shaved head and a tight-fitting dress shirt. The man had taken offense to Billy patting down his delicious, blonde girlfriend to find whatever valuables she was hiding. Yes, her dress was form-fitting, absurdly so. But one never knew, did one? She could be harboring some hard currency or the Hope diamond under there somewhere. The only way to be sure was a thorough inspection.

The action hero sat in stony silence, Billy's gun pointed directly at him. But the moment came when he could take it no more. Chivalry had not died. It had merely arrived late. The man came at Billy with moves likely seen during the mixed martial arts bouts on the telly, so Billy had fired his one shot into the man's chest.

BANG. It was loud. It hurt Billy's hand a little bit as the gun partially ruptured. But it worked. No more troublesome boyfriend. Finding and eliminating people like that could mean the difference between success and failure on a job like this. And after that, there was no trouble of any kind from the rest of the passengers.

The girlfriend had collapsed into an inconsolable puddle, and moments later became mute and semi-comatose. The action hero's dress shirt was ruined, Billy supposed. It was a nice shirt, probably from a high-end shop. That might have been the one downside to the whole incident.

"I'm going!" Ringo shouted.

Billy turned. He caught one more glimpse of Ringo, a young, fit guy in a blue wool sweater, with short, blond hair and a freckled face. His eyes were WIDE. He was in a full-on panic. You couldn't get good help anymore.

Outside the wide door, the dark land raced by. The train wheels shrieked along the track. Sparks were flying out there. The entire train seemed to lean now, like a sailboat in heavy weather. It leaned and leaned. Billy was hanging backwards, his hand still gripping that iron rung.

Then it leaned the other way, nearly pitching Billy out the door.

If they did derail …

"Don't," Billy said, but it was too late.

"Good luck," Ringo said.

He leapt through the open door and was gone in the night. Billy saw what he thought might be Ringo hitting the low stone wall legs first, crumpling, then flipping upside down. It was impossible to say if that was real, or if he had imagined it. It was too dark, and everything was moving too fast.

"Oh," Billy said, despite himself. "Oh no."

Why did he do that?

The train was no longer in their control. That was clear. Its wheels made strange, almost tortured, squealing sounds. There came a series of clunks and then a heavy shudder. The train leaned hard to the left again, then to the right.

They were halfway across the bridge. The curve steepened and steepened. This thing was going to crash. For a split second, he considered calling Jackson Mack on the radio one last time. But it wouldn't make a difference. They had just talked five minutes ago. Jack had no idea why the train wasn't slowing. The train driver he was holding at gunpoint had no idea, either. The whole system had been overridden. Whoever had done that was the only one who could stop it. The driver had tried to manually apply the brakes, only to have them snap from the sheer force being delivered to the wheels.

Billy stared out the open door. The cold night zipped by. He couldn't see anything out there, except faraway lights and dark shadows closer by. It was horrifying.

He took a deep breath, pushing it deep into his abdomen. There was one thing left to do, the same thing Ringo had just done. The thing he had told Ringo not to do. Abandon ship. Billy almost started crying at the thought of it.

"It's wrong!" he shouted. "It's wrong!"

People abandoned boats in storms all the time. Then the rescuers found the boats intact the next day, perfectly upright, and the people who jumped in the water were turned to floating corpses. But boats were built to weather storms. This train was not built to handle these curves at this speed.

"Damn you!" he screamed at whoever had hired him for this job. When the money had appeared in his account, he had barely even wondered who it was. Money was money. But it had all been a trick. "Damn you! Damn you! Damn you!"

Calm. Be calm. This won't hurt a bit.

He hesitated. He glanced back at the people in the dining car. They sat there frozen like poor, helpless sheep. They were lambs to the slaughter.

Just like Billy Lowman.

"God save me."

He leapt through the open space.

Then he was gone, too, just like Paul Ringo. But he was smarter than Ringo. Or maybe he had learned Ringo's lesson. Don't just *fall* out of the train.

Billy jumped high and far, hurling himself with the leverage from his hand on the metal rung. He flew out and over the stone wall below. He cleared it, moving very fast, the train rushing on behind him.

It was a nightmarish drop. He fell and fell, for what seemed like much too long.

Then: BOOM.

His legs hit the ground, a bone-crushing impact. It knocked the breath out of him. It felt like his legs were driven up into his chest. He bounced, turning head over heels, and something inside him broke. Searing pain cut through him like a dagger. Then he bounced again, and more things broke. Another bounce. Then another. He felt himself breaking into pieces. He was a bag of shattered glass.

I'm dead. I'm dead. That's okay.

All was darkness and silence. For how long, he couldn't say. He opened his eyes and gasped for breath. It hurt to breath, but what choice was there?

He lay on his back in the snow. A cloud of the soft white stuff, disturbed from a tree somewhere above him, fell gently down onto his face.

"Anh."

He swallowed hard. It hurt to swallow. It hurt to do anything.

He'd landed in a snowbank, and that had probably saved his life. But what kind of life would it be? He seemed unable to move.

No. It wasn't true. He could turn his head. It moved slowly, like an iron ball at the top of a rusty pike.

He turned his head to the right. The train had continued on its way. He watched the rear lights. In the reflection of the snow, in the night, the train shimmered. It was silver, topped with a purple-black sliver of sky. It turned along the sharp curve, revealing a row of golden windows.

It was as if Billy was dreaming. The windows were like eyes shining underwater, the sea lit by a cold, alien sun.

For a second, he thought the train was going to make the turn. That would render this jump very stupid. Now he was broken, in pieces, lying in the cold, with no chance of escape. Perhaps he was dying. And the train was fine.

But … no.

As he watched, the train seemed to bend at the middle, like it was made of some soft material, like taffy. A high-pitched screech sounded, like a vampire running his long nails on a chalkboard. The engines whined, then a loud shriek came, the loudest one yet, followed by a BANG.

To Billy's eyes, the train moved in slow motion. All the cars were turning sideways, turning, and sliding. The cars crashed, clanged, and screeched, the sound of metal scraping metal.

When the cars collided with the stone wall of the bridge, the train—which looked to Billy like a fat bubble now, like a cartoon train—burst apart. It almost seemed like a bubble was popping. Sparks flashed everywhere. Then flame from somewhere in the middle of the train leapt toward the sky. Maybe a fuel line of some kind had blown.

Does the kitchen run on gas?

The train cars, each one in turn, were hurled from the tracks and into the air. They flew off the bridge and landed on their sides, crashing one by one into the frozen ground. The sound was LOUD, louder than Billy's ears could bear. He would cover his ears, but his arms were in too much pain to move.

Pain. Pain is a good sign.

He closed his eyes and screamed instead.

Behind his eyelids, something flashed. He opened them again. He watched as a short distance away, one of the cars rolled down a wooded hillside on fire. A moment later, the forest all around it was burning. The air itself seemed to be on fire and reeked of diesel, smoke, and burning oil.

Billy tried to move again, but nothing worked. He couldn't lift his arms. His legs … he didn't know. But he was in a lot of pain, seemingly everywhere, and he welcomed it. If it hurt, that meant he still could feel it. He might survive this, and he might walk again.

He decided to just lie where he had landed. People would arrive soon. Rescuers. Firemen. He was dressed like the other passengers. *Maybe he could tell them he ...*

But it would be hard. They had left the passengers tied up. Those people had gone helpless into the crash. Anyone who was still on that train must be dead now. And Billy was out here, free, alive, not bound in any way.

And with a gun in his pocket.

He hadn't gotten rid of the gun. It could be traced to the crime. He thought of reaching into his pocket, taking it out, and throwing it as far as he could. But he couldn't throw it anywhere. His arms were broken, probably in several places. He couldn't move them at all.

Suddenly, he was very tired. His eyelids drifted down again, and he watched as the flames danced in the darkness. But that couldn't be, could it? How could he watch anything? His eyes were closed.

Somewhere in the distance, a siren began to shriek. More soon joined it. They were coming this way.

"God," he whispered. "Thank you, God."

CHAPTER TWO

2:30 pm Eastern Standard Time
New York City Police Department Counterterrorism Bureau
One Police Plaza
Lower Manhattan, New York City

"Who else knows you're here?" Missing Persons said.

Troy Stark sat in the uncomfortable wooden chair across the desk from Persons, in the tiny space that served as the former colonel's headquarters.

"Where? In your office?"

Persons's office. The place was a joke. It was narrow and long, more like a walk-in closet than an actual office. The desk was wedged in a cramped spot directly across from the door. Boxes were piled up on the floor around him. His laptop computer sat on a pile of paperwork.

The only thing this office had going for it was a wide, tall window behind the desk, giving a view directly out toward the Brooklyn Bridge. From Troy's angle, he could watch the afternoon traffic leaving and coming to Manhattan, far enough away that the cars were like so many buzzing insects.

"No," Persons said. "Not in my office. Here, in New York. Inside the United States."

Troy shrugged. "My mom. I'm staying with her. My brothers, and their wives, I guess. A few people who might have seen me out at a bar on Saturday night."

"How long have you been here?"

"I got into town Thursday afternoon."

It was now Sunday, two weeks before Christmas. He was still getting his mail at his mom's house. He didn't really care about his mail, and neither did his mom. It was just piling up. Sifting through it yesterday afternoon, he had come upon a letter from the office of the Sergeant at Arms of the United States Senate.

Troy's presence *was required* at a Senate select committee hearing regarding war crimes committed by United States military personnel.

The date was to be determined. *Please contact this office for scheduling and to obtain the necessary …* yadda, yadda, yadda. Troy stopped reading at that point.

"Are you here until Christmas?" Persons said.

Troy shook his head. "No. I'm going back to Europe tomorrow. I'm not on indefinite leave. I'm just nursing a few injuries from the most recent fiasco."

Persons nodded. "Good. Europe is a good place for you."

"I might come back here for Christmas," Troy said and smiled. "My fairy godmother granted me ten thousand euros in cash, so for the time being, I can flit about however I want."

Persons raised an eyebrow. It was the eyebrow over his one remaining eye. Persons said nothing about the money. This was the kind of loose talk that probably embarrassed him. He had sent Troy the money through their intermediary, Alex. Black budget money—a bonus for work well done. File it under Miscellaneous.

Troy watched Persons carefully, while also looking around the small room, pretending not to stare.

Colonel Stuart Persons. Retired. Former United States Army Special Forces. Former Joint Special Operations Command. Troy guessed he was in his mid-fifties. He was tall and slim, with sharp edges to his face. His singular feature was the black eyepatch that he wore, the band tight to his bald head. Nowadays, the patch was situated under a pair of rimless glasses. The new setup made Persons look older than his years.

Persons had never said what happened to his eye. Rumors had always abounded. He lost it playing racquetball without safety goggles. He was up against an exceptional player, and the hard rubber ball hit him squarely in the eye at a hundred miles per hour.

He lost it in hand-to-hand combat with a Nicaraguan Sandinista. The guy knew Persons was going to kill him, and in a last-ditch effort to save his own life, he gouged out the eye. He lost it to an untreated infection during a classified mission to take down a warlord with a child army deep inside the Congo. It could have been any of these, or none of them.

"Look Stark, I'm not telling you that you can't be here. You should see your family if you want. You've been doing a hell of a job over there. No one will ever thank you for it, but understand that inquiring minds are watching, and they like what they see."

"They just don't want me in the United States."

Persons shrugged. "No one knows which side you're on. Until you decide that, you're a wild card. People would prefer if you stayed where these summonses can't reach you."

"It reached me," Troy said.

Persons shook his head. "No, it didn't. You weren't here. You never saw it."

"Anyone who cares to look can find me."

"I know," Persons said. "And that worries me. I don't like to worry. I'm beginning to think we should have planted you over there under an assumed name."

"Is it really that bad?"

Persons pursed his lips and gave a slight shrug. "That all depends. How well did you know Enrico Morales? And what did you think of him?"

Troy didn't have to think long to answer that question. "Off the record?"

Persons didn't answer. Nothing was off the record in this world they inhabited. Troy decided to plunge on anyway. "Enrico was a sadist," he said. "He was a nutjob, and he was out of control. Maybe he was good earlier in his career. But by the time I met him, he had gone over the edge."

"Maybe he was just a bad apple?" Persons said. "In an organization that was otherwise clean?"

Troy paused. "I think the Metal Shop deliberately recruited people like Enrico."

When Troy spoke the words *Metal Shop*, Persons glanced around at the walls. It was a reflexive action, like a knee getting hit with a ball peen hammer and kicking outward. Persons didn't even seem to realize he had done it.

"He was the worst I knew of, but he wasn't the only one," Troy said.

"Nobody," Persons said, "and I mean nobody, wants you to say that."

"Well, I'm sure the media would want to hear it. Some of our crusading Senators would love it. Maybe the *New York Herald* would dig up some anonymous sources."

Persons clucked his tongue. "See, this is the kind of chatter …"

He trailed off. Troy knew how the sentence ended without Persons saying it. In fact, Troy heard the sentence finish in his own mind.

"… that gets people killed."

"Not that I would ever say anything like that," Troy said. "I liked the Shop okay. It took care of some very messy business. Someone has to do it. And anyway, I wasn't there that long. More of an ad hoc relationship than anything."

"You realize, don't you, that if you end up testifying before the Senate, you're going to have to say something? Being away in Europe makes that less likely."

"But it can't go on forever," Troy said. "If they want me to come and testify, they'll find me. And if they really want me, they'll send someone out to collect me."

"That's right," Persons said. "And that doesn't only pertain to the Senate."

Troy didn't like this. It was one thing to suggest that loose talk could get someone killed and not even finish the sentence. It was quite another to suggest someone might come to get him.

"Who else might it pertain to?"

Persons shrugged. "You know how our friends are. They prefer to nip problems in the bud."

"They might find their errand boys being nipped in the bud instead."

"Agreed," Persons said. "You would be a hard problem to nip, but it doesn't mean they wouldn't try."

"Is there something our friends would prefer that I do?"

Now, Persons broke out into a slight grin. "You're catching on. Not quite the babe lost in the woods that you used to be."

Troy didn't share the humor. "I don't want to look over my shoulder the rest of my life because of work I once did for our government. I did whatever I did because I was patriotic, and I followed orders. It doesn't seem fair, does it?"

"Life isn't fair, Stark. If you haven't figured that much out, I don't know if I can help you."

"What do they want, Colonel? This is your office. I assume you have it swept. Why don't you just speak plainly for once?"

Persons's eye glittered. Troy couldn't tell if it was with anger or some other emotion. This was the first time in their relationship that Troy had spoken harshly to him or accused him of anything, however obliquely. Usually their patter, even when it was hard-edged, was good-natured and teasing.

Persons took a moment before speaking. "Our friends are offering you a deal. All they want is firm agreement from you. You're on the team, and you're willing to play ball. The Senate knows you were on at least one mission with Morales. If you get dragged in to testify, you tell them that you never heard the term Metal Shop, or Shop, or anything along those lines. You're not aware of the existence of such a group. Yes, you served with Enrico Morales at Joint Special Operations Command. The mission or missions you performed are classified, so you're not at liberty to discuss anything about that. But you never witnessed anything that could be considered a war crime or a human rights violation. And as far as you knew him, Morales was a highly skilled, courageous, and upstanding man, the best of the best. If anyone failed in their duty, it was Veterans Affairs, who did not get him the much-needed mental health treatment for the PTSD he suffered as a result of his service to our country. His suicide is on them."

Persons shrugged. "If you need it, a script detailing all of this can be provided to you, so you can commit it to memory before destroying it."

Troy sat back. He watched Persons. The eye never wavered. The man's upright frame never changed posture. This man had been a mentor to Troy, and yet, it was almost as if Troy was looking at him for the first time. The things Persons knew, the intricacies of his networks, the skeletons crouched in dark closets, the bodies buried beneath remote cornfields … it was a lot to take in all at once.

"I'm just the messenger," Persons said. "I hope you understand that."

Troy nodded. "I do. And what do I get in exchange for being on the team, besides the privilege of remaining alive?"

Persons shook his head. "No one threatened to kill you, Stark. Don't take anything I said as a threat, veiled or otherwise. I was just sharing a concern."

It was baloney. Persons had passed on a threat less than five minutes ago.

"Okay," Troy said. "Do I get anything?"

Persons nodded. "You get everything, my friend. Full honorable discharge, with rank reinstated, and all accrued benefits. The insubordination charge isn't just dropped, it's erased. The incident in Syria becomes a letter to your file evidencing your bravery, leadership, and your initiative in saving the lives of more than a hundred non-combatants while under enemy fire."

"The enemy was the Turks," Troy said.

Persons smiled again. The smile didn't reach his eye. "They'll leave that part out." He waved his hand. "The mission was classified anyway."

Troy was breathless for a moment. He forced air into his lungs. In exchange for not telling anyone about their dirty little secret, they were going to give him his life back.

"Did Enrico really kill himself?" Troy said.

Persons became watchful again. "He disappeared into the desert. His wound appears consistent with a self-inflicted gunshot to the head."

More games. Another non-answer.

"What do you say, Stark? Do they have a deal?"

Troy took a deep breath. "I'll have to think about it."

"The Senate isn't going to offer you anything."

Troy nodded. "I know that."

"Well," Persons said. "Don't think too long."

Troy stood up to leave. This friendly conversation left him with a lot to think about. It also left a sour taste in his mouth.

"Colonel, it was great to see you, as always."

"You're doing a good job, Stark. If that guy Alex turns up, give him a listen. It's like you're talking directly to me. And please, call me Stu. All that colonel stuff ended some time ago."

Troy turned toward the door.

"It's an excellent deal, Stark. There's nothing more to think about."

CHAPTER THREE

December 14
8:35 am Central European Time
INTERPOL Headquarters
Lyon, France

"Let's call this to order," the man at the front said. "Order, please."

Slowly, the people in folding chairs throughout the large room quieted down. Up at the front, the presenter, a man with sandy hair and wearing a beige suit and wire-rimmed glasses, snapped the fingers of his right hand. In his left hand, he held a laser pointer.

Miquel Castro-Ruiz watched him closely. He looked like a man who, in a moment, was going to start directing that laser at people in the audience. The finger snapping didn't seem to be getting the quiet the man craved.

"Order, please!"

Behind the presenter was a large video screen. On the screen was a still image of the derailed train cars of the *Royal Highlander*, a couple of them blackened, burned out, and gutted, lying in the snow beneath the Glenfinnan Viaduct in the northwest of Scotland. The photo had been taken the morning after the crash.

Miquel had been called down here to Lyon yesterday afternoon, expressly for this briefing. He was invited to no other meetings besides this one. He and Agent Dubois sat side by side, in this room with about two dozen other Interpol officers. These officers were all either people at the top of the organization or people who ran their own departments or groupings.

Dubois was seemingly the only person here who didn't fit that bill, but as far as Miquel was concerned, she was his right hand. For years he had mentored her, but over time she had grown to be his equal, if not in rank, then in gravitas. She belonged here as much as anyone.

He glanced at her. She was dressed conservatively, for her, in a blue suit. Her hair stood up in an outrageous Afro, tied with a blue sash that matched the suit. She wore rings on every finger of both hands.

"Quite unruly today," she said. "It must be the movement of the stars."

Miquel didn't like coming here. He would much prefer to remain in Madrid and focus on his own work. He was a pariah within this organization now. There was no way around it. In the weeks since the CERN attack, it had become clear to him.

El Grupo had saved a lot of lives at CERN. But people had died, and tens of millions of euros in equipment and facilities had been destroyed. In a series of meetings just after the event had taken place, this had been impressed on him again and again. Lives were lost. Cutting edge equipment and facilities were destroyed.

Of course, tighter security to begin with might have thwarted the attack before it began. Better protocols might have meant that the loopholes the terrorists exploited never existed in the first place.

Miquel's superiors ignored these obvious facts. Instead, they pushed to discover how he knew the attack would take place at CERN on the exact date it did. They seemed to think he was holding intelligence back from them.

"I guessed," he had told them. "I didn't know anything for a fact."

It was an unacceptable answer, apparently. So, he tried again. "Everyone in this organization had the same information I did. I shared everything I knew. Anyone could have made the same guess I did. I warned you that I suspected the attack was coming. You granted me minimal resources to intervene, under very tight rules of engagement, and then sent me on my way. We are very fortunate that many more people didn't die."

He shrugged. "That's what happened."

And they either didn't believe him or didn't want to.

Now, in the large conference room, the audience finally quieted. He was surrounded by people, his colleagues, but he was apart from them. If Dubois wasn't here, he would've felt as alone as a man on a desert island in the middle of the Indian Ocean.

"Thank you," the presenter said.

Miquel had never seen the man before this morning. Miquel was an exile from these headquarters. For all he knew, the man gave group briefings every day.

"This meeting covers a forthcoming Interpol Orange Notice, warning of a potential threat to persons and property. What we know hasn't been made public, but aspects of it soon will be. For now, the information I'm about to share must be guarded with utmost secrecy.

17

The train disaster in the Scottish Highlands this past weekend is the worst such incident in Europe in nearly twenty years. There were forty-six people on the train, including passengers and staff. Of those, thirty-nine have died. In the immediate aftermath of the disaster, it was thought to be the result of a malfunction in the new guidance, control, and signaling systems the railroad has been using. It appears now that this is not the case, and that it is the result of a hijacking and robbery attempt gone wrong. Indeed, nearly everyone on the train, alive or dead, was immobilized through the use of plastic zip ties."

A low hum of muttering and whispered conversation broke out across the room. Miquel sipped coffee from his paper cup. He and Dubois glanced at each other. The announcement was not a surprise to either of them. If the crash had been a tragic accident, there would have been no reason to hold this meeting.

"To be clear, the disaster does not appear to have been intended as a terrorist attack. It will, however, warrant increased security at train and bus stations and at airports."

People were still talking.

The presenter raised his hand. "Please."

Two photos appeared on the screen behind him. One was a mug shot of a handsome, dark-haired man who looked to be in his thirties. Next to it was an image of a man in a hospital bed, eyes closed, face badly bruised and swollen, one wrist cuffed to the metal railing of the bed, and numerous machines positioned around him.

"The man you see boarded the train as a passenger from London named William Lowman. That isn't his name. DNA and fingerprinting have determined that he is Dean Carver, a forty-one-year-old Canadian citizen with a long criminal history, who has lived and operated in Britain, Ireland, and southern Spain for between ten and fifteen years. He has gone by at least six aliases besides William Lowman that we know of."

"And that's him in the bed?" a voice from the crowd said.

The presenter nodded. "It is. For the time being, he is one of the seven survivors of the disaster. He was seriously injured, with several broken bones, broken vertebrae, and internal injuries too numerous and complex to adequately describe as part of this briefing. More information about his condition will be made available once it is obtained. It is not clear at the moment if he will survive."

A number of hands went up and voices chattered.

"Carver was found lying in a snowbank at the site of the crash," the presenter said. "He seems to have leapt from the train just prior to the derailment. He was a few meters from a leather satchel holding tens of thousands of British pounds, along with smaller amounts of other currencies, and jewelry taken from the passengers. Other survivors have indicated that Carver was one of five hijackers who took over the train, subdued the crew, and robbed the passengers."

On the screen behind him, the image changed. Now the monitor was showing an odd-looking gun. The snub-length barrel, rounded body, and trigger mechanism were gray, with a dark blue grip extending away at an angle. The gun was unfamiliar, but very simple. It had no obvious markings on it, no sights, no safety, nowhere to slide in a magazine, and no revolving cylinder.

"An interesting corroborating point is that Carver was also found with the gun you see here, in his pants pocket. It's a so-called ghost gun, a 3D-printed, hard plastic, one-shot firearm widely known as the *Freedom Fighter*. The design for the gun was released by an anonymous party or parties to an open-source website about two years ago. The gun Carver had in his possession was sturdy enough that when he jumped or was ejected from the train, upon impact of landing, the gun seems to have cracked his pelvis."

More chatter broke out around the room. The man raised his hand for quiet again. On the monitor behind him, the image changed. It showed a snowy field, with a large white tent in the middle. Under the tent were bodies laid out on tables. In some cases, the bodies were not complete, or they were simply burned and blackened lumps. In the distance, derailed train cars could be seen at the base of the stone viaduct.

"Many of the corpses were badly damaged, and some were burned beyond recognition. Medical and forensic personnel are working to match dental records and fingerprints, where they exist, and DNA to the identities of passengers listed on the manifest. It's a slow process. As far as we can tell, the other four hijackers appear to have died. We are working to sort that out and determine their identities."

"Has Carver given any statement?" a voice said.

The presenter nodded. "He is under sedation at this time. But he was awake and alert for a period after he was first identified and arrested. He claimed that he did not know the other hijackers. He insisted repeatedly to the interviewers that he had been used and betrayed. He indicated that he had been hired to help carry out the robbery, and that the train was supposed to slow down, so the hijackers could jump off and escape. Instead, it speeded up and crashed. He claimed further that he did not know the man who recruited him. Bear in mind that Carver is a lifelong career criminal. We have little reason to take anything he says at face value."

"When will they wake him up again for further questions?"

The presenter shrugged. "He has brain swelling. He had to be sedated so his skull could be opened to ease the pressure. We have no idea when or if he's going to regain consciousness."

More chatter broke out. In Miquel's opinion, the presenter was not good at commanding a room.

"We can all see there is a great deal more that we would like to know. Some of it will come from the data stored by the train itself. The driver died in the crash, so we won't have any testimony from him. Personnel from the railroad say they lost contact with the driver soon after the train sped up, and that they were unable to slow it down from the control facility."

Miquel's ears perked up.

"We are operating under the assumption," the presenter said, "that the railroad control system was hacked. We don't have all the facts yet, but the analysis is moving in that direction. Which means other railroads could be vulnerable. There are hundreds of potential targets worldwide. Urban metros and undergrounds, suburban commuter rails, intercity high-speed rail, tourist trains. There are many, many systems."

"If they did it once," Miquel said, "they will do it again."

The presenter nodded his head just slightly.

"This is why we're issuing the Orange Notice, and why we called this preliminary meeting to give you the intelligence. We recommend you and your units carefully monitor the data available to you. This could have been a one-off robbery that went wrong, or it could be something more."

Oh, it's something more.

Assessing a blizzard of data that size would be hard if not impossible. There was too much information, too many variables, too many possible targets. By the time an attack became apparent, it would already be underway.

"There's a problem," Miquel said. "There's a giant amount of data to study, and it could take weeks to even begin to organize it. But the next attack can come tomorrow, or tonight, or could be unfolding right now."

The presenter nodded. "Yes, that's right."

"So, what are we doing to get out in front of the problem?"

The presenter almost seemed to smirk at Miquel. "We're preparing an Orange Notice to all partner police forces. We will soon go public with the information."

"It's not enough," Miquel said.

Agent Dubois reached out and patted Miquel's hand. "Miquel," she said, under her breath. "Stop."

"What do you suggest?" the presenter said.

Of course, Dubois was right. A meeting like this was not the place to stick his head out. It would be duly noted and just give them all more reason to one day chop it off.

But Miquel plunged on anyway. "Jumpstart the process," he said. "Rather than sift through massive amounts of data, look for obvious patterns and eliminate ninety percent of it right away. Force, or at least strenuously insist upon, shutdowns of the train lines that seem the most at risk."

Rather than a buzz of chatter, the room went silent. The presenter turned his head just slightly. He seemed pleased because he was no longer fighting for quiet. He had the attention of everyone present.

"We currently consider all train lines at risk," he said. "That will remain the case until we have a reasonable basis for doing otherwise."

Miquel glanced at Dubois again. Her face was expressionless, but there was something there in her dark eyes. *God, don't let it be pity.*

"It's too slow," he said.

The presenter shrugged. "It's how we work, Director Castro. I imagine you must know that by now."

CHAPTER FOUR

11:05 am Eastern European Time (10:05 am Central European Time)
Foinikion, Island of Carpathos
The Greek Islands
The Aegean Sea

The supreme art of war is to subdue the enemy without fighting.

"Sir, they just pulled up with Mr. Sokolov in the car."

Lucien Mebarak looked up from the book he was reading. The man standing before him was a brute, with a shaved head and broad shoulders, nearly two meters tall, with the dumb eyes of an ox. His upper body was overweight and soft. His legs were as strong as the trunks of oak trees.

He was a man who, if he fell on you, would probably squash you like a grape. He wore a light blue, collared shirt with short sleeves that looked painted onto his awkward body. He wore tight, green dress pants with pinstripes. He was one of Lucien's bodyguards, but if he was carrying a gun, it wasn't in evidence.

Lucien nodded. "Very good. Please see him out here to me."

The man nodded, then he turned to go and retrieve the mad dog killer who had come to visit.

Lucien was dressed informally today. He wore a black t-shirt and ripped, blue jeans. He had sandals on his feet. The sun was out and beginning to ride high, but the day was not hot. He put his book, *the Art of War* by Sun Tzu, and his reading glasses on the table in front of him, next to his blue mug of coffee.

Lucien was sitting on the patio of his modern, white stone house, overlooking the pale blue waters of the Aegean. The house was built on a rocky outcropping high above the water. It was designed to capture a sweeping southern exposure, facing down the coastline, but also out to sea and to the west as far as the eye could see.

From here, there was a wide staircase down to the pool deck. Two young lovelies, one blonde and one brunette, were wrapped in white robes on chaise lounges next to the pool. The pool was an infinity pool, made to trick the eye into thinking it was an extension of the sea itself. The day was not yet warm enough for the girls to reveal their bodies.

It was just as well. Sokolov was a dangerous man. It was fine to tweak him a little bit, perhaps raise some envy and frustration within him. But it wouldn't do to set him off or anger him.

Lucien picked up the coffee mug and took a sip. It had gone cold but still tasted quite good. He made sure his pantry was stocked with the best of everything, including coffee. Especially coffee.

Sokolov must be almost upon him. Lucien raised his arms, maybe to stretch, maybe to indicate victory. He turned in a grand sweep, taking in the house, the pool, the girls, the cliffs, and the surrounding grounds, all the way past the house up into the rugged brown hillsides that rose to the east. He rarely hiked those hills, but he did own them.

He sighed. Everything was beautiful here. Everything was perfect.

His life was perfect and getting better all the time. What could he possibly want that he lacked?

Nothing. He lacked for nothing.

"Hello," a man said. "Mr. de Klerk, I presume?"

Lucien nearly jumped, as if he'd seen a ghost. Anatoly Sokolov. The man had come out onto the patio and simply stood behind Lucien, saying nothing. And Lucien's bodyguards had left him here.

"I won't hurt you," Sokolov said. "You're my employer."

Lucien recovered himself and smiled. He extended a hand, which Sokolov shook.

"Anatoly, welcome. Yes, I'm Charles de Klerk," Lucien said, using one of his many aliases. "Of course, you wouldn't hurt me. I know that. I instructed my guards to see you out here so we could speak plainly."

He paused. The truth was, Sokolov had frightened him the slightest amount. Sokolov was not a large man, but he had *presence*.

He was perhaps fifty years old. His hair was dark but speckled through with gray-white. His eyes appeared to be black like a shark's eyes. The eyes of a man-eating predator. But a shark's eyes were lifeless, whereas these eyes were alert and aware and had a horrible intelligence. There were pronounced crow's feet around his eyes.

Sokolov had a day or two day's stubble of dark beard on his face. He wore a light blue dress shirt, open at the collar, with a new, white t-shirt underneath. The shirt sleeves were down to his wrists, hiding the tattoos that Lucien knew covered almost the entire upper body. Sokolov wore jeans and black work boots.

23

He was handsome, in a sharp-edged way. His face looked like it was carved from some dense, dark wood. His body was thin, but sinewy and strong. On some men, his clothes would make him look like he was a foreman at a job site or dressed for business casual. Sokolov looked like he was dressed for prison.

Indeed, he had spent much of his adult life in prison. As far as Lucien knew, he had done at least seventeen years in three different countries, including Russia, Georgia, and the United States. He had been an elite Spetsnaz soldier at one time, perhaps also a spy or a secret policeman, and an enforcer and assassin for mafia figures fighting for turf after the collapse of the Soviet Union. He was a hard man. He had likely killed a lot of people. He had probably tortured some of them first.

"Can we get you anything?"

Sokolov gave a gentle shake of his head. "No, that's very kind. I think maybe we should talk right away, so there are no misunderstandings."

Lucien nodded. "Good. Please join me at the table."

He swept his hand back to the white table and two chairs where he had just been sitting. The sweep of his hand caught the pool deck below the patio, where one of the two lovelies, the blonde, had moved into the pool. You could see from here that she was nude. For a brief instant, Lucien longed to join her. The pool was heated to a perfect temperature, and it was shaping up to be a cool but very sunny day.

"Nice view," Sokolov said, not giving away too much.

"I find it exceptional," Lucien said.

They sat down. Lucien gave Sokolov the view of the sea, the sky, and the girls. Lucien looked back at the many tall glass windows of the whitewashed house and the stark hills looming in the background. Lucien's view was undeniably nice. The view he gave to Sokolov was spectacular.

He was trying to impress the man. Maybe he was trying too hard.

"Istvan Gajdos," he said, naming the insipid Hungarian oligarch. Ten years ago, the man had been a mechanic, with a shop and perhaps five or six employees. During the bad old days after communism had collapsed and there was no fuel for automobiles, he had apparently worked on bicycles all by himself. But seven years ago, the current dictator of Hungary, Xander Racz, had emerged after a bloodless revolution and coup, likely sponsored by the CIA and certain unnamed Western investment bankers.

Gajdos and Racz were childhood best friends. In short order, Gajdos became the richest man in Hungary. He was now the sole owner of Hungary's largest television network. He owned Hungary's largest high-speed internet provider. He was buying up smaller TV networks, radio stations, newspapers, and popular websites. It was clear that his ownership of Hungarian media was in fact his friend Racz clamping down on free speech.

Last year, Gajdos bought a decrepit, communist-era diesel train system and began to renovate it with high-speed electrified trains. And in the past ten months, he had branched out of Hungary completely.

He bought a boutique hotel in Vienna, along with train lines that ran from Vienna, through the Austrian Alps, and all the way to Switzerland. He claimed that all of his train systems were now compatible with each other, and with the Austrian national train system. A person could conceivably board a train in Budapest and take it to Zurich without changing trains, without the trains swapping out power sources, with no inconveniences of any kind.

"East meets West," Gajdos had been saying in recent interviews. "Budapest is a great world city, like Vienna, Prague, and Zurich." In his mind's eyes, Lucien could see Gajdos raising a meaty forefinger. "When we say these names of great cities, the name Budapest must also be on the tip of our tongue."

Lucien had no dispute with that. Twelve million tourists visited Budapest each year. Lucien himself had been there half a dozen times, including once on a motor yacht trip along the Danube River. It was a lovely city, and Gajdos was trying too hard. His inferiority complex was clear for all to see. He and his friend Racz were tearing the country down and dragging it backwards into the past. They weren't building bridges to anywhere.

Sokolov lit a cigarette and took a drag. Lucien noticed that Sokolov did not ask, "do you mind if I smoke?"

Lucien suspected that Sokolov rarely asked permission for anything.

"Gajdos," Sokolov said, "is a fat, pompous ass. He's stupid. His dreams of incorporating a fascist Hungarian dictatorship into the western world are just that. Dreams. The westerners engineered his friend's takeover of the country, but they don't want these rat men like Gajdos and Racz to join their little club. They just want to thwart the will of the Hungarian people."

That was more or less Lucien's exact interpretation of the situation as well. Gajdos seemed as dumb as a rock. He had simply been handed enormous wealth and been told how to do his master's bidding. But he could not sense the weather. His newest venture was a luxury train, vastly expensive and only for European and global elites. It would run directly from the center of Budapest, high into the Alps. His inaugural voyage, for himself, his entourage, and hand-selected guests, was due to leave in a couple of days. Who but invited guests would bother to take such a ride?

"Are you and your team prepared?" Lucien said.

Sokolov did something like a nod, but also a shrug. "We are ready. But you must understand that my fee has gone up."

The black shark eyes met Lucien's. Lucien couldn't discern any emotion in those eyes. There was no aggression, no humor, no concern, nothing at all. But they weren't dead eyes, like those of a shark. They were alive and full of knowing.

"How much?" Lucien said.

"My fee is now an entirely reasonable ten million dollars. All of it payable in full up front. You've already paid me five, so it shouldn't be much effort to deposit the additional five."

"And your team?"

Sokolov's team consisted of four others, who he had known in his Moscow hitman days, and apparently again in his Brooklyn organized crime days. Maybe Sokolov had even done prison time with them. Lucien wasn't sure.

Sokolov shook his head. "Their money is enough. They don't know I'm here."

Lucien had deposited three million dollars in each of the four other accomplices' anonymous offshore accounts. Sokolov and his Russian countrymen had insisted not only on being paid up front but also on being paid in American dollars.

"May I ask why the increase in price?" Lucien said.

"I follow the news," Sokolov said. "It isn't lost on me that the train hijacking in Scotland was your work. It also isn't lost on me that all but one of those men, whom I presume to have worked for you, are now dead. And the last survivor doesn't look like he's doing too well, either."

"He's not doing well at all," Lucien said.

"He's a loose end at this point," Sokolov said. "Isn't he?"

Lucien said nothing to that.

Not for long.

"Why did you kill them?" Sokolov said.

26

Sokolov was an intelligent man. There was no sense trying to lie to him. "It was a test run," Lucien said. "A dress rehearsal for the real presentation. Those men were nothing like you and your men. They were expendables. I needed to see if my people could take control of a train. I needed to see if a small team could take control of the passengers. Mission accomplished."

"Why didn't you stop or slow down the train?"

Lucien shook his head. He was careful to show only a hint of irritation. "This has been explained to you. When my people take control of the computer system and start the high-speed run, the decision cannot be reversed. It's a failsafe so that someone like Europol, Interpol, or the CIA—or whatever other agencies might become involved—can't just step in and turn it off. The tie is severed. The train is out of anyone's control and gaining speed until it crashes. That's how it has to be."

Sokolov nodded and took a deep drag of his cigarette. He exhaled blue smoke into the sky. "I was told, but I wanted to hear it from you."

"On Gajdos's train, the first car is akin to the old locomotives," Lucien said. "That's where the electronic brain is. You can save yourself by manually decoupling that car from the rest of the train. The first car is smart, as they say. The rest of the cars are dumb. If decoupled, they will simply roll to a stop as their momentum peters out."

"And the parasite?" Sokolov said.

"Gajdos?"

Sokolov nodded. "Yes."

"He's a clown," Lucien said. "His train leaves from Budapest, and this he sees as his great publicity coup, but he won't even be on it. He and his people will stay at his hotel in Vienna and meet the train there. A mostly empty train will leave the great global city of Budapest."

Sokolov smirked. "It doesn't surprise me. And it won't be completely empty. I'll be aboard, waiting for him."

"He always travels with six to eight bodyguards, depending on the circumstances," Lucien said. "They carry semi-automatic handguns, Tasers, truncheons, and sometimes heavier weapons."

Sokolov knew this already, of course. But Lucien thought it important to repeat the facts. Sokolov had insisted from the beginning that he and his hand-picked team were enough to carry out this job. He was confident, Lucien would give him that. But confidence only went so far. And it troubled Lucien that Sokolov refused to name his men or what their individual tasks would be.

Sokolov made eye contact with him over the top of the cigarette. Dangerous, dangerous eyes. Sokolov gave a sort of half-smile.

"Why don't you let me worry about the security?"

Lucien shrugged and moved on. Why not? Part of Sokolov's reasoning was that with a small team, it was easier to sneak on board and hide. That made sense. As for Sokolov and his team overpowering and perhaps killing six or eight men … either Sokolov knew what he was doing, or he didn't. If Lucien really thought he couldn't pull it off, then he wouldn't have hired him.

"Gajdos will have to make the call from the train to release the funds," Lucien said. "I suggest you wait until high in the Alps to make yourself known. Certainly not before Innsbruck. That way you are isolated, and the authorities will know nothing. Have him call from the satellite phone we've given you. The encryption is very good."

Sokolov was watching Lucien closely. Lucien realized that few men probably told Sokolov how to run his operations. But this was Lucien's operation, and Sokolov was a paid employee. If Sokolov wanted complete autonomy, he should have built his own empire by now. So, Lucien plunged on, "Once he makes the call and once I know the entire ransom is paid, my people will alert you. At that point, do with him, and his entourage, whatever you wish."

Sokolov exhaled a long stream of smoke. "This is a suicide mission. I think you know that."

"If that's what you believe, then why the additional fee?" Lucien said. "You can't take it with you, as they always remind us."

"For my ex-wife and son."

"It doesn't have to be suicide," Lucien said.

He believed what he was saying. A man like Sokolov, with his training and his experience, could carry out the operation, ride the train cars to a stop, and disappear into the mountains of early winter. It would take an army of searchers to find him in the snows of the Alps.

"It's either suicide or a return to prison," Sokolov said. "We'll take that train, and you'll get your ransom. But I won't go back to prison. I'll die before I'll do that. And kill everyone on board if I must."

CHAPTER FIVE

Back in Europe. Thank God.
"How you doing, beautiful?"

Troy and Aliz Willems climbed slowly up the roughhewn stone steps of the trail. She was just a few steps ahead of him. It was a cool day at the tail end of autumn, a nip of winter's coming bite in the air. There were still some golden leaves on the trees. There was a mat of crunchy ones on the ground.

She looked back at him and smiled. The smile was like an arrow that pierced Troy's chest. She was beautiful, no doubt. Almost comically voluptuous and very fit, with long, blonde hair tied in a ponytail today. Her pale blue eyes caught the light in a way that made her look like a princess in a fairy tale.

She was wearing all weather hiking gear, light brown cargo pants with many pockets, a tight-fitting, light brown jacket, and breathable mesh boots. She carried hiking poles, which she used. It was almost as if she was cross-country skiing while she walked. Wraparound polarized sunglasses were perched on top of her head. She had a light knapsack over her shoulders in a sort of harness contraption. She probably had a thousand euros in high-end outdoor fashion on her body.

She could be posting photos of this online, along with a *Buy the Look* link to her millions of social media followers, each sale triggering a kickback to her. Except she was already rich beyond what most people could imagine, and she kept her private life very private. She wouldn't dream of letting countless strangers know where she was or what she was doing.

"I'm having a very lovely time," she said.

"So am I," Troy said.

He was dressed a little differently from her. He wore cutoff jeans shorts, LL Bean work boots, and a blue windbreaker jacket over a long johns-type t-shirt. Even though the day was chilly, he was sweating. The shirt was soaked.

Troy was a city person. It occurred to him that he probably got more exercise than ninety percent of the people in the western world, but he rarely did things like this for fun. And when he said *rarely*, what he meant was *never*. Just going hiking in the woods—it didn't happen.

Come to think of it, Troy was not a guy who had much fun. He wasn't even sure if "fun" is what he would call this. He wasn't sure what he would call it.

The idea was all Aliz's. She liked doing things like this. They weren't far from where she lived—an hour by car. She told him they called this region the Switzerland of Luxembourg, with its hillsides, sweeping open landscapes, forests, streams, and old market towns dating to the Middle Ages. It was an odd name. People from Europe were a riot. Was there also a Luxembourg of Switzerland? There was no Florida of Colorado, as far as he knew.

They moved upwards along the trail through a stand of impossibly tall trees. Then they passed through the narrow gap of a towering rock formation. Aliz's big, perky butt moved along just ahead of him. He resisted the temptation to give it a smack.

He could hear her breathing. They were climbing a steep uphill. They moved higher and higher through the enormous boulder field. A little higher, and they meandered up a carved boulder switchback. Soon, the trail leveled off, and they walked through some dense forest again. He felt pretty good physically—relaxed, at peace, maybe better than he had in some time. It was nice to be away from work. It was nice to have nothing on his mind. The problem was … he did have something on his mind, didn't he?

Just ahead, the trail was marked with a white and red sign. It seemed like another sign popped up every few feet.

"The Mullerthal Trail," Aliz had told him earlier today, "is perfectly signposted. The signs make it nearly impossible to get lost."

As if Troy Stark was worried about getting lost. The prospect of losing his way along perfectly signposted trails in Luxembourg didn't trouble him at all. He had taken a lot of wrong turns in this world, into some very bad places. And he had interacted with some very bad people while he was there.

His mind wandered as they hiked. The forest around him faded and was replaced by the interior of an old wooden building in Mexico. Outside this building was wide open scrub desert. The building was like a barn of sorts, with high rafters and birds flying around up there. It was hot and dim in here, with bright light streaming through cracks in the wooden slats behind them.

They weren't supposed to be in Mexico. But they were.

Mexico was a sovereign nation. It had its own laws, its own court system, jails, and prisons. It had its own federal and local police forces. It had its own military. It had borders that it considered sacrosanct, which needed to be respected. The United States was an ally of Mexico, a neighbor, a close trading partner, and a country that should respect more than just Mexico's borders, but all of its government functions.

The Metal Shop didn't care about things like that.

The Metal Shop only cared about getting things done. Sometimes, it didn't even seem to matter what those things were. Was this the official policy of the United States? Who even signed off on operations like this?

"You remember me, don't you?" Enrico Morales said. "You remember me, Manuelito?"

The thin man was chained to a chair. He said nothing. He was blindfolded, but even with the rag obscuring part of his face, it was easy to see that he was bruised and beaten. His mouth was swollen. His face was covered by sweat and some blood, and his white t-shirt was stained deeply. His bare feet were chained around the ankles. This person was Manuelito, apparently.

He nodded slowly. "I remember. Yeah."

A radio crackled. "*Federales*, five miles out and closing. Convoy of jeeps. Ten vehicles." The voice pronounced the word like "fedder-allays."

The federales were the Mexican federal police. There was no armed force in Mexico that wasn't corrupt, and there was no group that wasn't tainted by drugs and money. The federales were bad news.

"Your friends are coming, hey Manuelito? Those are your friends? Are they coming to rescue you?"

"We can't be here," one of Enrico's guys said.

His name was Damon, and he was a black guy from Harlem. He had been around the block a hundred times. He was probably thirty, several years older than Troy, but they had bonded a little bit over New York City and the places they knew. But Damon was a long-term member of the Enrico Morales's squad, and suddenly that was a very strange thing to be.

31

Enrico raised a hand without turning around. "Charlie Mike, man. We're only here another minute."

"More than that and it's an international incident," Damon said. "We don't want to be seen in a shooting war with Mexican coppers."

"Noted," Enrico said.

There were four Metal Shop operators on the ground. As teams went, it was lean and mean. Three men, Enrico, Damon, and Troy were in the building. Another guy—a tall, blond surfer-looking dude named Marcus—was outside.

They had come here in two Little Bird helicopters. They were small and fast, known for being maneuverable and for packing heavy weapons. They looked like flying eggs. They were favorites of American special operations.

Right now, one was on the ground, out on a cleared patch of dry, hard dirt fifty meters from the door of this place, the pilots keeping the engine running. The other was in the sky, watching the roads approaching this spot in the searing desert wasteland. The Pacific coast was less than ten miles away, but it might as well be on Mars.

The choppers had entered Mexico from over the water, flying very low, using nap-of-the-Earth techniques to evade radar. It had seemed to work, but now the cops were coming. And when they got here, what would they find?

To start, they'd find the man known as Manuelito, beaten to a pulp, and chained to a folding chair with thick, steel shipping chains. More, there were two other men, both chained to chairs in a similar manner, blindfolded, gagged, and both dead from gunshots to the head. Someone had executed them before Metal Shop even got here. Whoever did that was no longer around.

It must have happened a while ago. They were covered in buzzing flies. The blood from their ruined skulls had already dried on the dirt floor. Their shirts were saturated with tacky blood.

Manuelito had been sitting here with these corpses. How long had he waited like this? Did he know these guys? Did he speak to their spirits while he waited for the next questioners to arrive?

"I'd love to stay and talk," Enrico said. "But we're nearly out of time."

He took his sidearm out of its holster. He placed the muzzle against the left side of Manuelito's head.

"You feel that, Manuelito?"

"Yes."

"You know what it is, right?"

Manuelito nodded. "Yes."

Troy was new here. He didn't know any of these guys. He had done loans from the SEALs to Joint Special Operations Command before—and had even been on a couple of Metal Shop missions—but never with Enrico and his team of cowboys. It was a special assignment. Enrico was considered a hot shot, a guy willing to go all the way out to the edge. You might even say he was becoming a legend.

But this?

"Enrico, what are you doing?" Troy said.

"Shut up, kid," Enrico said, without turning around. "You're a noob, so you don't talk. Okay? You're hired muscle and that's it. You move when I say move. You shoot when I say shoot. Other than that, you keep your trap shut."

Troy looked at Damon.

Damon shook his head. "Be cool, man. Ain't nothing wrong. This is how they play it down here. You'll understand in time. Or you won't."

The radio crackled again. "Federales three miles out and closing. They are coming hell bent for leather, kids."

"You hear that, Manuelito?" Enrico said. "Must be that you've made some new friends, right? You're a man who seems to make a lot of friends. I used to like that about you. But you take it too far."

"Enrico," Manuelito said. "Listen to me."

Enrico shook his head. "There's only one thing I want to hear from you. Where's the money? You tell me that and then I haven't made a wasted trip. You tell me that, and I'll walk out of here and leave you to your friends, or whatever they are. Maybe they'll kill you, right? Maybe they'll run you for President. I don't know, and I don't care. It's up to you how they find you."

"I need to get out of the country," Manuelito said.

Enrico nodded. "Yeah, I know. That's gonna be a tall order, I'm afraid. The last thing I need is someone like you wandering around the United States, talking to everybody, running your mouth."

"Enrico! I would never ..."

Enrico jabbed him in the head with the gun. "Where's the money?"

Manuelito's teeth clenched.

"That's all I care about, my friend. It's the reason I'm here. You better tell me, or we have nothing more to talk about."

Manuelito shook his head. "It's gone," he said quietly, his voice so low that Troy could barely hear him. "They took it from me."

"Who?"

"Sinaloa."

Enrico grunted. He turned and looked at Damon. Damon just shrugged.

"Why are you even still alive?"

Now, Manuelito was crying. "I don't know."

For a few seconds, the four men were like statues, like standing stones at some medieval burial site, the three Americans standing over the chained and defeated Mexican. Their shadows moved away diagonally in the bleak half-light illuminating this corner of the wooden building.

Enrico banged the grips of his gun onto the top of Manuelito's head. It looked more like frustration than anger.

Manuelito was weeping now, his body shaking. New blood streamed down his face.

"Look, man. I have a family, okay? I got two kids, a wife. All right? I have people who need me."

Enrico said nothing to that. He just pointed the gun at the guy's head again.

"We need to get out of here," Damon said.

"Don't do it, man," Manuelito said. "Don't do this."

Enrico stood there for a long moment, the gun pointed at Manuelito's head.

"Don't do it," Manuelito said. "Please don't do—"

Enrico pulled the trigger, once.

BANG!

Troy snapped awake. He had been walking along in a daydream.

They were passing through a high, green meadow with an escarpment of stone rising to their right. They walked on for a bit, Aliz on the trail just ahead of him. The grasses here had grown tall, waist-high, just in time to die off for the winter.

On the far side of the meadow, the trail turned and hugged the edge of a cliff. They followed it to a rocky outcropping.

It was beautiful here. Breathtaking, a spectacle laid out in front of them—a green valley below them and on the other side, low foothills rising to steep rocky cliffs. Nothing was that tall—Troy had been to much higher mountains before—but the view here was spectacular.

Aliz turned to him. Her smile was like the sun shining itself. She slung her backpack off her shoulders and let it drop to the ground.

"I thought we'd stop and have a bit to eat here."

Troy nodded. "It's a lovely spot for a break."

She clasped her hands together. "Oh, I'm so glad you like it. I was hoping you would enjoy it as much as I do. It's my favorite place on the whole trail."

Troy returned her smile. "I love it."

She came and hugged him. "Our lives are magical," she said.

There was a lot of darkness, Troy realized, but there were also moments like this. Even if Enrico Morales was dead, there were more people just like him out there. But those people were for another time. They could wait.

Aliz looked up at him now, searching his eyes. "Aren't they?" she said. "Aren't our lives magical?"

"Yeah," Troy said. "They are."

CHAPTER SIX

December 15
1:15 am Central European Time
District 7
Budapest, Hungary

"Help!" the man screamed. "Help me!"

It did no good. It wasn't loud enough. It wasn't a true shriek. He had no air in his lungs. He was running too fast to breathe. He looked up at the darkened flats all around him. Nothing, no response, no lights coming on, just dead, blank eyes staring back.

"Shut up!" one of the men coming up behind him said.

His name was Georji. He was twenty-nine years old and worked as a bartender. He made good money as a bartender and had traveled all over Europe, and to other parts of the world, with this skill.

He was flashy. He was handsome. He could make nearly any drink and make it well. He could flip bottles before pouring. Girls loved him. They wanted to take him home. He got hired to work exclusive parties by very rich people. Private jets, yachts, mansions on hilltops. It was a job, but it was also a lifestyle.

And because of this, he was now running for his life.

He sprinted down an empty side street, flying, the pavement wet from a recent rain. He gasped for air, breathing so hard that his lungs hurt. He splashed through puddles. His shoes clacked on the ground as he ran and slid on the slippery stones.

They were expensive leather shoes. He remembered falling in love with them at first sight. He was a sucker for fashion.

Stupid. The men chasing him were wearing sneakers.

"Georji," one of the men said now, the voice low and menacing, almost below hearing. "There's nowhere to run."

How did they know his name?

Up ahead, at the end of this street, a car pulled up to the crossing with the much wider boulevard. A cop! It had to be a cop. What were cops doing this time of night? They were just sitting in their cruisers, waiting for something to happen. Well, this was happening. A man was being chased down the street by two other men.

That had to be worth a cop's attention, no?

No. It wasn't a cop. A man stepped out of the car, an older man with dark hair, and Georji instantly recognized the dark, remorseless eyes of the gangster. Georji had been around them enough to know the look.

Georji slowed to a stop. The man was holding some sort of metal canister with one hand. The canister was almost something he would use to water the plants in the garden.

"Georji," the man said. "Stop running. I just want to talk to you."

No, thank you. The men coming from behind were almost on top of him. The way forward was blocked by this newcomer. Georji looked left and then right. To the right, there was a narrow alleyway between buildings.

Georji darted down there. He had always been a good runner as a kid. Now, he flew along this alley, the buildings looming above. It was like running through a slot canyon. He had never been in a slot canyon, but he imagined it was like this. In a few of the windows, the lights of late-night TV watchers flickered.

He could hear the footsteps pounding behind him, but they couldn't catch him. As he ran, he grabbed a garbage can along his route and spilled it to the ground behind him. It made a sound of rattling aluminum cans and glass bottles breaking.

Good. That was good. Maybe it would wake someone up. Maybe it would call someone's attention away from the infernal television.

There was a wooden fence ahead, blocking the way. The details of it came to him all at once, sharp, wood pickets standing upright. A green, steel garbage dumpster was pushed against it, under some dim, yellow light.

He had to leap onto the dumpster, grab the top of the fence with both hands, and vault over it, no thought for what was on the other side.

He could do it. He was athletic as a boy.

The only sounds were his breathing, the breaths of the men behind him, and the rapid footfalls.

Here came the dumpster.

He leapt, like he was an Olympic hurdler.

His first leg was up but slid across the top of the dumpster. The surface was corrugated, uneven, and a pain went through the inside of his upper leg. A pulled muscle, it must be. No matter. He had to move.

He was straddling the dumpster, one leg hanging off back into the alley. He pushed himself up to a standing position.

"Ah!" His leg really … he had done something to it.

The first man was already here, a gorilla in a blue tracksuit, the uniform of hired thugs all over Europe. Georji turned to the fence and put both hands on top of the sharp pickets. He would get splinters in his hands, but he didn't care. He was running on jet fuel now. It would be a story to tell others, how he escaped a …

The man had him, grasping him around the ankles. He pulled Georji back. For a second, Georji gripped the top of the fence. He was suspended in the air. His body was in a tug of war between his own hands and the man who had his ankles.

"No!"

The man was too strong. He yanked Georji fiercely, with incredible strength. Georji's hands ripped away from the fence, and he fell straight forward, his face and chest crashing into the metal surface of the dumpster.

He did shriek then. Someone must have heard it.

The man pulled him backwards, across the dumpster and off of it. Now Georji fell to the pavement. His face hit again.

Teeth. He lost front teeth. He felt them break. He put a hand to his mouth. It came away bloody.

"Ah."

The other man was here. Two criminal thugs had captured Georji, and he had no idea what they were going to do with him. He didn't know them. He had never seen them before. He didn't know what they wanted.

He should scream again. He was at the back of a dark alley. No police would come here of their own accord. He had to scream so that someone knew what was happening. He gathered himself for one last attempt.

A strong hand clamped over his mouth.

"Shut up!" one of the men hissed. "You shut up, or I'll kill you right now."

They were Russians. He recognized it from how they spoke. They were his brothers. He had originally come from Belarus. But there was no sense trying to convince them of that. In these days, brotherhood was dead.

The thugs held him to the ground, crouching over him. They faced him back down the alley, the way he had come.

The third man was just now arriving, walking slowly. He was well-dressed in a black collared shirt, tan slacks, and black, leather shoes. Georji noticed these things about people. His sleeves were folded up a quarter turn, showing a tangle of tattoos on both arms all the way to his wrist line.

The man seemed to saunter, as if there were no rush at all. He was still carrying that large can, as if he would water the flowers. But a smell was coming from it now, a horrible smell that Georji recognized instantly. It was the smell of raw gasoline.

"Georji, look at me," the man said quietly.

One of the thugs tilted Georji's injured face upward to look into the man's eyes. The eyes were dark, and hard, but not the brutish eyes of the typical mafia thug. Oh, Georji had met many of them in his line of work.

Every country had them. They seemed to surround rich and powerful men. Their eyes displayed about as much intelligence as the eyes of a barnyard animal. More than a cow, maybe, but less than a pig.

But this man wasn't like that. His eyes were sharp and reflective. His dark hair was peppered with gray. He was thin and fit, but probably middle-aged. Not typical of a gangster. They usually grew fat as they aged.

"Do you know me?" the man said.

The thug's heavy hand was still clamped over Georji's mouth. Georji shook his head. He moaned involuntarily.

"Let him speak," the man said to the thug. "Don't even think of crying out," he said to Georji.

Then the thug's hand was gone.

"Do you know who I am?" the man said.

"No," Georji croaked.

"Never seen me before?"

"No."

"But I know who you are, don't I?"

A few funny ideas for answers occurred to Georji. *It seems that way. I dated your sister, right?* He was usually a wise cracker, often enjoying a witty back and forth with the customers. But this man was not a customer. And it seemed that he didn't have a sense of humor.

"Yes," Georji said simply.

"I know who you are," the man said. "And I know everything about you. I know where you live. I know where you go and who you see. I know where your mother lives. There's no way to avoid me. Do you understand?"

"Yes."

"I know that you have a job coming up. You're going to tend the bar aboard a train traveling from Budapest to Switzerland. A full night and the following day. A sort of party train, owned by Istvan Gajdos. Rich people on board. Big tips, I imagine. This is true, yes?"

There was no sense trying to deny it. "Yes."

"You're not going to work on that train."

Georji nodded. "Okay."

He saw that there might be some light left here. These men didn't want him to work the bar on a train to Switzerland? That was fine. Perfect. He probably stood to make a few thousand euros. Five thousand, tops. A nice payday, but not something to die over. He would call in sick. His face was ruined anyway. There was no way he could get his teeth fixed before that train left, not even in a temporary, cosmetic way.

"You're going to call your employers the morning the train leaves. You're going to tell them you're not well and cannot make the trip. And you're also going to tell them that you've already secured a replacement. She is an exceptional bartender, as good at mixing drinks as you are. No one will notice a difference in quality."

Georji doubted it. He tended to think of himself as among the very best bartenders on the continent. This was why he found himself pouring the drinks in Ibiza, Berlin, Cannes, and anywhere else the beautiful people went.

But he didn't say that. "Okay," he said again.

"Her name is Helena. She is going to replace you on that trip."

"Yes," Georji said.

"Say the name."

"Helena," Georji said.

"That's right. Say it again."

"Helena."

"You're going to call them that morning, and tell them what?"

"Helena," he said. It hurt to speak, and his mouth made a sort of whistling sound from the broken or missing teeth. He didn't like that sound.

"Helena is what?"

"Replacing me." *Replayshing me. Oh God.*

"What will happen if you don't make that call?"

Georji knew the answer without even having to be told. "You'll kill me."

"That's right. You're a fast learner. We'll kill you. Even if you run, we'll find you, and we'll kill you. If we don't find you, we'll kill your mother. Okay?"

Georji nodded, but suddenly he was crying. They were evil. They were terrible. Gajdos was a bad man. Georji had known that, and ignored it, because Gajdos paid well. But he had these terrible enemies too. Bad men had bad enemies. He had to remember that and live by it. Bad men would beat you and kill your mother for no reason.

"So, what are you going to do the morning of the train journey?"

"Call. I'm going to call and tell them Helena is replacing me."

His whole body shook.

"That's right. Or what will happen?"

"You'll kill me."

He couldn't bear to repeat that they would kill his mother.

"Correct. And do you know how we'll kill you?"

"Shoot me," Georji said without even thinking.

"No. That would be too easy."

The two thugs holding Georji down stood and moved away from him. He sat there, facing the ground, garbage strewn all over, and wondered if they were just going to shoot him anyway. After all this, the chase, the useless talking, maybe they would just kill him in this filthy alleyway.

A fluid splashed down on him as the man upended the canister. The stench of petrol was overpowering. Georji nearly retched from it. He couldn't breathe. It was the worst smell in the world. The gasoline flowed down over his head and onto his shoulders. It soaked into his shirt.

"Oh. Oh no. Please."

"Look at me, Georji," the man said.

It was everything Georji could do to meet the man's gaze. The man had a cigarette in his mouth and a lighter in his hand. He flicked the wheel and held the flame to the tip of the cigarette. Then he inhaled deeply.

The man was playing with fire and Georji was soaked in petrol. He moaned again, a sound deep in his chest and throat.

"Don't forget," the man said.

He turned, and then the three of them simply walked away, leaving Georji alone on the ground.

CHAPTER SEVEN

1:45 am Central European Time
Engel Castle
Engeldorf-Pont, Luxembourg

"Troy? Are you all right?"

He had noticed Aliz's voice the first time he met her. Even in English, which was her fourth or fifth language, she spoke with the accent of the upper class.

He wasn't sure what it was about her voice that gave it away. But instantly you knew she had lived in the best places, had gone to the best schools, and was exposed to the very best people.

She skimmed over the top of the world like an exotic bird, landing here and there, but only in places that were pleasing to her. She had never taken a long and unpleasant bus ride. She didn't wait in lines. She didn't experience unavoidable delays. Somehow, her voice let you know all that.

"Yeah. I'm okay."

Troy stood in a pair of boxer briefs at the large bay window in her bedroom, looking up at the medieval stone castle that commanded the hillside above them. There was a wide stone wall around it, with a narrow bridge across to a gate. There were spiral towers with giant windows. The whole place was lit up in the darkness. The lights reminded him of torches burning through the night a thousand years ago, instead of the modern electric lights they were. Maybe they were designed to look that way.

They were in the old mansion where she lived, at the base of the rocky outcropping the castle stood upon. The house was huge by the standards of most people's homes. It was the tidy, modest cabin of a pauper compared to the sprawling ancient wreck that loomed on the hill.

"Why are you standing there like that?"

He shrugged. "I'm just digging that crazy castle. Every time I look at it, I think of King Arthur and white knights on horseback. It's an amazing sight. It's even more amazing that you own it."

"Well … it's in the family trust."

She often used little misdirections like that. The family this, the family that. She seemed to hope this would give him the sense that she was somehow once or twice removed from the issue at hand, as though her ownership of vast resources was something as impersonal as the weather.

"The trust you control?" he said.

"Yes."

"Hmmm."

He turned and looked at her. She was lying on the wide bed. It was larger than king size. The lights in the room were all off, but he could see her in the light cast from the castle, which was shining through the window. It created a play of light and shadow that he enjoyed. They were in the gloom, but he could see pretty well. She was leaning back on several pillows, and she had the covers pulled up to her chin.

Her hair was tousled. There was an empty bottle of white wine on the bedside table. There were two empty glasses as well.

It was cool in here, bordering on cold. Outside, the early winter was beginning to settle in. The house was old, not nearly as old as the castle, but probably late 1800s. He hadn't asked her the exact age. But it was old enough that it had little drafts and cracks that let the cold air in. To her credit, she didn't hunt them down and eliminate them. She let the house be what it was. It was a charming, old house of a vastly wealthy family, and it had its quirks.

He sighed. He liked it here.

"I got a text from work tonight. I didn't want to bring it up and kill the mood. But I have to be back in Madrid tomorrow. We have a meeting, and my presence is requested."

"Requested or required?"

He smiled. "What do you think?"

"So that's what's been troubling you?" she said.

It wasn't. Not really. He knew he was going to have to go back to Madrid soon enough. He'd been mostly out of work the past month, nursing his injuries. He'd spent a lot of that time here, as well as the past few days in New York. You could only live the fantasy so long. So, he felt fine about it.

What bothered him was Enrico Morales. The man had killed himself, and that was his decision to make. Or maybe someone had done it for him. Whichever it was, it was fine with Troy. The world was a better place without Enrico in it. The truth was, Enrico was a sicko, people knew it, and he commanded troops in the field for years.

"You got a problem with me, *pendejo*?"

Troy nearly laughed. Enrico had just called him the Spanish word for pubic hair. It was a slur and an insult, to put it mildly.

Troy was sitting at the bar in a rundown watering hole near Fort Bragg, which was the home base of a nonexistent special operations group called Metal Shop. It was where Enrico Morales was stationed.

It was the middle of the afternoon. They were back from Mexico, and Troy was about to be separated from Metal Shop and sent back to Coronado. He had been brought in for an individual debriefing before separation. Enrico shouldn't have access to the transcript from that, but—of course—he had his ways around these things.

Troy supposed he should have realized there was no way Enrico would allow reports about him, positive or negative, to happen without him finding out what was in them.

Troy took a sip of his beer. There was no sense denying it.

"Yeah, man. I got a problem with you. I think you're a nutjob. I asked them not to assign me to you anymore. I told them I think you're unfit for command."

Enrico sidled up next to Troy. There was almost no one in the bar. He didn't need to come that close.

"Listen to me, Stark. You don't decide what happens. I decide if I want you or not. I'll get you assigned to me whenever I want. You want to tell these head shrinkers you saw something bad out there? You're gonna see it again and again."

Troy shrugged. "I'm on loan from the SEALs. I don't have to come here. You and I both know that. I can decline."

"I'll make your career a living hell."

Troy turned and looked at him. "Get out of my face, Morales."

Enrico smiled. "What are you gonna do, pendejo? You gonna punch me? You gonna fight me? I don't think so."

"I'm not stupid," Troy said. "You outrank me."

Enrico shook his head. "No ranks today, my friend. Just you and me. Ain't nobody else even here. Civilian clothes. Civilian location. Nobody has to know."

Troy raised an eyebrow. "Yeah? You mean that?"

There was nothing Troy would like more than to put this bastard on the floor. Then clean the floor with his face. But first, he had to know the opportunity was real.

Enrico nodded. "Yeah. It'll give me great satisfaction to bust you up after what you did today."

Troy slid off his stool. Enrico did the same.

"I'm going to take you at your word," Troy said.

"Please do."

Suddenly, the bartender came alive down at the far end of the bar. Until now, he had been watching some afternoon TV talk show. The bar was on the far outskirts of town, but still close enough to the base that he must have known what came next.

"Guys! Don't do that in here. Outside. Please."

Enrico's eyes drifted to the bartender for a moment.

BAM!

Troy punched him in the face. It was a hard right. He followed it with a left hook, and then another right. Enrico's head went right, left, right.

He came back to center just in time to catch a knee to the balls. Troy tilted him back and delivered a head butt, the hard part of Troy's upper skull connecting to the soft parts of Enrico's face.

Then he pushed Enrico backwards over the stool and onto the grimy floor of the bar. The back of Enrico's head hit the floor. No brakes, nothing to even slow it down.

His teeth chattered when he hit.

"Buddy!" the bartender said. "I said don't do that."

Troy didn't turn around. He raised a hand. "My fault. I didn't mean it."

He looked at Enrico on the floor. Then he crouched down low next to him. He kneeled on Enrico's chest. Enrico's eyes were open, but the lights were out. His nose and mouth were bleeding, but not enough, not yet. A small dagger appeared in Troy's right hand, like a magic trick. Troy enjoyed sleight of hand like that. He gripped Enrico's head by the black hair and put the knife to his throat.

"Hey!" the bartender shouted. "I'm calling the cops."

"Don't pick me for your dirty missions anymore," Troy said to Enrico, ignoring the bartender. "Because if you do, I'll kill you."

Enrico was beginning to focus again. "Kill me," he said. "Do it."

Troy sliced the knife along Enrico's cheek, drawing a line of blood there. It was a deep cut. He flayed the skin open like he was filleting a fish.

Enrico shouted in pain. That really woke him up.

"Annnh!" He gritted his teeth, his eyes suddenly on fire. There was an unspoken threat in those eyes.

Troy put the knife to Enrico's throat again.

"Cheap shots," Enrico said. "They told me that about you."

Troy nodded. Why argue? "I'll kill you in your sleep," he said. "I'll kill you when you're on the toilet. You need surgery? I'll kill you when they put you under. Because I don't care about you. Pick me again, or mess with me at all, and you better have eyes in the back of your head. Eyes that never close. You understand?"

Enrico stared at him.

"Yeah," Troy said. "You understand."

He dropped Enrico's head to the floor again, stood up, turned to the bar, and finished his beer. The bartender had the landline phone in his hands, but he hadn't dialed anything. He just stared across at Troy.

"Sorry about that, bud."

"You didn't kill him, did you?"

Troy shook his head. "Nah. Next time."

Then he walked out. As far as he knew, Enrico Morales led at least a dozen more missions for Metal Shop over the next few years until he retired. He was the worst Troy ever worked with, but he must have been what the brass wanted.

At least he never picked Troy again after that. If he tried to hurt Troy in some other way, Troy never heard about it. And to his credit— the only thing to his credit—Enrico was as good as his word about the bar fight.

"Yeah," Troy said, now to Aliz. "It's a bummer to just get back and have to leave again."

She smiled, but it was a wistful smile, and she shook her head. "I don't believe you."

Troy arched an eyebrow. It was a trick of his. Not everybody could do it. "You don't believe me?"

"No. You've been very distant since you returned. It's as if you're here, but you're also somewhere else. Not Madrid. Somewhere in the past. I'm intuitive, you know. I can sense these things. And I want you to know that you can tell me, whatever it is."

For a moment, he considered doing that, spilling the beans on the whole story. Enrico Morales. Metal Shop. But it was a never-ending story, because those two things were hardly isolated from the rest. They were bad, but there was plenty more. Troy had spent nearly his entire adult life in combat, much of it the dirty kind, black operations. How to describe it to her?

How to even begin to explain it? It was a world where Enrico Morales could be a superstar, and Troy Stark had to *disobey orders* to rescue innocents.

Why? What was it for?

No. Better to leave it penned up. Opening the floodgates would serve no one.

"I'm fine, sweetheart. I'm really just ... eh ... not looking forward to going back just yet. I'd rather be here with you."

The wistful smile was still on her face. "Okay. If that's how you want to play it."

He nodded. "It is. For now, anyway."

She held out her arms to him. "In that case, come here. Let's not waste the time we do have."

She was right about that. He went to her and slid under the covers.

CHAPTER EIGHT

2:45 pm Central European Time
Headquarters of the European Rapid Response Investigation Unit (ERRIU)
aka El Grupo Especial
Outskirts of Madrid, Spain

"Banker's hours, Agent Stark?"

"Thank you, Agent Dubois. It's lovely to see you too."

In fact, it was lovely to see her. She was not hard on the eyes. She wore a blue jumpsuit, which Troy would almost call electric blue. The suit hugged her curves. She wore high heeled shoes and a bandana in her hair that matched the color of the jumpsuit. Her thick, curly hair was high and wide and tamed only by the blue bandana. Her red lipstick was a deep, dark red. She looked like she was going to be in a music video shoot or had just come from one.

She smiled at his comment, but it was a sly smile. Troy sipped coffee from his El Grupo coffee mug. He and Dubois had been paired up from the beginning, but it hadn't gone smoothly. He was black operations, a former Navy SEAL, and had seen a lot of combat. Sometimes, he went straight to violence as a sort of preemptive tactic.

He knew that about himself, but there wasn't much he could do to corral it. He was a gorilla, both by training and temperament. Meanwhile, she was a police officer, an investigator, a career civil servant, you might even say. During her years at Interpol, before she met Troy Stark, she rarely had a reason to draw her firearm.

Not long ago, it seemed like Agent Dubois was going to hate Troy, perhaps permanently. She claimed he was going to get her killed. For the moment, her anger appeared to have gone by the wayside. Maybe Miquel had given her a raise. That made as much sense as anything. These police budgets were moving targets. If he had learned anything so far, it was that.

This was Troy's first formal meeting in a long time. He had been gone for most of a month. Troy had been seriously injured during the CERN operation. That was how the agency described him: *seriously injured.* He supposed he had been. He came away with a cracked skull and six knife wounds, including five defensive stab wounds to his arms and one slice along his jaw line. If that last cut had been a few millimeters deeper, he might have bled out right there.

"I was under the impression that the meeting is scheduled for 3 pm," he said.

Her smile broadened. Now, she was showing very white, perfectly aligned teeth. "Oh yes," she said. "That's true. It's just that some agents arrive for a full day's work, instead of magically appearing just before a meeting starts."

Now Troy smiled too.

They were in the conference room, Dubois sitting, Troy standing. The room was spare, with a long, black table at the center. It had replaced an oval table that had been here previously. The old table had been a "dumb" table, with no technology of any kind. This seemed to be a "smart" table, with electrical outlets and data ports.

Troy hadn't brought his new laptop into the conference room, but it didn't matter. They had him covered. There were small tablet computers on the table at intervals, standing upright on little tripods. There was a large video screen mounted on the wall at one end of the room—with a low, black table below it, piled with snaking wires and stacked processing units, red and green lights blinking.

He had come in late this morning from Luxembourg. He hadn't booked a flight ahead of time, things were mostly sold out, and the scheduled commercial flights from Luxembourg to Madrid that remained were not good. Fly from Luxembourg east to Berlin for a two-hour layover, then fly west and south to Madrid. Or fly north to London for a six-hour layover, then fly back south to Madrid and appear here later this evening. In the end, Aliz had simply booked, and paid for, a private jet to take him here.

When he had asked her how much it was costing her, she smiled and waved the very idea away. "Oh, don't give it another thought. It's silly to fly to Berlin to go to Madrid. This is much better."

It was an odd feeling, to have such things handed to him. He was accustomed to working hard for everything he got.

"May I come in?" someone said.

Troy turned and Carlo Gallo was standing in the doorway. He didn't have any computer equipment with him, either.

"Carlo Gallo," Troy said. "The international man of mystery."

Gallo stepped into the room. He made quite an impression. He had a perfectly white beard framing his face and a shock of white hair on top of his head.

"Please. Call me Carl."

He stood about six feet tall and was very tan, with broad shoulders. He wore a tight, leather jacket, tight, blue jeans, and boots. For a man in his fifties, he was very fit. His eyes were wild but also jolly. He looked a little bit like a muscled-up Santa Claus.

"That's all right," he said. "Don't bother to get up."

"Okay," Dubois said. "We won't."

The most obvious thing about Gallo now was the long vertical scar that went down the right side of his face. Gallo was ex-CIA, if there was such a thing, and he claimed to have been Special Operations Group. Troy didn't buy it. The CIA didn't just let those guys walk away into the sunset.

Either way, whatever he was really doing, Gallo had hung his own shingle in Amsterdam as a security expert for hire. Miquel had brought him on as an intelligence consultant right before the CERN operation. Apparently, they were old friends who had infiltrated Basque separatist cells together way back in the 1990s.

He had to give Gallo some credit. He acted like this consulting gig was really a field agent position. He put himself right in harm's way and took a gunshot to the face. Troy had heard that Gallo had already been through three surgeries on it, with a few more to go. So, he had courage, and he was rugged. He could take a licking and keep on ticking.

But he had to subtract credit away from him too. He had disappeared during CERN and had never explained to anyone where he went, what he did, and how he got that gunshot wound. Troy had the sense that Gallo was going to be one of these people who might be good in a tight spot, or he might evaporate.

Troy didn't trust him. That's what it all came down to.

"How's your face?" Troy said, ever one to kick a sore spot.

Gallo shook his head seriously. "I don't know. How does it look?"

Troy stared at the scar. "Well, you weren't that beautiful to begin with."

Gallo smiled. It was genuine. "You never saw me when I was young."

Okay. He had to give some credit back to him. He had a thick skin. In Troy Stark World, that went a long way.

Jan Bakker came sidling into the conference room, a black laptop tucked under one arm, a mug of coffee in his free hand. He wore a dress shirt and khaki pants that were tight to his body. Bakker was huge. Tall, for one thing, but almost impossibly broad as well. His wide shoulders just about fit through the door.

He was a genetic anomaly. Guys like this often went to chub as they reached their thirties. As big as Jan was, he didn't seem to have an ounce of fat on him.

He looked at Troy. "Agent Stark, back from holiday, I see?"

These people were too much. Troy had been stabbed. He took a rifle butt to the skull. Bakker hadn't even been anywhere near the action. Because as big and strong as he was, he wasn't a field agent. He was an intelligence analyst. He was exceptionally good at that, and indeed, everybody said he was the best. But you'd never find him out there in the midst of the chaos.

Miquel Castro-Ruiz finally came walking in. He was the reason Troy was back in Spain, so he might as well show up for his own meeting. Miquel was the reason for the whole thing. He was the reason for this headquarters out in a far-flung suburb, and he was the reason they were all hanging around CERN when the terrorists hit it. Miquel was, very quietly, a sharp guy and a shrewd operator.

He held a hand out to Troy. "Agent Stark."

Troy took it and shook. "Director Castro."

Miquel was several inches shorter than Troy. He was a small, middle-aged guy. He had a thick head of mostly black hair spotted with strands of gray. The last time Troy had seen him, he was clean shaven. Now, he had grown a salt-and-pepper goatee. He was dressed in a blue suit that fit him well, but he was not in the same condition as his friend Gallo, and certainly not the same as Troy or Agent Dubois.

"I see everyone's here," Miquel said. "So, let's begin."

They took their seats at the table.

"I'm not going to make a big presentation about this. Jan has prepared a dossier for everyone to read more when the meeting is over. Agent Dubois and I were in Lyon yesterday. You've all heard something about the train crash in Scotland, yes?"

Everyone nodded. Troy had seen something about it on TV. He hadn't paid much attention to it. There had been some sort of malfunction. A bunch of people had died.

"It wasn't an accident," Miquel said. "It was a hijacking that went wrong. The train line had recently been converted to electric power and networked to a central computer system. The power could be controlled from the cockpit of the train, or in an emergency, from an external control room. Someone hacked the system and took control of the train. Then they sped it up to the point where it could no longer handle the turns and it derailed. Meanwhile, a group of hijackers on the train robbed everyone on board. They also committed at least one murder."

"It was my impression," Troy said, "that nearly everyone on the train died."

Miquel nodded. "They did."

"Did the hijackers escape?"

"No."

"So, they died too?"

"There appear to have been five of them," Miquel said. "Four of them died in the crash. One survived and was airlifted to a hospital in Edinburgh. He's in critical condition. His name is Dean Carver. He's Canadian."

"Do they think the crash was a mistake?" Gallo said. "I mean, why would they hijack a train only to have it crash and nearly all of them die?"

"They don't know if it was a mistake," Miquel said. "But I tend to think that it wasn't. Jan can explain why I think that. Jan?"

Bakker nodded. His laptop was open, and he was staring into it as if he was about to read from something there. "To hack the train's computer and make it speed up is a relatively simple affair. Increase speed? Yes or no. Yes, in this case. I've investigated the security that was employed when the system was developed, and it was rudimentary. It doesn't take much thought to see why. Who would hack into a moving train? Just to speed it up? Why would they pick this train system specifically? The answer, if you're developing this train management system, and you're hoping to control costs to some degree, is they wouldn't. There is no good reason to hack the train. This is especially true because the central control room would likely notice the hack in progress and seize back control of the train immediately."

"But that didn't happen?" Troy said.

Jan shook his head. "No. As soon as the train's control system was overridden and the train began to increase speed, the control room was hit by what we call a denial-of-service attack. And it was very large. What that means is a computer system suddenly receives so many automated requests for information, or for tasks to be completed, that it is overwhelmed and is unable to respond. It is like the system becomes plugged with mud and it slows to a crawl. The central operators were unable to regain control of the train. They weren't even able to contact it. Moments later, it crashed along a sharp curve on a viaduct."

"Why didn't the driver deploy the manual braking system?"

Jan nodded. "The evidence we have suggests that he tried to do exactly that. There was too much energy compelling the train forward. The brakes simply snapped from the immense force they were subjected to."

"So, you're saying the crash happened on purpose?" Troy said.

"Yes, I believe so," Jan said.

"The hijackers were on board, but the hacking was coming from somewhere else?"

Jan nodded again. "Yes."

"Could it be a coincidence? It doesn't make sense."

Miquel was shaking his head. "The little bit they got from Carver before he had to be sedated was that he believed the train was going to slow down so they could get off. The hijackers were double-crossed. To me, it only makes sense if this attack was just practice for something more important."

"Get hijackers on board undetected," Gallo said. "Then hack the train system. It worked. It's a proof of concept. The real attack can move forward. So now everyone on this train becomes expendable, including the hijackers."

Miquel nodded. "Exactly. Especially the hijackers."

"How many train systems are there?" Troy said.

"In Europe?" Miquel said.

"Sure. For starters."

Miquel looked at Jan.

Jan shook his head. "Oh, I would need to research that a little bit. If you include urban metro systems, commuter rail systems, intercity rail, international high-speed rail, and sightseeing tourist trains like the Scottish train ..." He trailed off.

"Hundreds in Europe alone. There are almost too many to count, with no obvious method for vetting them."

"The man in Scotland is under sedation?" Dubois said.

"For now," Miquel said. "He was badly injured, and they had to open his skull."

"But he's expected to survive?"

Miquel shrugged. "I don't think they know that yet."

"Well," Dubois said. "We're an investigative arm, are we not? Maybe we should take a trip up there in case he wakes up. If he does, we can have a little chat with him, as the English say."

Troy liked where she was going with this.

"Maybe we should wake him up ourselves," he said.

Miquel nodded, but he also raised a hand. "I need to talk to my bosses first. We will need permission to speak with the man, not just from Interpol, but probably from the UK National Crime Agency, the local police, and the hospital itself."

"How long will all that take?" Troy said.

"Could be tomorrow," Miquel said. "Could be a month from now."

CHAPTER NINE

"He's right up here."

The three men, dressed in blue surgical gowns and gloves, masks covering their faces, walked the darkened hallway to the isolated area of the ward where the prisoner was being kept.

Two of the men were gangsters from Manchester. The third was an actual doctor, and he worked here at the hospital. Ray Greene was one of the gangsters, although that was not his name. It occurred to him that the doc must be getting paid quite a bit of money to take on a risk like this. Either that, or the doc was the most confident man in the kingdom.

A fat policeman sat in a metal chair at the far end of the hall. He was supposed to be guarding the prisoner. The way he sprawled there suggested the uncomfortable chair was interfering with his sleep. It was not that late, but this end of the hospital was deathly quiet. There were no patients down here except the train hijacker, and no one was coming to visit him. The dibble looked like he'd much prefer to be home, asleep on his couch with the telly playing in the background.

He looked up, bleary-eyed, as the three men approached.

"I'm just going to show these gentlemen the patient," the doctor said.

The dibble nodded. He rose from the chair that was so bedeviling him.

"I'm gonna go down to the café. Get a cuppa."

"We'll be just a few moments," the doctor said.

The fat bluebottle didn't say anything. He just nodded and walked off down the hallway, the way they had come. For all Ray Greene knew, the cop was being paid off too. He certainly took a powder as if their arrival was his cue to leave.

With the policeman gone, the three men went inside the room. It was dark in there. The window shades were pulled down. Dean Carver lay flat on the bed, asleep. He was the only one there.

He looked very tired. He looked like he was a hundred years old. His face was swollen and discolored, and yet somehow, he seemed drawn, as if he had lost much of his bodyweight. With his eyes closed, he could be dead, the victim of a severe beating. Both of his arms were in casts. His right leg was in a cast from high on his thigh to his ankle. There was a cast stabilizing his neck. His head was shaven, and a wide scar ran over the right side of its crown. He wore a transparent, plastic bag over the top of his head, like a shower cap.

Also, he was secured to the bed. His right wrist was fastened to the metal rails of the bed with steel handcuffs. His left ankle was bound in the same way. Even if he somehow woke up feeling healthy and energetic, he was almost completely immobilized. He wasn't going anywhere. Various machines monitored his vital signs.

The doctor walked straight to Carver's bed. He positioned himself near Carver's bare feet. For an instant, Greene wondered if the man's feet were bare as a punishment. It was chilly and drafty in this old hospital. Greene wouldn't put it past the police to deny the man socks just because they didn't like him.

After all, Carver was the most hated man in all of Britain at the moment. A few politicians must be breathing a sigh of relief that someone worse than them had appeared on the scene.

The good doctor took out a disposable syringe, peeled the paper covering away, and removed the cap.

"Morphine and fentanyl," the doctor said. "It'll do the job fast." He made a brief gesture, a hand flick, at Carver. It was a gesture of dismissal. "In this case, I doubt anyone will investigate too closely."

He looked at Greene and the other gangster, a man calling himself Simons.

"I wonder if you gentlemen will give me some assistance?"

"That's what we're here for, doc," Simons said.

*****

Three men entered his room.

They were quiet, almost silent. There was a sudden change in the light as they came in. The weak light from the hallway flooded into the room, but then disappeared again after the door closed.

It didn't matter. The light didn't awaken Dean Carver. He was already awake.

He didn't want to sleep. Not at a time like this. He had been prescribed powerful painkillers for his many broken bones and internal injuries. He had been prescribed a drug that would make him sleep.

But he couldn't afford to sleep. The train robbery was a set-up, a double cross. Whoever had hired them didn't want them to live. And that meant there must be a price on Dean's head now. There should be a phalanx of police protecting him at all times, and there wasn't. They were setting him up to be killed.

He was being careful. He didn't refuse the painkiller or the sleeping pill. He palmed them. And when the nurse left the room, he slipped them into the top of his thigh cast. He was running out of room in there.

He didn't refuse the IV morphine drip, with the controller placed into his hand. In fact, when the pain became unbearable, he gave himself a dose. He could just about move his thumb enough to press the button. But it was rare that he did so.

He had to stay alert. Lying in this bed, he hovered in a state beyond agony. At times, the pain became surreal, and he seemed to float above his body where it lay. At those times, he thought maybe he was already dead. It would be a relief to be dead and to escape this tormented and broken body.

On the other hand, he believed in the reality of God and the Devil and in Heaven and Hell. He had done some very bad things during his time here. He feared for his immortal soul. If he died now, there was no doubt where he was going next.

He breathed deeply, his chest rising and falling. One eye was open, just a slit. The button for the IV drip was pressed into his palm. There was another button, red in color. It was hanging on the bed frame. It was a call button he could use to alert the nurse's station in an emergency. He would have to reach for it, and he had a hard time moving at all. He could see now, only in retrospect, his mistake in allowing the nurse to drape it over the railing. That was the button he should have in his hand.

The three men approached the bed. They were dressed in medical gowns, gloves, and masks. Carver watched them through his tiny sliver of sight. If they were medical personnel, they would have turned on the lights. The only part of them that was visible was their eyes, which would make them hard to identify.

But they're on video. Don't they know they're on video?

One of the men went to the foot of his bed.

Of the other two men, one went to Dean's right side, and one to his left. The man at the bottom pulled out a syringe. In the dim half-light, Dean watched him hold it up and remove the cap. A tiny pop of fluid squirted out.

Dean didn't know if he was going to be able to move. One of his feet was tied to the bed frame. One of his wrists was also. Everything else was broken and battered. It was going to take every ounce of energy he had to stop these men.

"Morphine and fentanyl. It'll do the job fast."

The job? What job? Were they going to kill him? He steeled himself for a gigantic effort of will. He had heard that people in extreme desperation could lift small cars off of toddlers. At the vest least, he could reach for the emergency button.

"I wonder if you gentlemen will give me some assistance?"

"That's what we're here for, doc," said the man to Dean's right.

"You see that button he's holding? It's also morphine. Please press his thumb down on the button."

One of the men took Dean's hand. The men were wearing surgical gloves. They would leave no fingerprints.

"No," Dean croaked. His voice was barely louder than a whisper.

"He's awake," said the man who was holding Dean's hand on the button.

"Sshhhhhh," said the man at the bottom of the bed. He nodded at the man holding Dean's hand. "Go ahead, then."

The man next to Dean depressed his thumb on the button that controlled the morphine drip. It was that easy, and they had him. In a few seconds, the morphine was coursing through his bloodstream. The pain began to subside. The beautiful feeling began to overtake him, the feeling where he didn't care about what happened.

As he watched, the man at the foot of the bed spread his two middle toes and administered the shot. Dean barely felt the needle go in. The man fully depressed the plunger and then he looked up at the two other men.

"That'll do it."

"That's all?"

The man down by his feet gestured at the morphine drip again. "Give him another go with the morphine drip, just to make sure."

The man next to Dean pressed his finger to the button again.

The man at the bottom stepped back. "Won't be long now."

Dean floated above them. They no longer seemed important. Resisting them was not on his mind anymore. He gazed down upon his battered body. It looked like the body of a stray dog hit by a lorry, dead by the side of the road.

Time passed. It was hard to say how much time. Dean looked again at the three men who had murdered him and was surprised to see that they were no longer there. It was just an empty room now, with a dead body on   a   bed.

CHAPTER TEN

God, this hurts.

Lucien lay on his back on the wide bed. Across from him, the double doors were thrown open, and he could see the bright disk of the moon high over the water. It was a very cool night, which he enjoyed.

He and his two lovelies lay nude under soft, heavy blankets. They were asleep on either side of him, nestled against his strong body. But in another sense, he was alone. They were young women, of course, but in terms of maturity, they might as well be small children. They knew nothing of the work he did and the risks he took to provide this venue where they could bask in their youth and beauty and childlike innocence.

They knew nothing of the psychic pain that he endured.

A small digital device lay on top of the blanket. A white wire extended from it to a tiny earphone in his left ear. The sounds of the recording could only be heard by Lucien.

"While my mother was very pregnant with me," a female voice said, "my father impregnated another woman, Imane, an Algerian who worked as a domestic at our home in Paris."

It was his sister speaking, in fact his half-sister, Aliz Willems. Lucien kept her medieval palace of a home in Luxembourg under surveillance. Sometimes, he could infiltrate workmen who bugged the place, and sometimes, they were able to infiltrate again to retrieve the bugs.

He never tired of listening to Aliz. It was fascinating to him, the way some scientists must be fascinated by the insects they find under rocks.

Aliz was everything he did not want to be—spoiled, entitled, self-centered, self-aggrandizing. She was at the absolute center of her own universe. She was the heroine, perfectly good, of the adventure story she had been telling herself since childhood.

He hated listening to Aliz speak of his beloved mother. He hated it, and yet was mesmerized by it at the same time. He couldn't stop himself.

Get my mother's name out of your mouth.

This was all the more embarrassing because on this recording, she was obviously drunk, and she was confessing these things to the American spy, double agent, or whatever he was, Troy Stark. Stark's female partner at Interpol was also in the room. It was the night before they went to Lucien's old convent in the champagne country of France and massacred Lucien's men.

Aliz prattled on, "My father was at the embassy there. Of course, he never acknowledged the child publicly, but he did provide for both mother and child. Luc was born Lucien Mebarak and grew up in a Paris high-rise, a building full of doctors and lawyers and other professionals. Luc and Imane never wanted for anything—Luc went to very good schools. But they didn't have ..."

There was a brief pause.

"All of the comforts that comes with being a Willems. The best schools, the best homes, the luxury, and the mingling with the elite of Europe. Luc did not experience these things. But he knew what he was missing."

He did know. He had always known. She was right about that much. He was a bright boy, and the signs were impossible for him to miss.

"I'm afraid Luc hates me," Aliz said.

Did he hate her? He couldn't say. He had feelings for her, certainly. And they were intense feelings. He loved her, in his way. And he delighted in tormenting her when he could. He would not mind destroying her. No, he wouldn't kill her. But if he could completely demolish her reputation, strip her of everything she loved, and leave her desolate and humiliated, he would do it.

Then perhaps he would bring her here and comfort her, hiding from her that he was the very source of her destruction.

"He has the meanness and the greed that has defined my family through the centuries," Aliz said. "The Shadow. He has it. He is it."

The Shadow. She used the contrived, simplistic, and likely plagiarized central concept of her book, or graduate thesis, or whatever it was, to define her own brother. She had no access to any other ideas.

It was mortifying to listen to her. And it did hurt him. She was twisting the knife now.

Lucien was the bastard son, and Aliz was the darling daughter. The facts never left him. They traveled by his side always and overshadowed everything he had ever done. All these years, he had worked hard, nonstop, and had taken mad risks, all to build the fortune he now enjoyed. But it wasn't enough. He had to have more. He must dwarf not just what Aliz did (he had accomplished that long ago), but what the entire Willems lineage had done through the centuries. He was going to beat them, all of them, just to finally prove that he was one of them.

Aliz still spoke to him and about him. Her rich voice probed deep into his brain. "Luc has become involved with very dangerous people over the years. Sicilian and Russian mafias. Mexican cartels. Afghan warlords. Maybe darker than these. He seems to have a boundless appetite for dealing with the worst people on Earth."

She thought of him as a monster. He knew that. Perhaps he had turned himself into a monster, all in search of an acceptance that would never come. Or maybe she was the monster, though she would never consider it. In her mind, she was his victim.

"Luc has computer experts at his disposal who leave trails across the dark web, and the internet proper, that lead back to my foundation. He has mocked my work to my face, and through his actions, he makes a mockery of my hope to have our money help the world. He mocks it even further by tangling up the foundation in his web of lies."

Lucien had heard enough for tonight. He turned off the digital player, took the ear bud out, and placed the earphones on the bed.

She was right. Over the years, he had sought to undermine her charitable foundation and point out to the world her hypocrisy and the hypocrisy of their father. It had never worked. The Willems family were too wealthy, too well-connected, to be stained by even a hint of wrongdoing.

And she was right that he had computer experts at his disposal. The latest trick they had developed was to hack into the computer systems of modern train lines and speed up the trains themselves until they went out of control. The hack had been explained to him as a rather simple procedure that exploited an obvious fault in the networks.

The designers hadn't considered that an outside party might have reason to increase the speed of a train, then sever anyone's ability to slow it down again. Such a thing wouldn't have been possible in the long era of diesel locomotives, or even just ten years ago, in the era of manually operated electric rails. And why would anyone do it anyway?

Istvan Gajdos was why. The man was more than just an oligarch whose closeness to the Hungarian dictator brought him wealth and power beyond measure. He was also a thief, practically a common criminal.

Gajdos was a silent partner in an eastern European cryptocurrency exchange called FiSafe. The exchange was anything but safe. Gajdos had his own hackers, and more than a billion euros worth of crypto had gone missing from FiSafe in the past year. It appeared that Gajdos had funded the exchange merely so he could steal from it. Lucien had a grudging admiration for that.

The missing crypto was the domestic coin of FiSafe, a currency optimistically called SafeCoin. It had collapsed in value since the theft, down perhaps eighty percent. But that didn't mean it had no value. Interest had waned, but SafeCoin was still traded. Twenty percent of a billion was two hundred million. And given the wild fluctuations of the crypto market, there was a very good chance the price would rise again.

Lucien was going to take the crypto, and Gajdos was going to hand it over to safe his own skin. Gajdos was going to make Lucien richer than the young Lucien had ever imagined, richer than any Willems in history.

The European authorities would not know, or likely care, that it had happened. Gajdos would be the victim of a robbery, and he would lose the untraceable crypto that he himself stole. Who was he supposed to report this to?

Would he even live to report it? Anatoly Sokolov had no love for the oligarchs of former communist countries. And Gajdos would be at his mercy.

It was better if Sokolov killed Gajdos. Lucien saw that perfectly. And it would be even better if Sokolov died, too, taking everyone with him. Sokolov was a dark force, and it would be troubling to have him loose in the world, wondering if Lucien Mebarak had underpaid him.

A new idea occurred to Lucien.

His sweet sister Aliz had betrayed him and had now taken Troy Stark as her lover. How did she not see that Lucien and Stark were enemies? She must see it. She probably took delight in it. But what if there was a way to eliminate Stark? Surely that would crush Aliz.

What if Troy Stark was on the train with Gajdos? And what if Sokolov made good on his promise to destroy the train and everyone on it?

Stark was with Interpol now. To be more precise, he was with a secret offshoot agency of Interpol. They were almost certainly taking part in investigating the train crash in Scotland. Knowing Stark, he would want to be on a train that was speeding out of control high in the Austrian Alps. He would want to be the hero that stopped the train. Maybe Stark had a death wish. Maybe he would like nothing more than to die in a fiery train wreck. Lucien could oblige him.

It would not take much to leak the hijacking, or even just drop a hint about it, to the small police group that Stark had joined. Just a little morsel, first to call their attention to it, to whet their appetite, then hook them and reel them in.

It would be a betrayal of Sokolov, but Sokolov would likely never find out. If the timing was right, Sokolov and Stark would face off against each other only after the crypto transaction was completed.

Risky, yes. But Lucien had taken many risks before now. And how glorious would it be for Lucien to become filthy rich and put an end to Troy Stark, all in the same day?

Troy Stark was like a common criminal in a hospital bed in Scotland—not very bright and just a loose end to be snipped off.

Lucien picked up the phone from his side table and dialed a number. This call was secure. It was to the man who ran the computer operation.

"Yeah?" the man said. Not pleasant, but Lucien had no qualms about calling him at this hour. The man was awake. It was his job to be awake.

"I want you to alert a certain agency to our activities," Lucien said. "I want you to make it look like someone is probing our Hungarian friend's network for weaknesses. I want the agency to see this."

"It doesn't make sense," the man said. "We've already pierced the Hungarian's network. We can assume command any time we want."

"Right, but can you make it look like you're probing it?"

"We can make it look like someone else is."

"So do that. I want it obvious. I want you to call their attention to it."

"What's the agency?" the man said.

Lucien told him.

The man sighed. It was a long sigh, like a mechanical device running down and dying. "You're playing a dangerous game."

"Yes," Lucien said.

"There's a lot of money at stake."

"Have you been paid?" Lucien said. "Have I paid you?"

"Yes," the man said. "Very well. Exceedingly well."

Lucien smiled. No risk, no reward.

"Then do what I ask and let me worry about the money."

CHAPTER ELEVEN

December 16
5:45 am Central European Time
Just before dawn
Keleti Rail Yard
Budapest, Hungary

"Uncle Joe?" someone whispered near him.

Anatoly Sokolov was not asleep. He was not dreaming. He was in a sort of fugue state between asleep and awake. He knew where he was. He was lying under a tarpaulin on a flatcar parked in a bleak train yard. He was wedged between large wooden crates that would soon be shipped somewhere.

"Joe?" the voice said again. "Joe!"

Now, the person poked him.

Sokolov sighed. Uncle Joe, Stalin's old nickname, was his code name for this train hijacking and this robbery of Gajdos. As Sokolov came back to the present moment, the weight of the years that had passed seemed to fall onto his shoulders in a second. After all this time, he was still working and still risking his life. Was it worth it?

Was it worth what? There were no rewards at all.

He had been a failure as a husband. He was a miserable failure as a father. He had spent long years in prison, and his boy was growing up without knowing him. And yet, it was almost better that way. Sokolov was a bad person. He had killed many people, and he couldn't even claim that the ends justified the means. None of it had amounted to anything.

He pulled the wool cap off his face and opened his eyes.

A man was crouched there, his head perfectly bald. Sokolov happened to know that he shaved it because it was already so far gone with male pattern baldness. There was no sense keeping the little bit that was left.

For this job, the man was calling himself Ivan, as in Ivan the Terrible.

"Yeah?" Sokolov said.

"The train is here," Ivan said. He had sincere eyes, like a baby seal. He looked like someone who could get his feelings hurt. He couldn't, but that was how he looked.

"It's time to move."

Sokolov nodded. A moment later, he watched the train yard from under the tarp. The place filled him with dread. It was a vast yard, covered in melting snow and dirty mud puddles. The grounds were not paved. Steam rose. It had snowed yesterday evening, but the temperature had warmed up overnight.

Countless lines of track twisted, turned, and led off toward the horizon in what seemed like every direction. The rails glittered, reflecting the brightening morning sky. Yard lights were blinking here and there. Some of them were night lights that would go off soon. Sokolov could hardly make sense of any of it. He had slept only fitfully on this flatcar, and he could use a cup of coffee and a smoke. There was no time for that now.

To the left, a few freight cars were standing. Everything over there was still. In front of him, and snaking off to the right, was a monstrous freight train, easily one hundred cars long, probably more. Many of the cars were tall, two stories high. Three cars in a row carried small mountains of coal in the open air. The train moved slowly, with a stolid, solemn rhythm. The front of it was already far away.

Sokolov noticed that the ground was shaking. The train was so heavy that it made the Earth tremble.

A man in coveralls and work boots passed, carrying a lunch pail. The morning was chilly, in the sense that the chill got into a person's bones, and the man's body seemed to hunch against the cold.

Sokolov watched him cross several tracks until he reached a group of men, maybe a hundred meters from here. The men all wore coveralls and stood in a rough circle, talking, smoking cigarettes, and drinking from thermoses. There must be a shift change taking place.

"Where is our train?" Sokolov said.

"Hard right," Ivan said. "Near the washing station."

Sokolov looked to the right. There was an old, wooden roundhouse over there in the medium distance, steam rising from all of its entrances and exits, as if it was on fire. It seemed to sit in the middle of a small lake, the ground reflective all around it.

A sleek, modern train was moving slowly away from the roundhouse. The train was brightly painted in red, white, and green horizontal stripes, the colors of the Hungarian flag. The colors seemed garish, loud, and presumptuous compared to the muted browns and blacks and rust colors of the rail yard and the trains found there.

Looking closely, Sokolov could see that the train was nearly all windows, smoked, and painted over with the colors. It was a shiny thing, this train, positively gleaming, a young trophy wife compared to the old battle axes lurching through the rail yard. This train wanted to be the center of attention. It was eager for your lustful gaze.

Gajdos must be very proud indeed. Without him, the train would not exist. He had caused it to be made, and it matched his personality.

Sokolov was going to kill this train.

"It just had a bath, eh?"

Ivan nodded. "Probably it will have one more at a train yard in Vienna before the guests board."

"Where are Peter and Vlad?"

Peter was named for Peter the Great. Vlad was named for Vladimir Dracul, also known as Vlad the Impaler, the medieval Transylvanian prince who tortured and killed many of his peasants and who was thought to be the original model for Count Dracula.

Ivan, here with Sokolov, was the smart one, logistics, and he also happened to be able to drive the train. Peter and Vlad were younger guys, big and strong, intimidating and remorseless. They could break your arms and legs, or they could murder you. It would make no difference to them. And of course, the inside "man," on this crew, so to speak, was the lovely and talented Helena of Troy. Much hinged on her getting herself aboard and blending in unnoticed.

This group would be nothing without its sense of humor. It was a good team, and Sokolov had worked with all of the individuals involved before. He trusted them to do exactly what he asked of them.

"Peter and Vlad are hidden two cars down from us," Ivan said. "When they see us pass, they will wait another few minutes, then move to their position aboard the train."

Sokolov nodded. "Okay. Good job. Let's go."

Ivan poked his head all the way out from under the tarp and looked both ways, like a careful child about to cross a busy street. He slipped out from the tarp, climbed over the side of the rail car, and dropped to his feet on the ground. Then he reached back inside and got his gear bag. It was like the bag in which a hockey player would carry his equipment, except it was gray and unexceptional in any way.

Ivan slung the heavy bag over his shoulder. Then he reached back under the tarp and came out with his own lunchbox. They would be hidden inside the train for most of a day. They would each need to eat. He began walking toward the train.

From the back, Ivan looked like a man you might expect to see walking through a rail yard. He wore jeans, heavy work boots, a dirty rain slicker, and a gray wool hat on his head. Carrying that bag and his lunch, he thoroughly faded into the background. He was just a guy here to do a job.

Sokolov glanced at the real train workers, congregating at the other side of the yard. They didn't seem to have noticed anything about Ivan. So, Sokolov slid out from under the tarp on the flat car, much the way Ivan had done. He reached back, got his gear bag and his lunch box, and followed Ivan.

They both walked with a certain nonchalance, as if they belonged here and were in no hurry. Up ahead, Ivan passed through a valley between the flatcar and a pile of railway ties, for a moment rendering him invisible to onlookers. Sokolov followed him through there.

As Ivan exited the valley, he looked both ways again. That was the only movement that might possibly give him away. A seasoned rail worker probably knew where the trains all were just by the sound.

From behind them came the sound of metal hammering metal. The ground shook again, with each hammer blow, as if a pole was being driven into the earth. The ground here probably shook quite a lot. Then a new sound came, SSSSS, the sound of compressed air being released. It was nearly ear-splitting.

Sokolov was much closer to the Gajdos train now. Ahead of him, Ivan walked straight to an open passenger door, climbed the stairs into the car, and disappeared. *Voila!* Magic. Now you see him, now you don't.

Sokolov crossed the open space. It was the most vulnerable moment, where he was clearly visible to someone who might be watching. Who was he? Who did he work for? What was he doing here? What was his task?

There were no good answers to these questions. If someone discovered him this close to the train, then that person would have to die.

Somewhere behind him, a whistle blew. It didn't mean anything. It was just a typical train yard sound. No one yelled. No person came running.

Sokolov reached the passenger door. Like Ivan, he didn't look around at all. He simply climbed the steps and into the train. He turned left at the top. Ivan was standing in a narrow hallway, grinning back at him.

He had a long, metal tool in his hand, which he had used to open a trapdoor in the floor. The door opened away from Sokolov, giving the gap in the floor the effect of an open mouth facing him.

"Into the bowels," Ivan said.

Sokolov didn't hesitate. He walked up to the hole, turned around, and climbed down the short ladder that was bolted there. When his feet touch the bottom, he unslung his bag and pushed it into the tunnel under the floor. Then he bent and crawled in behind it. Ivan's bag was already down here.

A moment later, Ivan came down the ladder and yanked the trapdoor closed behind him. A lock mechanism engaged as he pulled the door shut. Instantly, the space became almost completely dark, the only light coming from outside the train through tiny narrow slits where metal met metal, and from a series of ventilators in one wall.

Sokolov took a deep breath. It was a close space, like being buried in a tomb.

"We're locked in," Ivan said.

Sokolov nodded. "I feel that," he said. "It's like being back in prison, when they put you in the hole."

"I always liked the hole," Ivan said. "It gave me time to myself, time to think. A man with education, with a life of the mind, can last a long time in the hole."

Sokolov smiled. "I feel that too."

CHAPTER TWELVE

6:50 am Central European Time
An Apartment Block
Outskirts of Madrid, Spain

"What floor?" Miquel said.

The old man who served as the building superintendent wore dirty, green workpants and a heavy rain jacket that was caked in black grime along the bottom. His face was lined with white whiskers on his chin. His dark eyes were deep set and mournful.

This was a sad, dead-end place to live. It was probably even worse to try to run it.

The group stood outside, in the courtyard of the high rise in the dark, early morning, an hour and a half before sunrise. There was the super and a squad of four door kickers from the Madrid Policia Municipal. And there was a second squad from El Grupo, the usual suspects—Miquel, Troy, Dubois, and Gallo. The call had come in during the night—a hacker group was trying to attack the Madrid Metro train system.

Steady, cold rain was falling. Only Miquel and the old man were talking.

"Siete."

Seven. Even Troy Stark understood that much.

"Elevator?"

The old man shook his head. He raised one finger. *"Solamente uno. No funciona ahora. Esta en reparacion."*

"There's only one elevator," Miquel translated. "And it's not working. It's being fixed."

Troy stared up at the gray, wet building looming above them. It was tall, probably twenty stories high. And the elevator was out. That might be funny, except there were probably old ladies and handicapped people of various kinds living in there, trapped on the fifteenth floor. It didn't matter if you were talking about the Bronx or Madrid, or probably Mumbai for that matter, there were always plenty of old and handicapped people in a building like this one.

The elevators were always out, but in the process of being fixed. It could be a long process. Right nearby, there were ten or fifteen more buildings in a ring, just like this one, and in the same state of disrepair.

Places like this, tucked away out of sight on the far edge of Madrid, maybe ten miles from downtown, were a bit of a disgrace. They put the lie to the myth of Europe as some beacon of progress, prosperity, and openness. Troy had been here only a short time, but he could see that much already.

His small but elegant apartment in La Latina, and the fancy restaurants and museums he went to with Aliz, were a world away from here. The runway models and footballers doing fashion shoots and laughing it up on nighttime TV talk shows might as well be on another planet.

On the edge of this development of high rises, and all around it, was a large shantytown of tumbledown shacks and dirt pathways, turned to brown mud on a day like today. The people inside the buildings were the lucky ones. At least they were warm. They had electricity. They were out of the elements.

The whole area was a warehouse for Gypsys from Eastern Europe, refugees from wars in the Middle East, and new immigrants who had made the boat voyage across from North Africa. The place was a breeding ground for crime, and possibly, terrorism.

Miquel seemed to believe the Atocha train bombers had planned their attacks from this neighborhood. That might be why he insisted on being in on this raid. He didn't need to be awake and out here in the rain. None of them did—Miquel had told his group, again and again, that their role today was as observers from Interpol. They were to offer assistance only in an emergency.

Then why bother coming out? Maybe Miquel was trying to fix something that was permanently broken. He was certainly acting like he was in charge.

"Ellos estan aqui?" he said. Are they here?

The man nodded. *"Si, senor. Quatro o cinco."* He shrugged.

Troy understood well enough. There were four or five of them.

The man opened the heavy, steel door to the building with his key. The door let them in a back way, where there was a concrete stairwell. The police clambered up the stairs silently. The element of surprise was important here. The only sound was their boots on the stairs, and even that sound was muted.

Normally, Troy might seek to take the lead here and be the first in the door. But that job was going to the Madrid cops. This was their show. El Grupo was not supposed to engage with the subjects. That was fine with Troy. He didn't want to engage.

"How many people have you killed in your life?" Aliz had asked him the other day.

How many had he killed? It was a hard question to answer honestly. He had probably killed close to twenty people in just the past couple of months. Since the terror attack on the tourist attraction in New York City, and the original call from Missing Persons, he had been stacking up bad guys like wood for a fireplace. How many? Three or four in Luxembourg. Five or maybe more at the old convent in France. The guy on the Brooklyn Bridge. A pile of bodies at the human trafficking auction in Algiers. A bunch of terrorists at CERN, including three people who died in a helicopter he shot down. Was he missing anyone?

Oh, yes. Dozens of enemies he had killed in war zones.

"I don't know, sweetheart," he said. "But I do know this. I've only ever killed bad guys, people who are out to hurt other people, usually innocent people."

That was true, probably, or close to true. It was the best he could do on the fly.

Now, they stood completely still in the dim, yellow light of the seventh-floor hallway. The group was positioned in a stack along the corridor. They had trudged up the stairs and reached their destination while Troy was busy daydreaming.

Troy was the last in line. His gun was out, and his back was pressed to the wall. Just ahead of him, Dubois stood in almost the exact same pose as his. In front of them were Gallo and Miquel, and then the four helmeted and flak-jacketed Madrid cops. They had split up, two and two, on either side of an apartment door.

Everywhere in the building seemed dead quiet. Everywhere, but on the other side of that apartment door. Inside there, a TV was on. Male voices were shouting over it. The inside of that apartment was a wall of sound. So much so, that eight cops could walk right up to the place in the early morning without fear of being discovered.

Up the hallway, about five meters further on, not far, there was a dark spot on the far wall. Troy stared at it for a long second, wondering what it was. Gradually, it coalesced into a small camera, pointed straight at the door to this apartment.

It was just a little webcam-type camera, placed in a spot where there was a lot of shadow. You could pass it a hundred times and never see it. It could be a large spider there, or a smudge caused by a dirty hand, only it was too high up the wall for anyone to reach.

Two Madrid cops stepped up with a heavy battering ram. It was a swing-type, an officer holding the handle on each side. They didn't say a word. The team leader held up his fist. His index finger appeared.

That was one.

Troy was still staring at the camera. There was a recess for a light bulb in the ceiling above it, but the light was out. Someone had removed the bulb.

Middle finger. Two.

They know we're here.

"Wait!" Troy said.

Ring finger ...

The two men reared back and swung the ram. BAM!

The door exploded inward as the rammers ducked back and discarded the ram. The two others burst in, screaming in Spanish. Weapons out, the two cops who manned the battering ram were the next in.

El Grupo followed on Miquel's lead. The guy was a former Madrid commando. He probably was nostalgic over an action like this. Gallo went in after him.

Troy followed Dubois in, gun poised over her shoulder, left hand on her back. They moved room to room. The place was like a maze, an underground rabbit warren.

There were computers everywhere—laptops on nearly every flat surface—some closed and stacked five high. Desktops parked in corners, a massive TV set across a small living room from a long, sunken couch. Wires snaked all over the floors. On the giant screen was a first-person shooter style video game, the game not paused, instead continuing on without the player. There had been no time to even press pause. Male voices were screaming inside the game.

Where are these guys?

Dubois and Troy moved through a dining area, little more than an alcove with a white Formica table pushed against the wall and some chairs around it. There were empty cardboard food delivery boxes, aluminum containers, plastic utensils, and empty soda cans all over the table. Some of the food was half-eaten, like it had only recently been opened. The table looked like it hadn't been cleaned off in days.

"I don't see anyone," Dubois said.

"I don't like it," Troy said. "They had a camera in the hallway."

"Why didn't you say anything?"

"I only saw it at the last second."

All the Madrid commandos were gone, moved on ahead to other parts of the apartment. Their voices sailed back here, calling out to each other. No shots had been fired in the apartment. Behind them, on the TV, far away on the internet, people were shooting at each other.

"Stark, what do you see?" Miquel said through the headset.

"Clear," Troy said. "It looks like they were here a minute ago, and they just left. They knew we were coming. Somebody should check to see if they all jumped out a window."

"Dubois?"

"I'm with Stark. All clear. No one here."

Across the room from them, there was a large, heavy tapestry hanging on one wall. At first glance it was red, but then Troy noticed there were many colors in it. It was complex in its design, shapes and lines interweaving. Red was the dominant color, along with various blues and greens and yellows.

The tapestry hung behind a long, black table. The table had a few pieces of electronic equipment on it, but not much, not like the literal piles of electronics in other parts of the room. These electronics almost seemed like they were there for show.

The table was made from some cheap wood, like pressboard. It would be an easy table to move. A person could almost retreat to the other side of that tapestry, through a doorway, then reach back and pull the table into place with one hand.

"Dubois?" Troy said, very quietly.

"Stark?"

He tapped her on the shoulder and pointed at the tapestry.

"There's a hole in that wall," he whispered.

Indeed, the tapestry was rippling the smallest amount, almost an imperceptible amount, probably from air flow between the two open spaces. There was a door there, or maybe ...

"I think someone cut it," he said.

Dubois saw it now. "Should we alert the Madrid ..."

"No."

"What's going on guys?" Miquel said through the headset. "We're coming back."

"Okay, good," Troy said out loud. "We'll wait." He practically shouted it, not that he imagined whoever was behind there understood what he was saying.

"Pull the table away," he whispered to Dubois.

They went to the table. Dubois walked around to the far side and grabbed the edge with her free hand. She looked at Troy. Their eyes met. He nodded.

She pulled it back with ease. It didn't really make a sound. Troy stepped to the edge of the tapestry and yanked it away with his right hand.

Sure enough, there was a large hole in the wall, narrow, not tall, but similar to a door. They had cut a hole between two apartments.

He burst through the hole, his gun in his left, non-shooting hand.

A young guy was there. He wore a white soccer jersey with Emirates Fly Better in dark letters on the chest. He was kneeling on the floor, doing something to a couple of laptops, pulling them apart maybe. He jumped up as Troy came in. He was holding a screwdriver.

Troy punched him in the face. Once. Twice. Both were hard right hands. The guy's eyes were dazed, but he was still on his feet. The screwdriver was still in his hand. Troy could kill him just for holding that screwdriver. Instead, he pulled it away and threw it across the room. Then he slid a foot behind the guy's legs and shoved him onto the floor.

"Dubois!" he shouted.

"Right behind you!" she shouted in return.

"Arrest that guy!"

He caught a shadow image of Dubois jumping on top of the guy and rolling him over onto his chest.

There was a hallway to the right. Troy moved down it, going fast. Hallways were vulnerable moments. His gun was back in his right hand.

He reached an open room. He put himself against the wall, checked a room at an angle. No obvious people in there. He moved in. It was a room with a long, white table against the wall. There were half a dozen desktop computer screens, with tower-style CPUs on the floor. No one here. No closets to hide in.

He moved on.

"Stark?" Miquel said. "Where are you?"

"Behind the tapestry in the living room. There's another flat back here."

He was approaching a turn in the hallway. Somewhere up ahead, a child was screeching. Maybe it had always been doing that, but the video game noise from the other apartment had obscured the sound of it.

Where there was a baby, there was bound to be an adult.

"Show yourself!" Troy shouted. "Come out!"

A Spanish phrase came to him.

"Ven aqui! Ven aqui!"

Come here!

A very young woman appeared from around the bend in the hall, carrying a baby in her arms. She wore a black hijab on her head. She froze when she saw Troy's gun, her eyes locked on it. It was pointed right at her.

He lifted it and pointed it toward the ceiling.

"Go! Vaya! Vaya!"

She ran past Troy, her mouth an O of fear, tears streaming down her cheeks. Troy guessed she was a teenager, barely older than sixteen. Babies having babies.

Troy made the turn where the girl had just come from. It was another long hallway. The layout of this place was impossible to understand. Someone had gone through and changed both of these flats since the building went up, tearing out walls and putting up others. It was a drywall fiasco in here.

"Behind you," Dubois said.

He could feel, rather than see, her there.

There was a door straight ahead, down at the far end of the hall.

"Follow me," he said.

Surprise was gone. Speed and force were all that was left. There were supposed to be four or five guys in here. So far, they had found one guy and one girl. The rest of the guys had to be somewhere.

Troy took a deep breath and sprinted at that door.

He accelerated into it, hitting it without slowing down, giving it his left shoulder, blasting through it. The door exploded into pieces. It was a cheap door, made out of wood chips and glue.

Troy came crashing into the room. He lost his balance and rolled to the ground, head over heels. There were people in here.

He still had his gun.

He came up on one knee, gun in a two-handed grip, looking for a target.

There were three young guys in here, all skinny, all wearing jeans and soccer jerseys. One of them had a gun. He pointed it at Troy.

Troy hesitated, when he should have gunned the guy down. But the guy was a kid, a fresh-faced, young kid. A long second passed, too long, a time during which the kid could have fired.

How many people have you killed?

"Drop it!" Troy screamed. "DROP THE GUN!"

The kid's hands were shaking. His eyes were wild. He screamed something at Troy. He took a step closer, then another one.

The other two guys were standing, knees bent, hands out, as if they were waiting for Troy to throw them a ball.

"Drop it or I swear to God I'm gonna kill you."

The two gun barrels moved closer, closer. The kid screamed again. His eyes were going to pop out of his head.

"DROP IT!" Troy shouted.

He was gonna have to kill this kid. There was no more time.

A dark shadow flew into the room from behind Troy. It reached the kid and kicked his gun sideways across the small room. The gun hit the wall with a heavy CLUNK.

Dubois.

In an instant, she had the kid on his back and was on top of him, her own gun in his face. She shouted something at him in rapid Spanish, then in another language, Troy guessed Arabic. The kid went limp, all the air going out of him like a slashed tire.

Dubois rolled him over, pulled his wrists together, and zip-tied them. She glanced back at Troy.

"These guys don't speak English. You know that, right?"

Seconds later, the room filled with large men in storm trooper outfits—the Madrid cops. They grabbed the other two young guys, spun them around, put them on the floor, and handcuffed them.

Troy worked his way to his feet.

Dubois had removed her helmet. She was sweaty under there, a dark purple sash keeping her crazy hair at bay. She was still kneeling on the kid.

"Pretty nifty moves there, Agent Dubois," Troy said.

"Pretty nice restraint shown, Agent Stark. You didn't shoot anybody."

Troy smiled. "I'm turning over a new leaf. It's like going on a diet. Every day I don't kill somebody is a good day."

"Stark!" a voice said.

Troy turned. Miquel and Gallo were just entering the room.

"I was wondering when you guys were going to get here," Troy said. "Dubois and I took down the bad guys for you, such as they are. The whole thing is over."

"We're supposed to be observers," Miquel said.

CHAPTER THIRTEEN

12:55 pm Central European Time
Boutique Hotel Gajdos Exclusive
Innere Stadt
Vienna, Austria

"Who do you see as the market for a train ride such as this?" a young man using his mobile phone to record the conversation said. The man was thin and tall with wispy, blond hair, and big, bright eyes that gave him the look of a deer about to be hit by an oncoming truck.

Stupid people. I'm surrounded by very stupid people.

Istvan Gajdos hated the Austrian media.

He hated the German media. And the Swiss media. Also, the English media. Actually, he disliked English people in general. Their newspapers were sensationalist rags which were best used to wrap fish. He had no love for the French media, or the Dutch media, either.

The Americans were okay, though the news there rarely covered him. American people seemed to have little interest in what went on outside their own borders. There were no Americans at this press opportunity, for example. That was their loss. But some in America were beginning to follow and cheer on the career of Racz, and with good reason. Istvan predicted that before too much longer, the Americans would start to fall in love with him as well.

Of course, the media he liked the most were the Hungarian media. They were the best. Certainly, he owned most of the large Hungarian media now, and he hoped to own all of it one day. He was in the newspapers and on TV quite a lot, and he received the best possible coverage. There were a few small newspapers and radio outlets that were critical of him, and of Xander Racz, but they were in the process of being stamped out. Most of the coverage was positive and much of it was enthusiastic.

And why not? The things he was doing were the best possible things. He was putting Hungary back on the map of the world and in a big way. If Western reporters sometimes gave him unflattering coverage, it was because of envy. Not necessarily envy on the part of the reporters—who, let's face it, were mere peons in the scheme of things—but by the owners of the media outlets for which they worked.

Istvan Gajdos was coming on hard, and he was bringing Hungary with him. There were elites in Western Europe who were not happy about that.

"Well," he said, "it's a luxury train, one of the most exclusive and expensive trips in the whole world, and it travels to some of the most beautiful places in Europe. Every detail has been considered. The meal service compares to the finest restaurants in Paris and New York City. Every whim of our passengers is catered to. So, the market for it certainly isn't newspaper reporters."

A wave of laughter went through the group of reporters and onlookers and carefully placed members of his entourage surrounding him. Istvan was known to many as a bit of a comedian, and he relished that reputation. He was quick-witted, sharp-tongued, and larger than life. Indeed, he stood a little over two meters tall, and so he towered above nearly anyone near him.

His imposing physical size gave him a dominance that he relished as well. Was he ugly? He supposed he was, though that had never stopped him from capturing the attention of women. Was he fat? He weighed about 135 kilos, which while large, was not terrible for his height. He was big, as a general rule. His hands were the large hands of a workman, which he was for decades before his current good fortune. His feet were big. His arms, his legs, everything. He liked to think that he was as well hung as a southern African bull elephant. He was a literal giant and not necessarily a gentle one.

He and the reporters were standing in the gleaming chessboard lobby of Istvan's new hotel in Vienna. The first floor was all Calacatta marble from Italy, polished brass and giant, plate glass windows fronting the street. It was one of the best addresses in the city, just a short walk from St. Stephen's Cathedral, and the Christmas Market ongoing now in St. Stephen's Square.

Elegant appointments, concierge service, a twenty-four-hour front desk, hot stone and Swedish massage, airport shuttle, room service, and a la carte breakfast. There was a modern fitness room and a rooftop terrace offering commanding views of the surrounding neighborhood. There were only thirty-two rooms, making it a special place for only the finest people. And it was full. It was always nearly full.

"Isn't this a great hotel?" he said, although it had nothing to do with why the reporters were here. He had gathered them to tell them about the train and then lead them on a tour of it. But the hotel was catching his attention right now.

"I mean, look at it. I think it's the best hotel in Vienna. There's never an empty room."

Everyone was laughing again at this sudden non sequitur. Istvan didn't mind. This was supposed to be fun.

"Istvan," another reporter said. This one was a female, wearing large, red eyeglasses. Istvan encouraged everyone to call him by his first name. It would be amazing if one day, people all over the world associated the rather common name with him alone. When someone said "Istvan," anyone, anywhere, he wanted people to picture him.

"If the idea is to link Budapest in the popular mind with the West, then why begin your train trip today in Vienna?"

Stupid. It was a stupid question.

He supposed, however, that stupid questions led to what one world leader used to call teachable moments.

"Several reasons," he said. "One: I can't get enough of this hotel, and neither can my people. Two: a couple of my girlfriends wanted time to shop at the Christmas Market here before we leave. Three: I'm already the most famous man in Hungary. I don't need any more coverage there."

Everyone laughed again.

"The most famous?" someone called out.

Istvan sighed. "Okay. Second most famous after my great friend Racz. Anyway, everyone there knows about the train. I want to give you all a chance to experience it."

"Are we invited to accompany you to Saint Moritz?"

Now everyone was having fun. This was what it was all about.

"Unfortunately, all the rooms are booked for this trip. But next week, you can certainly take the ride. I call it a bargain price at thirty thousand euros."

"You also say it's the fastest train on Earth."

Istvan nodded. "Yes, I do. We will take our time traveling through the Alps, but the train itself can go up to 400 kilometers per hour."

"The fastest trains now top 500 kilometers per hour. Did you know that? The Chinese are said to be developing one that will approach 550 kilometers per hour."

550 kilometers per hour? Istvan didn't know what to do with that piece of information. It was an absurd speed. An impossible speed.

"No matter what the Chinese do, ours will always be faster. Even if we have to ask our friends the Americans to bomb the Chinese railway."

It was a great meeting. He was winning them over. He was smart, he was entertaining, and he controlled vast resources. He was building a business empire to rival anything in the West. These people felt privileged to obtain this audience with him.

"Istvan," the original doe-eyed, tow-headed reporter said. It was likely that he alone was not having a good time. "What would you say to those who believe that you and Prime Minister Racz are dragging Hungary backwards into the authoritarian dark ages?"

Istvan stared at the young man. "I'm sorry?"

The man's eyes got wider and wider as he spoke. He probably thought that Istvan was going to reach down and choke the life out of him in front of all these people. There was no reason to think that. If they were alone, it would have been a different story.

"You must be aware that Hungary's Global Democracy Score has dropped to 3.2 on a scale of 7. Its Democracy Percentage Score has fallen to 41.5 out of 100. Its Human Development Index has dropped to a par with some other Eastern European countries, and countries in parts of southern Asia, from where it once was, just below countries like Denmark and the Netherlands. All of this has taken place in the past five years, and is closely associated with the steep drop in freedom of the press which has happened during your consolidation of—"

Istvan had heard enough. "Do you see this suit I'm wearing?" he said, cutting the man off mid-sentence.

Istvan held the lapel of his suit jacket.

The young man said nothing. But he had stopped talking, which was good. Istvan's anger could be like an approaching storm. It had frozen the poor lamb in his tracks.

Istvan looked at the other members of the crowd. Some of them were his own people, who would be taking the train ride with him.

"Do you see this suit?" he said to the group.

"Yes!" a few people shouted.

"It's a fancy suit, wouldn't you agree?" Istvan said.

"Oh, yes."

"It has no brand name on it, do you know why? I'll tell you. Because it was hand made by a master craftsman, for me alone, to perfectly fit my body. It cost ten thousand euros, but I don't care, because I only get the best. In fact, I ordered three more suits from the same man."

He looked at the young reporter again. The man was dressed in jeans and a black jacket that might have been leather. The jacket had a fur collar against the cold, which might have been real fur but probably wasn't.

"Do you understand?" Istvan said.

The man shook his head.

"You, my friend, are what some call a crab in a bucket. You cannot climb above your circumstances, so you try to pull others down to your level. But I, and my true friends, the people who are with me—and yes, that includes Prime Minister Racz—we are flying to the stars. We are going from strength to strength, and we are achieving great things. Everyone in Hungary loves us. Everyone. And we are integrating with the other great countries of Europe. Remember the great history of Austria and Hungary together."

Istvan felt pride welling up inside him. He was a man of enormous passions and animal drives. He felt love, he felt there was a future right of front of him and everyone who stood with him, a future of wealth and success without limit.

The young man found his voice again. "The Austro-Hungarian Empire lost World War One, the empire was destroyed, and the two countries were severed. Soon after, Austria became complicit with Nazi Germany. Hungary was overrun by the Nazis, and almost its entire Jewish population was wiped off the face of the Earth. Then it was overrun by the Red Army, and the country lived under communism for more than forty years. Is that the great history you're speaking of?"

Istvan had been a child and a young man under communism. There was nothing in this world—nothing—that he hated more than communism. He hated when people uttered the word. This young man, who Istvan had benignly tolerated until now, had brought Istvan's hate and anger upon himself.

Istvan pointed at him. "Crab in a bucket," he said. "Negative energy. And that's why you're not coming to see the train with the rest of us. In fact, I don't even want you in my hotel. We're going to have coffee, tea, and cakes now, before we all go to the train station, but not you. I want you out."

Istvan glanced at two of his bodyguards, who had been standing near the front doors of the lobby, at the edge of the group. They were big men but had rendered themselves nearly invisible until this moment.

That was part of their job. They were here to protect but not necessarily to intimidate. Only if necessary.

"Out," he said to them. "I want him out of here. This is a private hotel, and he's not welcome. He's causing a disturbance."

The men waded into the crowd, seized the young man by his arms, turned him around, and walked him toward the glass double doors. The reporter seemed to have lost his voice again.

"Beat him to death in the street for all I care."

Of course, they would never do it. It was just theater for Istvan to even say such a thing. But there was something he wanted everyone to know.

"I do not bend," he said. "I do not break. Not for anyone. I'd sooner die."

There was a moment of silence as Istvan and the group looked at each other. It could become an awkward moment if it lasted much longer.

Suddenly, from a far corner, another one of Istvan's bodyguards began to clap. Then a couple of his girls did. Then more of his entourage in the crowd did. They were clapping for him. And that was because he had done the right thing.

"I'm sorry you had to witness that," Istvan told them all, his loyal people and these reporters, these fence sitters from countries other than his own.

"We are, all of us together in this room, on our way to the top."

CHAPTER FOURTEEN

4:25 pm Central European Time
Headquarters of the European Rapid Response Investigation Unit (ERRIU)
aka El Grupo Especial
Outskirts of Madrid, Spain

"How much do you want to bet that's the guy?"

"The guy?" Dubois said.

They were in Dubois's office on the second floor. Troy's office was just two doors down the hall. Dubois's office had plate, glass windows that gave a view of the parking lot, some low, brown hills beyond it, and in the distance, the highway, with thousands of cars, headlights on, zooming past on their way in and out of Madrid.

The day was fading. It was almost time to join all those cars out there and go home. Troy welcomed it. He was tired. They'd gotten up early today, for what turned out to be no good reason. The hackers they hit were just a bunch of Moroccan kids trying to steal credit card information from the Madrid train system. In the three months they'd been at it, they'd made an amount of money the banks would consider a rounding error.

A kid had pulled a gun too. Troy had been one second away from killing the kid.

The Madrid cops had determined the gun was a CZ 52, made for the Czech military sometime in the early 1950s. A collector's item. No one had fired it in at least three decades, including the kid himself. He had never even tested it. But the cops did.

Misfire.

Now, a few minutes ago, Troy had been in his own office, scanning video feeds, and killing time before the day ended.

He was not an investigator. It was really that simple. Dubois might study reports from police agencies all over Europe and the world. Jan Bakker might analyze data flowing by from computer systems he had infiltrated or intercept emails from suspicious individuals and organizations. These approaches were not available to Troy.

They had been talking about flying up to Scotland to interview the last surviving suspect from the train hijacking there. Interviewing suspects and persons of interest was something Troy was very good at. He could sink his teeth into it, even if the people around him might become concerned about his interviewing methods. But the suspect had died in the night.

The policeman assigned to watch the guy during the overnight said nothing out of the ordinary had happened. But it also turned out that the security cameras in that wing of the hospital had been non-operational for months. So, while there was no evidence of murder, there wasn't really any evidence to the contrary. A person of interest to interview now would probably be that cop, but no one was going to allow the likes of Troy Stark to go do that.

So, he watched the news instead. And something interesting happened. Several stories about the same incident came to the top of his news feed. It must be a slow news day, because apparently this event was the most important thing happening.

A man in Vienna had been giving some kind of press conference in the lobby of a hotel. He was a rich guy from Hungary who owned a train line. He was surrounded by reporters. Then he did a funny thing. A reporter said something he didn't like, and he had the guy thrown out onto the street.

The whole thing was filmed from multiple angles by people who were there. Two big goons appeared, grabbed a young, blond-haired guy, and marched him outside. One of the goons took the guy's cell phone and smashed it on the sidewalk.

Troy watched the videos with fascination. Then he watched it again. There was something compelling about the man at the center of it. He reminded Troy of an ogre from a childhood fairy tale.

So, Troy brought his sparkling, new laptop, with the video on the screen, to show Dubois. Agent Dubois was eye-popping this afternoon, in a bright yellow bodysuit, with a heavy, black belt around her waist and black combat boots, with hair just gone absolutely wild.

This bodysuit was not her typical jumpsuit. It was more form-fitting and made of some stretchy, clingy fabric. Troy had a childlike urge to grab a bit of it and pull it out as far as it would go, then let it snap back. Just to see it happen.

"He's a rich guy," Troy said. "He's going on a long train ride with his rich friends. He's also a bit of a jerk. If I was someone organizing train hijackings, I think I'd probably hit this guy."

On the screen, they were showing the train now. It was long and sleek, super modern. It bore nearly zero resemblance to the idea of trains that existed in Troy's mind. New York City subway trains rattling into concrete stations underground. Coal-burning steam-powered trains from the 1800s. Freight trains a mile long chugging by slowly while you waited impatiently at a road crossing. Worn-out passenger trains in Central American dictatorships.

This thing looked like a spaceship if a spaceship was like a snake. It looked like a future that hadn't arrived yet. It must be twenty cars long. The top of each car was red, the middle was white, and the bottom was green, and that went all along the entire length of the train. If Troy had to guess, those were the colors of a flag, probably the Hungarian flag. In the white part, at the front of each car, were the words *Gajdos, Ltd.*

"I like it," Dubois said. "Let me talk to Miquel."

Half an hour later, they were all in the conference room, Miquel's brain trust. Dubois, Troy, Jan Bakker, and the newest addition, Carlo Gallo.

"Istvan Gajdos," Jan Bakker said.

Jan was sitting at the long table with two laptops in front of him. Everyone else was spread out around the room. Dubois was sitting at the far end, beneath the video monitor. Miquel, Troy, and Gallo were all standing, but in different parts of the room. They made a rough triangle.

Jan moved back and forth from screen to screen, pulling up reports and jumping between them at a rapid pace.

"He's fifty-eight years old, and likely the richest man in Hungary. It's hard to calculate his assets because not all of them are transparent, and some of them have unclear value. What is clear is that he has benefited greatly from his friend Xander Racz becoming prime minister. A creeping form of dictatorship has taken over the country, and it seems that Racz is looting public coffers and passing the resources to Gajdos."

Miquel looked at Troy. "And why do we think his train might be the one that is hijacked next?"

Troy shrugged. "Call it a hunch if you like. They attacked a luxury train last time. It was a sightseeing train, with a relative handful of wealthy passengers, who would be easy to control. The train was traveling through an isolated and mountainous region, where people might not notice right away that something was wrong with it. That might have been the practice train. This one might be for all the marbles. Instead of sticking this guy Gajdos up for whatever he has on him, you stick him up for things you know he has, but which he's hiding."

"Interesting," Miquel said. "But suppose I was playing the devil's advocate? Why would it not be the right train?"

"That's easy to answer," Bakker said. "Gajdos is surrounded by armed bodyguards at all times. He will have his guards with him on the train. To hijack the train, you would have to kill or overcome these guards. The hijackers in Scotland did not have to worry about this. Also, they infiltrated that train by pretending to be passengers. From what I can tell, everyone who will take this ride with Gajdos is a friend of his, a member of his entourage, an employee, or a prostitute. It is likely he knows everyone, or almost everyone, who will be on the train."

"What if we just told Gajdos we're concerned about him?" Troy said. "And you did an analysis of his cyber security?"

Jan shrugged. "His maiden train voyage leaves Vienna tonight. Were we to contact him now, if he responded at all, his first answer would be that he has the best cyber security in the world, even if he has none at all. Have you seen interviews with him? Everything he does is always the best."

"Anyway," Miquel said. "We are on a short leash, I'm afraid. We would have to make official contact with his organization through Interpol headquarters. By the time the bureaucratic back and forth was over, the trip would be over."

"I guess that means raiding the train is out," Troy said.

"Same problem," Miquel said. "And even worse. Gajdos would publicize it and turn it into an international incident. It would fit perfectly into his favorite narrative. Western elites hate him. Now he's being harassed by secret police agencies funded by western governments."

"Infiltrate?" Troy said. "Get on the train under cover?"

"Are we assuming this is definitely the train?" Miquel said.

Troy shrugged. "Maybe we're just thinking out loud. Call it an intellectual exercise. They sent us to raid a bunch of children playing in a sandbox this morning. This can't be much dumber than that."

"Point taken," Miquel said.

"Gajdos enjoys girls," Jan said. He stopped, then looked sheepishly at Dubois. "Women."

She rolled her eyes. "Thank you."

"He keeps the escort services in Eastern Europe humming. His need for this service appears to be boundless. Perhaps the only people he might not know on the train will be escorts. Prostitutes, if you prefer."

Gallo looked at Dubois. His face was expressionless, but his eyes seemed to be smiling. "We've done this before," he said. "In the CIA. We've deployed prostitutes, certainly, but we've also deployed agents as fake prostitutes. You might be surprised the places you can gain entry to like this."

"Why are you looking at me?" Dubois said. She glanced around the room at the rest of them. "Why is everyone looking at me?"

Gallo smiled. "The way you're rocking that yellow outfit, girl, you'd put the highest-class call girls to shame."

Troy shook his head. "You can't say things like that."

Gallo shrugged. "I just did. I'm a dinosaur. Sue me."

"You're a dinosaur sinking into the tar pits," Dubois said.

Now, everyone was looking at Miquel. It was going to be his call, of course. There was no way Interpol would authorize it. If El Grupo were going to put someone on that train, it would have to be a rogue operation.

"I need to see more evidence of a threat," Miquel said. "It can't just be a hunch."

"Said the man who plays his hunches all the time," Troy said.

"This isn't my hunch," Miquel said. "It's yours. But it is my agency. And it's my neck if it's wrong." He looked at Jan. "So, find me some evidence, no matter how flimsy, that this might be the one."

Jan nodded. "If there is any."

"And if there isn't?" Dubois said.

Gallo smiled. "Then we have an easy day tomorrow."

CHAPTER FIFTEEN

10:25 pm Central European Time
Aboard the *East Meets West*
Vienna Central Station
Vienna, Austria

"Joe," someone said. "Are you awake?"

Sokolov's hands were behind his head. He stared up at the ceiling that was right above his head. It was dark in here. In fact, the dark was so total, it didn't matter if he opened or shut his eyes. The ceiling that he stared at was invisible to him. He was staring at nothing.

He lay still, feeling the hard, metal surface of the flooring underneath him, the vibration of the train as it rolled slowly down the tracks, and the occasional jolt as it hit a switch or some imperfection in the track bed. He could hear something above him now, where before it had been silence.

It seemed that he was inside a coffin, like a dead person. One day he would be dead, perhaps one day soon. Did being dead matter? Did being alive matter? Did the dead dream? If so, what did they dream about?

He took a deep breath. The air was so close, he had some trouble breathing in here. He had been smoking since he was a child. He remembered how he would beg his father for a drag from the cigarette when he very young, maybe six or seven years old. And his father would give him one. That, and a sip of vodka.

That's how you become a man.

Time passed in the coffin, and Sokolov must have fallen asleep at some point. He knew it was later now because he could feel the train moving. As they rolled along, Sokolov noticed some things about his surroundings. He could breathe easily again. Fresh air was getting in from somewhere. In fact, a bit of a draft blew in. The train was not perfectly sealed. But he knew that already.

He could also see. If he held up his hand, he could just make out the lines of it—he wasn't in utter darkness anymore. Light was getting in from somewhere.

"Uncle Joe?"

In his mind, he could see a gloomy, overcast day, gray skies, gray snowy streets—everything had the same bleak color. He was riding high in an armored truck, his upper body sticking out of the turret. He had a heavy machine gun in the turret with him.

The tank moved through the streets, into the center of the city, Grozny, the Chechen capital. It was one in a convoy of many such tanks and trucks. The farther they traveled, the worse the road became.

There were leftovers of the recent fighting everywhere—buildings half destroyed by rocket fire, buildings pock-marked by a thousand bullets, buildings on fire. There was rubble everywhere. Gunshots sounded in the distance.

The winter trees were bare, and new snow was mixed with mud. They passed into an area where the buildings were completely destroyed, crushed, and smashed as if by an angry giant. It was downtown Grozny. He stared at the wreckage. He had been too young to go to Afghanistan. He hadn't seen a war up close before.

The convoy stopped at a plaza in the center of the city. Sokolov's tank parked near a large tree with massive, naked branches spreading out to the sides. He looked around and soon noticed something lodged between the branches. It wasn't one something—there were several of them. At every crook of the bald tree, one of these things had been carefully placed. He stared and stared at them, trying to make out what they were. They were round, like bulbs on a Christmas tree, but smeared in a dark color, like a deep brown. They were not festive. They were not bright.

Sokolov looked again. The things in the trees were human heads.

They were the cut off heads of Russian soldiers, plastered with mud and blood. The faces were young—they had been boys just recently. The Chechen bastards had cut their heads off.

A feeling of helplessness so profound that he could never explain it to anyone passed through Sokolov's body. Everything, his entire life, had been harsh and unforgiving. But nothing had prepared him for these heads. Wanton cruelty like this should not be possible. But there was the evidence of it, right in front of his eyes. It was a cold world, colder than he had even imagined.

"We'll kill them," he said quietly. "We'll kill them all."

"Joe!" someone hissed.

Sokolov opened his eyes.

Ivan the Terrible was near him in the cramped space beneath the train compartments.

"What?"

"The train is moving again. We've just left Vienna station. We're going very slowly, but Gajdos and his ilk are on board." Ivan smiled at that news. His eyes almost seemed to glow.

"Okay," Sokolov said.

He could hear and see the change now. There was music, talking, and laughter coming from above their heads. Lights of some kind were flashing, and some small amount of that penetrated into this crypt space through seams where metal met metal.

"You told me to inform you. We should be at Innsbruck by dawn. After that, a short break there, then St. Moritz in maybe three more hours."

Sokolov nodded. There was still time for a little sleep. He felt like he hadn't a proper sleep in days.

"They're partying. Do you hear them?"

The sounds came drifting down to him.

"Yes," Sokolov said. "How many?"

"I got a text from Helena a few moments ago," Ivan said. "She boarded without a problem. There are six bodyguards. Only six. Perhaps forty people in the rest of the entourage, including some whores, a banker from Switzerland, and the French pop star Calment. Some others. A dozen service workers, including the train driver, a chef, a cook, three other kitchen staff, four waiters, and two cleaning staff. There may be more joining the train at Innsbruck."

Sokolov thought about the banker and the pop star, but only for a moment. A rich person and a famous person … did it matter? Not really. He remembered Calment. The man was middle-aged now and long past his era of hits. He was a nostalgia act for people who remembered the 1990s fondly. He and the banker would live or die with everyone else. Their presence would make the incident more fascinating to the tabloid readers. That was all.

"Is everyone aware of the situation?"

Ivan nodded. "Everyone is aware and ready."

"All right," Sokolov said. "Good. If I'm asleep, wake me again as soon as we stop at Innsbruck."

"Will that be enough time?"

"For me?" Sokolov said.

"Yes."

"It's more than enough."

Ivan crawled off through the dim space again. In a moment, he was gone. It was no longer pitch dark in here, but it was still dark enough that a man a few meters away could disappear. Sokolov was thankful that Ivan knew enough not to crowd him.

The train rattled along now, gaining speed. It must be leaving the city center. It was going to become cold inside this compartment as the train climbed into the mountains. That was okay. Sokolov didn't mind cold.

From above his head came the thump of music. Gajdos was having his party. Men like Gajdos were always having their parties. But in this case, the party was almost over.

Sokolov lay back, his head on his bag. The bag was lumpy and hard, but better than the flooring.

Where was I?

He stared into blank space for a long while. The movement of the train was soothing, almost like a rocking chair.

In front of him now, there seemed to be seven small, round dolls. They were Matryoshka nesting dolls, the very symbol of Mother Russia. Each doll had bright eyes, pink cheeks, and cherubic faces. They wore traditional peasant costumes. They were all girls, nearly identical, except each one was a different size. The biggest one was at the far right, and they made a line, each one becoming smaller in size until they reached the smallest one, quite tiny, at the far left.

He closed his eyes as if he would sleep, but each time his eyelids drifted down, the dolls seemed to move. He didn't like that. He got the sense that they might creep up on him. His eyes popped open again.

Then there were six dolls. The smallest doll was gone.

He watched them carefully. But he was tired. He couldn't stay awake. His eyelids drifted down again.

Sudden movement. He opened his eyes. Now there were five dolls. The smallest ones were disappearing, being swallowed by the larger ones.

He shook the dolls away. It was too disturbing.

"I'm   just   dreaming,"   he   said   to   no   one.

CHAPTER SIXTEEN

"Casimir Skolnick," Jan Bakker said.

"What is that, please?" Troy said.

"It's the man who will get you all on board that train."

They were sitting in the staff kitchen lounge. It was the group Troy was coming to think of as the usual suspects—himself, Jan, Dubois, Miquel, and now Gallo. They were all tired. It was late. The lights were off in most of the building. Miquel had just made a fresh pot of coffee.

Troy drank a cup of it. The coffee was good. Miquel insisted on quality in a lot of things, and coffee was one of them. He was a bit of a coffee snob, in fact, but Troy didn't mind things like that.

They'd ordered in some sandwiches from a local place earlier tonight. Troy had napped on the floor of his office for maybe an hour. The office was carpeted. The carpet was new. It smelled like something unpleasant—a frog being dissected in a high school biology class. Troy rolled up his jacket, used that as a pillow, and tried to put the smell out of his mind.

Now, Jan was sitting at a table with his laptop. Troy was across from him, feet up on a chair. Gallo was ten feet away, lying across a table. Dubois was sitting on the floor, her back to the wall. Only Miquel was standing.

Large train systems with millions of passengers were being watched carefully. That was good, as it should be. But if Scotland was practice for another attack, the Madrid Metro, or the Paris Metro, or the London Underground, were not the next victims. Gajdos. Someone like Gajdos had to be it. Arrogant. Wealthy, but not necessarily well protected. A big, fat, easy target.

"Skolnick is a pimp," Jan said. "He's also a drug dealer. He operates across Eastern Europe and has been doing so for decades, even before the fall of communism. He runs a boutique, door-to-door service, very hands on, and the large mafias leave him alone. They don't lose any business because of him, and he's sort of a mythical figure. He brings people nostalgia for an earlier time. He was known to operate a bordello and marijuana lounge in Sarajevo during the Bosnian War. He has been provisioning Istvan Gajdos for three or four years."

"How do we know he's provisioning Gajdos on this trip, though?" Gallo said. "Gajdos could have packed all the drugs and prostitutes he needs onto the train already."

Jan shook his big head. He looked at Carlo over the top of his glasses. "I tracked Skolnick's whereabouts. He's under nearly constant surveillance by half a dozen police and customs agencies, so he's easy enough to find. He and three women arrived together in Innsbruck this afternoon. Austria is outside his normal travel path. It seems like no coincidence that Gajdos's train will arrive in Innsbruck early tomorrow morning."

"He's bringing more prostitutes," Dubois said.

"Yes," Jan said. "A second shift, you might say. And an informer reported to Polish customs agents that Skolnick is carrying half a kilo of cocaine in his luggage."

"But they didn't intercept?"

Jan shrugged. "Skolnick is well-insulated. He's been in business so long that he knows everyone. No one touches him."

"And how does he get us on the train?" Dubois said from the floor.

"He claims that you're one of his escorts," Jan said. "He claims that these two are henchmen, or bodyguards, or chaperones in his employ. He is known to accompany his girls on assignment. Yes, they're his investment, and he doesn't want them damaged, but reports I've seen indicate he is also genuinely concerned for their welfare."

"He's a pimp with a heart of gold," Troy said.

"It would seem," Jan said. "I suspect that if you speak with him, you can convince him to allow you to take his place on that train."

"But is there any reason to suspect that the train will be attacked?" Miquel said. "That's the primary question I want answered. As you know, no one above me is going to authorize the operation you're talking about. To take a risk like that …"

"I've been monitoring the Gajdos train network computer system since late this afternoon," Jan said. "Human hackers or automated bots appear to be probing the system. This sort of thing goes on all the time. I've tracked the location where the operation is coming from. It's a very small office building along a strip on the outskirts of Sofia, the capital city of Bulgaria. Numerous front organizations are headquartered in that building. The Bulgarian Mafia is known to be well versed in cyber attacks."

"So, someone is attempting to hack that train?" Miquel said. "That's what you're telling me?"

Jan raised his hands. "The train? Maybe. Is someone trying to hack Gajdos's computers? Yes, absolutely. Are they being successful? Not at the moment. Are they the same ones who hacked and controlled the train in Scotland? I couldn't say. It would seem like the Scotland hackers were more sophisticated, but I don't even know if that's true. I haven't seen the data. Apparently, the Scotland train was a low-security environment."

Miquel seemed to be staring at the wall. For a long moment, no one said anything.

"The train leaves Vienna tonight," Jan said. "It arrives in Innsbruck in the morning. From there, it's just a few hours to St. Moritz. Then it's another seven hours through the mountains to the final destination in Zermatt. It seems to me that an infiltration team could inspect the train for hijackers and be satisfied as to whether any are on board by the time the train reaches St. Moritz. Meanwhile, I could monitor for a more concerted cyber attack. If nothing happens, the infiltration team simply exits the train as mysteriously as they arrived. The day ends early."

"Am I supposed to have sex with the clients?" Dubois said.

Jan shook his head. "No. That would be a lot to ask."

Troy nearly laughed. He was overtired, and once again, Jan was demonstrating his complete lack of humor. The man just could not detect sarcasm.

"Good. Because I'd prefer not to."

"Of course," Jan said. "And if your cover is revealed for any reason, we can always report that we suspected there was drug trafficking and prostitution taking place on the train, and we were investigating. A mandate of El Grupo Especial is to detect and disrupt drug and also human trafficking networks."

"What if there is an attack?" Miquel said.

"In that case, I try to block or reverse the hack from here. One advantage we have is that I'm waiting for the attack. In Scotland, no one knew it was happening until it was too late. I also have a friend at the Bulgarian State Agency for National Security. I spoke with him earlier tonight. If we need, he can send a team to raid the office where the hack seems to be taking place. Meanwhile, the team on board the train either stops the hijacking or calls in the local authorities. The hijackers, if they exist, are confronted by the police. If that had happened in Scotland, the hijackers may well have just surrendered."

"The train would still have crashed," Miquel said. "If you can't stop the hack, or the Bulgarians cannot, how do our agents get off safely?"

Jan also had an answer for that. Troy didn't know if it was a reasonable answer.

"Jump off," he said.

"Jump?"

Jan shrugged. "If the agents can get to open air, either through a passenger doorway, or up to the roof of the train, they could jump off the train."

"That sounds like fun," Troy said. "Jump off a speeding train. This is a combination special operation and trip to the amusement park."

"It is a decision that would have to be made quickly," Jan said. "If the train wasn't going too fast yet, it could be done. The agents are trained in surviving crash impacts. Considering that they would be landing in snow, most likely, which is often a soft and forgiving surface ..." He trailed off.

"And the passengers?" Miquel said. "Do our agents simply abandon the passengers in that scenario?"

Jan had a better answer for this. He met Miquel's eyes with his own soft ones. Jan Bakker was a study in contrasts. A huge mountain of a man, immensely strong and imposing, and yet he did not seem to have an aggressive bone in his body. He wasn't arguing. He was simply stating the facts as he understood them.

"If the train is hijacked and the agents don't board the train, the passengers have very little chance of survival on their own. Only a handful of passengers survived the Scotland disaster, all of them with serious injuries. If our agents do board the train, it's possible they can stop the hijackers. They can alert me, and I may be able to thwart the hack and stop the train. It's possible they can work with local authorities, or even Gajdos's bodyguards, to get the passengers to safety. It's possible they can get some of the more able-bodied passengers to jump as well. Either way, escaping would be an emergency measure to save their own lives, only if all else failed."

Miquel thought for a long moment. "All right. Do it." He looked at Troy, Gallo, and Dubois. "But only reveal yourself as agents of El

Grupo if absolutely necessary. If there is no attack, I don't want to read about us in the newspapers."

CHAPTER SEVENTEEN

December 17
1:25 am Central European Time
Aboard the *East Meets West*
Traveling west of Vienna, Austria

The world is mine.

Istvan Gajdos was drunk. But he was more than just drunk. He was reaching a pinnacle, a peak state, not just of drunkenness, but of everything. He was rich, richer than anyone even knew. He was famous, in his home country, yes, but more and more he was famous everywhere. He could have anything he wanted. No, he could have *everything* he wanted. And that was good because he wanted everything.

He had a bottle of Beluga Gold Line vodka that someone had given him in one hand. The bottle was chilled almost to freezing. He had a lit cigarette in the other hand. One of his arms was draped over a pretty, young, blonde-haired girl from Belarus. The other arm was draped over an earthy, sensual brunette from ... somewhere. Turkey, maybe, or Armenia.

Her hair was curly and black. Her eyebrows were thick. Her lips were dark red, like a ruby. Her body was trying to burst out of her blue mini dress. She was so ... carnal. He couldn't come up with another word for it. If there was a heaven, she was earth. She was made by God for a certain kind of action, like an animal. He would take her to a stateroom but not yet. He wanted this buzz to go on a while longer.

Istvan was dancing, in his way. His suit jacket was unbuttoned. His shirt was open at the collar. His tie was gone. He was moving to the music, swaying, and bouncing along with the movement of the train. He was sweating. He could feel the sweat soaking through his clothes. That was the cocaine, making him do that.

The disco car was packed. Of course it was. He had picked the right people for this trip. People who liked an all-night party, which lasted through the next day. There was a DJ up at the front, on the little raised stage. He had an earphone pressed to the side of his head, and he bounced, too, while he manipulated the digital music machine in front of him. He was a popular DJ in Hungary, up and coming, and he played techno music, the music of all-night raves, the music that brought people together.

Istvan brought people together. Was it not clear yet?

The train car was dark, colorful laser lights firing among the dancing and bouncing people. A black light strobed in time to the bassline, making it seem as if people were stopping and starting to the music, like dancing robots. It was like some strange flash photography. On one wall, a giant screen was showing fast-moving drone footage crossing a cold ocean with ice floes on the water. You could immerse yourself in this imagery, or you could focus on the strobing lights and forget it entirely.

"I win!" he shouted. "I win!"

No one could hear him. It was too loud in here.

Nearby, the banker Lars Lanstadt was dancing through the crowd, moving closer to Istvan. He was blond, tall, and thin. He had all his hair. Istvan liked that about him. Lars was Swiss. He was rich in his own right, a high-level client relations person with ZuriBank. He was also one of the few true westerners on this train. Istvan had hoped more would come, but it didn't matter. They would come eventually. Everyone was going to come to Istvan.

Almost without a doubt, Lars and ZuriBank were hoping to take Istvan on as a client. Well, they would have to make it worth his while, wouldn't they?

Now, Lars was right here. He was nearly as tall as Istvan, but much slenderer. He didn't have nearly the presence Istvan had. He didn't have the *displacement*.

His eyes were blue, like crystal, warm waters. They were amazing to look at. Istvan wanted beautiful people around him. Lars qualified.

"Istvan!" he shouted. "May I speak with you a moment?"

Istvan took a drag of his cigarette. "Now?"

It didn't seem like the time.

Lars nodded. He leaned in close, practically screaming in Istvan's ear. "They've called me back to Zurich for a meeting in the morning. Unfortunately, I must exit the train at Innsbruck. I would very much like to have a brief chat with you before …"

His words trailed off. He indicated the party going on all around them. The party had been going on at Istvan's private penthouse suite at the Vienna hotel. Then it had moved to the train station on large, luxury buses. Now, it was on the train.

Before what? Before Istvan became too drunk and high to talk business? That had already happened. Before the international police raided the train and arrested everyone? Was that why Lars was really leaving? He was worried about the police?

"Before I must go," he said.

Istvan nodded. He hated this timid approach to life. The police were not a worry. The police had been generously taken care of from here all the way to St. Moritz. There would be no raid. There would be no embarrassed, prominent Swiss banker being frog-marched from the rolling cocaine party and den of prostitution, while sensationalist media photographers snapped his picture. It wasn't going to happen.

But Lars was getting off the train in the morning, the party was ramping up again, and he wanted to talk business before things went too far. Okay. Istvan could understand that. He might as well see what ZuriBank wanted to offer him.

He nodded and gestured toward the far end of the car, where a closed door led to the quiet wine bar.

He unwrapped his arms from the two girls. He leaned in to the dark-haired, lusty one. "Wait for me," he said in English. "I will return in a few moments."

She nodded and looked up at him with big, dark eyes. *Oh my God.* She was a gift. Her eyes, and her body, were promises. Istvan was moving to a place, a dangerous place, where he was becoming all-powerful. Disaster often awaited in that place, but it was difficult to stop.

He followed Lars, winding their way to the far end of the car. They went through the door to the wine bar.

The bartender was a woman. She was thin, wearing a white dress shirt and black pants. The outfit served to hide her figure. Her dark hair was pulled back, tight to her scalp. Her skin was very white. She was pretty, and she was also a brunette, but she was everything the Turk was not—serious, careful, completely self-contained. You might even say she was mousey. She wore a simple, gold wedding band on the ring finger of her left hand. She was here to do a job and then go home.

She saw the bottle in Istvan's hand and brought out two shot glasses without having to be asked. Then she retreated back and away to the corner. Good girl. Istvan liked service people who quietly excelled in their work.

Istvan poured he and Lars both a shot of vodka from the bottle of Beluga.

"Drink."

Lars nodded. He picked up the glass and raised it high. "To what shall we drink?"

"To the *East Meets West*," Istvan said.

"A lovely train," Lars said.

"The best train on Earth. And the best concept, the very best philosophy."

They clinked glasses and knocked back the shots. Istvan enjoyed the smooth fire sliding down his throat and hitting his belly. Wonderful feeling.

"What can I do for you, Lars?"

Lars looked at him with what he must have thought were shrewd eyes.

"Have another."

Istvan shrugged. Having another shot of vodka was no hardship for him. He poured two more. "What shall we drink to?"

"New friends," Lars said. "Good friends. New relationships." Clearly, he was drunk. Maybe he was also high.

They drank the shots.

Lars looked at Istvan and smiled. "We've done the research, Istvan. The bank." He pointed at Istvan. "We have a cyber security firm as a subsidiary."

"You do, yeah?"

The banking institution had an in-house spy agency. Istvan was hardly surprised. Everyone had a spy agency now, or soon would. Money was wealth, certainly, and power. But in the modern day, the real power was information.

Lars nodded. "Of course we do. In our business, we need it. So, we know some things, things that others do not know. For example, we know the billion-euro crypto theft from FiSafe was your organization. We know that you're a quiet partner in FiSafe. We know you're a billionaire, if not at this moment, when the market for SafeCoin firms and the price comes back up."

This was news. It wasn't news Istvan wanted to hear. He shook his head and pursed his lips. "My friend, I have no idea what you're talking about."

Lars kept smiling. "Of course you do. Who else could have done it, Istvan? Who else was close enough or knew the trading platform well enough? I need to impress upon you that we know you did it. We are not making an educated guess. Once we suspected it was you, we took steps to confirm our suspicions. I wasn't sent here to tell you we're not sure. We know what we know."

"Who else knows this?" Istvan said. "Who else has heard this rumor that you think you know about?"

Lars shook his head. "No one. A handful of people at the bank—the people, like myself, who need to know. The people who have your best interests at heart."

Istvan stared at him.

"You must understand," Lars said. "I'm sure you do. A windfall like that ..." He shrugged. "But it's not money yet. You know crypto is unstable. When the time is right, you will need to move it into real currencies. Euros, dollars, pounds. You need to turn it into money you can use. You need to transform it into real wealth, physical investments all over the world. And you need to do it without attracting attention. There are regulators interested in where that money went. They are watching carefully. There are also organized crime networks who are interested. A few of them are dangerous people indeed."

Istvan put his shot glass on the bar. This was quite an incredible invasion of privacy, wasn't it? Was Lars threatening him?

Lars must be very drunk. The drink had loosened his tongue.

"You are walking on a tightrope," Lars said. "We can help you navigate it successfully. We can guide you and do it very quietly. This kind of thing can't be allowed to become public information."

Did Lars and his overlords really think they had something on Istvan Gajdos? It seemed that way. It seemed that the offer here was to launder cryptocurrency through ZuriBank or suffer from some exposure with unknown consequences.

Istvan's thick right hand shot out and grabbed Lars by the throat. His fingers dug into the flesh on both sides and pulled Lars's skinny body closer. Suddenly, Lars's pretty, blue eyes were very big indeed. His hands went to his throat. He tried to pry Istvan's fingers away, but Istvan's hand was too strong. Istvan had spent most of his life as a workingman, not like this ...

Insect.

"Would you like me to kill you?" Istvan said.

"No." Lars could barely shake his head.

"I will kill you and throw your body out in the snow. Do you understand?"

"Yes."

"Tell this to your masters at ZuriBank. I don't know what you're talking about. I was not involved in any crypto theft. I may be a billionaire, but that is because I own successful, legitimate businesses. And I don't require the services of a money launderer at this time."

He shoved Lars away, again by the throat. They stood a couple meters apart. Lars put a hand to his neck. The skin at his throat was bright red. He looked at Istvan with aggrieved but not angry eyes. If anything, Istvan would call those eyes thoughtful. Well, he'd better not have too many thoughts. Zuribank was not going to blackmail Istvan Gajdos, not in this lifetime.

Istvan picked up the bottle of vodka.

"Enjoy the party," he said, and he turned to go back to the dance floor.

***

"Bartender," the tall, blond-haired man said, gesturing with one hand. The other hand was gently massaging his throat, right where Istvan Gajdos had only recently been choking him.

The bartender came over. She looked at the tall man. His eyes were blue. He wore nice clothes. He was very good-looking and appeared to be rich. He was exactly the kind of man she would expect to see at a party thrown by Istvan Gajdos.

"What's your name?" the man said.

"Helena," the bartender said. It wasn't her real name, of course.

"Helena," the man repeated.

"Like Helen of Troy," she said.

"I like that," the man said. "It's a very pretty name for a very pretty woman."

Helena allowed herself a smile. What difference did it make? In the end, it would make no difference whatsoever.

"Can I get you something?"

"How about your mobile telephone number?"

The man had bounced back quickly from being choked by a deranged oligarch. Only a moment had passed, and already he was hitting on the bartender. Good for him. He was resilient.

She held up her left hand, showing him the ring there. "What does that tell you?"

He smiled and shook his head. "It tells me you wear a fake wedding band so that men riding this train won't try to seduce you."

He was smart too. A good-looking man, who was probably rich, was resilient, and who saw through ploys easily.

"What about a drink first?" Helena said. "I don't know you at all. One of my rules is not to give my number to strange men I don't know."

He held his hand out, and she took it. He gave her a gentle pump. "My name is Lars. I work for ZuriBank in Switzerland. I work out of the Zurich office, but I travel a great deal. I'm here because Istvan is an important client of ours."

Now, Helena's smile broadened. So, Lars was indeed rich. "I saw him choking you before he left. He must be a very important client."

"He's a passionate man," Lars said. "We hope to deepen the relationship." He looked directly into her eyes. "And personally, I hope to deepen my relationship with you. It's crazy, I know, because we just met. But I feel strongly we're going to know each other better."

"How about that drink?" Helena said.

Lars shrugged. "Of course. Vodka and tonic, the best you have, with just a twist of lime. On the rocks."

She turned her back to him and went to the counter in the corner. Of course, he would order the best. They only had the best, and everything on the train was free. She took a scoop of ice and put it in a glass. In almost the same motion, she opened a drawer, grabbed a knife, and sliced a lime into quarters, then eighths.

As she did that, she slipped a small white pill onto the counter and crushed it with the palm of her hand. She brushed the dust into her other palm and dropped it into the glass with the ice.

She poured a heavy shot into the glass and finished it off with the tonic and lime. Then she stirred it until the dust from the pill was completely absorbed.

Lars was a silly man. He was silly to think that his money, or his looks, was going to get him anywhere with her on a night like tonight. He probably made these silly overtures to women everywhere he went, and they probably worked. He wasn't just looking for a woman. There was no challenge in that. After all, as a guest of Istvan Gajdos, Lars could simply have one of the prostitutes on the train.

No, Lars was a man who valued the hunt.

Helena had to admit it was kind of fun. But there was no time, and Lars's interest in her, however fleeting, could prove to be a distraction.

He was going to sleep anyway, like most people on this train, so he might as well start now. Helena guessed that given the amount of alcohol he had already ingested, if he didn't lapse into an overdose coma, he would fall asleep sometime in the next twenty minutes and stay that way for at least twelve hours.

She passed the drink across the bar to him. He picked it up and sipped it.

"Lovely," he said. "Delicious. Just like you."

She smiled. "Better drink up."

He did. He drank deeply. "Well Helena, where are you from?"

"Does it matter?" she said.

He shook his head. Was he already growing sleepy? His eyelids seemed heavy. He must have had a lot to drink.

"No. It doesn't matter."

"Are you married?" Helena said.

Lars smiled. "Does it matter?"

Helena shook her head. To her left, two more customers, a man and a woman, came in from the dance floor car. She might as well put them to sleep too. It was time to begin. The more people asleep when the time came, the easier this would be. Istvan Gajdos had to be awake, but other than him, the whole train could take a long winter nap.

"No," Helena said. "It doesn't matter if you're married."

Nothing about Lars mattered at all.

CHAPTER EIGHTEEN

4:05 am Central European Time
A guesthouse
Flusspromenade (north bank of the Inn River)
Innsbruck, Austria

"Casimir," Gallo said. "Wake up."

Troy watched the man in the flickering semi-darkness of the bedroom.

Casimir Skolnick was asleep under heavy, flannel blankets in a king-sized bed. There was what appeared to be a young woman under there with him, her blonde hair tousled and sticking up over the top of the covers. They had left several lighted candles going on plates and saucers around the room. The shades were drawn, blocking the light from the streets outside.

It was cold here in Innsbruck. Just driving into town from the airport made Troy feel cold. Looking at how the snowy Nordkette Mountains rose steeply from behind these apartment blocks sent a shiver down Troy's spine. The river already had ice on it.

And it was chilly in this flat. The building was old. The radiator was knocking a bit as steam heat began to rise from it. There must be a timer somewhere, telling it to start taking the chill off at 4:00 am.

"Casimir," Gallo said again.

Gallo, Dubois, and Troy had made the flight to Innsbruck in about ninety minutes. Casimir was an international pimp, and one of his clients was Istvan Gajdos. It was no coincidence that Casimir was here on the morning the Gajdos party train was due to arrive.

The woman woke before Casimir.

She startled at the sound of Gallo's voice and pulled the covers down from her face, her eyes wide. An instant later, she was up and moving. Troy took two sideways steps and got in front of her, hindering her attempt at escape. He grabbed her with both arms. She was wearing a tiny, leopard-patterned chemise.

"No!" she shouted.

It was too early in the morning for shouting. She could wake up everyone in this building with a little more of that.

He put his hand over her mouth. She struggled against him like a wild animal caught in a net. She was small but strong, with raw energy. She bit the palm of his hand, digging her teeth in deep. He grunted in pain but also annoyance.

He looked around for something to stuff in her mouth. Dubois appeared from the shadows in the corner of the room. She was holding a red ball gag in one hand. It had a strap to fasten it to the back of someone's head.

"Fun and games in here," Troy said.

"Yep," Dubois said. She held out her other hand to him. That hand had a pair of silver handcuffs, lined with some furry material.

"Perfect," Troy said.

He removed his hand from the woman's chompers, and Dubois quickly fitted the ball gag to her mouth. Then she tightened it around the back of the woman's head. Finally, she reached behind the woman and clasped the cuffs on her wrists.

Troy steered the woman to an elegant accent chair that was against the wall. He pushed her into it, gently but firmly. Then he held her there with one hand on top of her head. She stared up at him, ball in her mouth, hands behind her back. Her eyes were both aggrieved and sleepy.

Troy looked back at the bed. The man named Casimir was finally rolling over. He was a jowly, heavyset guy. He was mostly bald, with a little bit of gray and brown hair around the ears. He was wearing a white, sleeveless t-shirt.

He looked at Gallo standing over him and didn't seem at all surprised. He sighed and turned to look at Troy, Dubois, and the bondage queen now sitting quietly on her throne. The woman had a sort of electric energy in her body. She was moving and jittering and squirming, though she made no attempt to stand.

Casimir said something in a language Troy didn't understand.

"What did he say?" Troy said to Dubois.

Dubois was smiling. "He said, 'What is it this time?' I guess he's grown accustomed to this type of thing."

"Police," Troy said. "You understand police? English?"

Casimir nodded. He waved a hand. "Ya. I know. Police. It's all paid already."

Troy shook his head. "No. It isn't."

109

***

"It's a terrible idea," Casimir said. "I don't think you understand how terrible."

He was a slovenly guy in a pair of flannel pants, slippers, and now a stained, blue sweatshirt. He had a wide belly and skinny legs. His face was pock-marked, possibly with some ailment like adolescent acne from decades before. He was sitting in the chair that his girlfriend had recently vacated.

Once she realized there was no danger, she had been happy to go back to bed, still with the gag in her mouth, and the handcuffs on. She wasn't going to be any trouble for anyone. She just wanted to get back under the warm covers.

Troy didn't blame her. He'd gotten up early to raid a flat in Madrid yesterday morning, and he hadn't slept since.

Casimir smoked a cigarette. They had given him a cup of instant coffee from the kitchen of this flat. Casimir knew he was in a difficult position, and no matter how it played out, it wasn't going to be good for him. He seemed to be trying to decide which option was worse.

"If I let the police take my place," he said, "I'm ruined. I might as well be dead."

"They're not going to know we're the police," Troy said. "They're not going to know who we are."

Casimir shook his head. "YOU cannot go. I told you already. They'll know you right away. You look like Special Air Service, Spetsnaz, any of these. A commando, you understand? No one will believe you're coming from me. I don't send gorillas. I like to stay on good terms with the clients. If I can do that ..."

He shrugged. "Then I don't need gorillas."

He gestured at Gallo and Dubois. "These two, maybe they can go. She's perfect, exotic, beautiful." He looked at her. "You'll have to find some game, my darling. Some trick. Gajdos is a man of great appetites. He's a greedy man. He wants everything in the world, you know? When he casts an eye upon you, he'll want you right away. I guess you won't share the feeling."

Dubois shook her head and didn't smile. "No. I won't." She turned to Troy, her face a grimace at the mere thought of it.

Casimir jerked his chin at Gallo. "You. If you put glasses on your face, a bigger coat, clothes that are loose fitting, make you look weaker.

110

You're old enough. You look like someone I send. You could pass, I think."

He gestured at his own cheek. "The scar helps. You got knifed. It looks right."

"Thanks," Gallo said. "I'll take that as a compliment."

Casimir sighed again. "It's a terrible idea. I could be killed for this."

"We have you crisscrossing fourteen countries in the past year," Gallo said. "We have anonymous payments passed to you. We have emails, voice recordings, hotel stays. We have video of you boarding airplanes and boats with females known to be prostitutes."

Casimir shook his head gently. "Nothing you say sounds illegal. I'm an EU citizen. I may travel as I like."

"There's a bag under the bed with half a kilo of cocaine in it," Troy said. "Everyone in this room knows that. It has a tag on it with a red number 7. That's how the cops and custom agents on the take know not to touch it."

Casimir looked at him grumpily. "What is this? On the take?"

"Corrupt. Paid off."

Casimir nodded. "Ah."

"You brought that bag from Poland here to Austria. In other words, international cocaine trafficking. If we take you in now, what's going to happen? My guess is you'll breathe fresh air again maybe in five or ten years. You're a little old to spend that kind of time in prison."

Casimir sighed again. "You put it there. You put the cocaine in my bag."

"Casimir," Gallo said. "We intercepted the mobile phone call where they told you to bring the coke. We have the x-rays from when your bag went through security at the airport in Warsaw. It's clear enough."

Casimir looked at Gallo. "They'll kill me."

Gallo shrugged. "So, go to prison. I don't really care. If you weren't so stupid, you'd see we're trying to save your friend Istvan's life, not arrest him. We won't reveal ourselves unless something bad happens."

Casimir shook his head. "He's not my friend. He's just a client. And if something bad happens, I don't think you can stop it."

Troy tended to agree with that assessment. He was having second thoughts about all this. If the plan was to thwart a hijacking, Dubois and Gallo were going to need him on the train. He was the best fighter in the group, by far. How were Dubois and fifty-year-old Gallo supposed to take down a group of armed men?

Casimir stared at the floor. For a late-middle-aged pimp who just a little while ago was in bed with a beautiful young woman, he seemed about as world weary as a man could get.

"I'll do it," he said. "I'll tell them I'm sick, and I will vouch for you. You will have to accompany the other two girls on board. The real girls."

"Where are they?" Dubois said.

Casimir gestured with his head. "In the next flat. They give you a cover story. They can get to work, and you can hide in a room. Like a ghost. Make yourself go away. Maybe the clients will forget about you."

"I don't like it," Troy said.

Gallo and Dubois looked at him now. Gallo raised an eyebrow.

"You don't like what? We're infiltrating, exactly according to plan. We need two to board, and one for support, just like we talked about. You're the support person." He indicated himself and Dubois. "We're the boarding team."

"And if you get in a scrap?" Troy said.

Gallo shrugged. "We're both pretty good in a scrap. As far as I've seen."

Troy looked at Dubois. "I thought you were worried I was going to get you killed. What happened to that?"

Dubois nodded. "That's right. I was worried YOU were going to get me killed. I'm not worried about Carlo. He's not going to overreact and cause a sudden massacre."

Ouch. That stings.

Dubois and Gallo seemed to have become a little too familiar during Troy's absence. "You two are going to engage the gunmen on your own?"

Dubois shook her head. "If there's a hijacking, we are going to contact you to alert the Austrian authorities. As planned. And then you can contact Jan to detect, block, or reverse any remote hacking that's happening. Gajdos also has bodyguards on the train. We can team up with them if need be."

"What if you can't?"

She shrugged. "The drug bag has to come on the train. We'll put two guns inside of it and smuggle them onto the train too. If we have to fight on our own, we'll fight on our own."

"What if Jan can't stop the hack and the train is going out of control?" Troy said.

"It's like we talked about. If we have to, we will simply get off the train."

"And leave hostages behind?"

"We'll rescue whoever we can, by whatever means is available to us. You know that. And all of this assumes there are any hostages. This could just as easily be an undercover training exercise. Practice, so to speak."

"I don't like it," Troy said again.

Gallo stared at him. "What's the matter with you, Stark? Fear of missing out? Can't stand to be the towel boy on even one operation? Your manhood's not at stake here, buddy. Nobody's trying to steal your mojo. Casimir knows these people. He knows his business. He says they're not going to believe in you, so you're on the bench. We need you on the outside, doing your job."

Troy stared back at Gallo. For a moment, Troy couldn't come up with a single thing to say. Then he did think of something.

Troy Stark doesn't ride the bench.

But he didn't say that.

Gallo went on. "This is probably going to amount to nothing. The whole day could be over by noon. So, take it easy, okay?"

Towel boy. Bench warmer. Take it easy.

This guy was a piece of work.

Gallo looked down at Casimir again. "Let's go, buddy. We need you to introduce us to the other two girls. Don't, under any circumstances, tell them we're the cops."

"The girls will know what you are," Casimir said. "They know me. I am never sick. If I say I'm going to accompany, I accompany. I protect them. My rule is you cannot hurt the merchandise. I have many, many relationships in many countries. Even a man like Gajdos respects this."

"I'll protect them," Gallo said. "I'm your representative on that train. But if they think I'm a cop, they can't tell anyone that."

Casimir shook his head. "They won't say nothing about you. They're good   girls.   Very   quiet   country   girls."

CHAPTER NINETEEN

6:10 am Central European Time
Aboard the *East Meets West*
Innsbruck Central Train Station
Innsbruck, Austria

"Who are you?" Stanislaus Lepke said.

He stood at the top of the steps at the passenger entry door. He was big and broad. There was no getting past him. Outside, the sun was just giving the frigid early morning sky a bit of weak light. From here, on the other side of the station, he could catch a glimpse of the snow-capped peaks right outside of the town.

Stanislaus, or "Big Stan" as they sometimes called him, was one of the bodyguards for Istvan Gajdos. At thirty-five years old, he had only come on Istvan's security detail in the past three months, but he had been a guard for most of his adult life.

Diamond traders, pop stars, footballers, Big Stan had worked for them all. At one point, he had spent more than two years as a body man for the Serbian techno DJ who called himself Red Dawn. Red Dawn had been massively popular, and Big Stan had traveled all over Europe and North Africa in the kid's entourage.

Big Stan and eight or ten other guys, all armed, would sometimes have to form a wedge around this skinny kid with spiked hair and tattoos everywhere, who was swimming in an extra-large, green and white striped Glasgow Celtic football jersey. Or a custom-made, red jersey with the hammer and sickle on it. Or the infamous Arkan's Tigers jersey that caused such a stir in the western newspapers. Red Dawn's signature football jerseys were always like tents on his bony frame.

They had to force their way through swarms of people that seemed desperate to touch him. Moving through a mega-nightclub in Berlin or a warehouse rave in Belgrade to the kid's turntables was like fighting a ground war in the mud.

Red Dawn was some kind of strange Messiah. And he went out just like a modern savior should, hooked on opiates and dead from an overdose at the age of twenty-three. His death left Big Stan in the lurch, a little bit. Pay was always a month or more behind with Red Dawn, which was fine when the entourage was traveling and it was all paid for—hotels, food, transportation, drugs, hookers, and everything else. But with no DJ, the never-ending tour came to a sudden halt.

And Big Stan never did see his last paycheck. So, he was in free fall for a while, bleeding money, until he signed on with Istvan. The pay was good, but it was an uncertain gig. Istvan's moods were more variable than those of a teenage girl. People came and people went. Istvan could fire people while walking past them in a hallway. Something about them would catch Istvan's eye, something that displeased him, and the person was gone right then and there.

"You're out," he would say. "Okay? No argument. You're done here. I've had enough of you. Call us in six months. Maybe I'll take you back. But I don't know. Maybe I won't. I wouldn't bet your mother's farm on it."

Big Stan had seen it happen exactly that way. He was starting to think that he might have caught on, though. Three months and he was still here, working night and day now. The trick was to anticipate Istvan's needs and stay out of his line of sight. The best thing about this run was Istvan's pay deposits came right on time.

Even so, it couldn't last forever. Big Stan knew that. He was hoping to stumble onto another Red Dawn type soon.

The guy down on the platform was older, maybe in his fifties or sixties, with a white beard and white hair under a wool hat. He wore a heavy coat of gray wool. He carried a walking stick of white ash or some other wood. He had a prominent scar on his cheek. His face and hair were old, but his eyes were sharp. And his body looked strong. He could probably do some damage with that stick of his.

Plumes of white came out each time he breathed. It was cold in Innsbruck. And the guy was breathing a lot. He was becoming impatient. He had tried to board with three young whores, who Big Stan had let pass and were already behind him on the train. One of them, the pretty, black girl with the big Afro, was carrying the bag with #7 on the tag. That was an important bag.

"Who are you?" Big Stan said again.

The guy gestured into the train with his chin. "Casimir sent me to look after the girls. He told me to take them to the door of car number three. So that's where we came. And now we ran into you."

Big Stan shook his head. "Why didn't Casimir come?"

"He don't feel good," the man said. "He came down with something, maybe the flu, maybe just a bad cold. But he doesn't want his girls alone on the train. Your boss has a reputation, I'm sure you know about. Casimir likes his merchandise to remain intact. Gajdos isn't the only customer in Europe."

"I don't like it," Big Stan said. "This is the first I heard about it. Why didn't Casimir call?"

The man shrugged. "I don't know. Maybe he didn't feel like it. He's not as young as he used to be. I can tell you, when people start getting old, sometimes they just don't feel like doing things. You'll see. Maybe."

The man's hawk eyes looked Big Stan up and down. "If you live long enough."

Up the platform, the train whistled. Somewhere in the train station, a pleasant tone sounded. An announcement began on an overhead intercom. From here, Big Stan couldn't make out what was being said.

"Listen, you going to let me up there? If not, then send the girls back out. The train's about to leave."

"Who are you?" Big Stan said again. He'd already asked three times.

"My name is Gallo, like the cock crowing."

The old man pronounced his name "guy-yo," the Italian way.

"Italia?" Big Stan said.

The man nodded. "Yeah. Born in Sicilia. Moved to America when I was a kid. Casimir told me to look after the girls. Is that so hard to understand?"

The appearance here of this man put Big Stan in an uncomfortable position. Istvan had told him to come down here to greet the old pimp Casimir and the girls he was bringing on board. The girls were good, high-quality, especially the black girl.

She was something else. Very, very pretty. It was hard to tell with the winter layers on, but Big Stan was willing to bet there was a nice little body hiding under there too. In fact, he was hoping to sample her before anyone else noticed. It was lust at first sight.

But now this guy was here, and Big Stan either needed to let him on board, or go see Istvan in his stateroom, where he had retreated with a couple of girls an hour or so ago. Waking up Istvan—or worse, interrupting him—was not a strategy that would bring Big Stan long-term employment. Encountering a problem, and making an executive decision to fix it, was how you stayed on Istvan's good side.

"I need to talk to Casimir," Big Stan said.

The man shrugged again. "So, call him. You need his number?"

"No. I have it." He held up a hand. "Just wait."

"I don't want to get stuck on this platform with the train gone and the girls on the train. If that happens, I promise you're gonna lose your job. Because Casimir will never deliver another thing. You know what the girls have in their suitcases, right?"

Big Stan sighed. He had nearly forgotten about the coke. It had been a long night, after several long days. Life with Istvan was a constant party, and even though the bodyguards were supposed to stay sober, it was hard to say no to everything.

"Wait. One minute. He better answer."

Big Stan took out his phone, found Casimir's number, and hit the button. The phone rang three times.

"Casimir," the voice said. It certainly sounded like him.

"It's Stanislaus. I'm at Innsbruck train station. Why aren't you here?"

"I'm sick. It's a little flu, or something. I don't know. It's been coming for days, finally took me down."

Casimir's voice was raspy, and he sounded like he was mostly asleep.

"Who is this person you sent with the girls?"

"Gallo? He's okay. He works for me. I got him to come here in a pinch. You should thank him. If I didn't have him here, I wouldn't send the girls. I'm too sick to be there."

Big Stan shrugged. "All right."

"There's a black girl," Casimir said. "She's getting over what I have. She should be fine if you let her sleep for a couple of hours."

This was getting crazier and crazier. "Casimir, if she sleeps for a couple of hours, she misses the whole thing."

That wasn't true and Big Stan knew it. If she went to sleep now, what she missed was Big Stan.

"No, she doesn't," Casimir said. "She has medicine with her. Just let her take some and then nap for a little while. She worked last night here in Innsbruck, okay? She's tired, and a little bit sick. She's a good girl, but you have to give her a chance."

Big Stan sighed and shook his head. "Is she going to make the guests sick? You gonna cause a whole epidemic on my train, Casimir?"

"Oh, is it your train now? I thought it belonged to that big Hungarian illiterate. Anyway, no. She's not gonna make anyone sick. She's past that. Just give her time to rest, okay?"

"Okay, okay. But you're going to end up talking to Istvan about all this."

It didn't really matter at the moment. A lot of the guests were asleep anyway. It had been a blowout party night, and several guests didn't even make it back to their rooms. They just passed out on the furniture in the various lounges. One man had fallen asleep on the floor in front of the giant fish tank.

"That's fine," Casimir said. "I've been around a lot longer than Istvan. I'll still be here after he's gone."

Big Stan smiled. Every word of that was probably true.

"Okay, Casimir. I'll talk to you."

Big Stan hung up the phone and waved the old guy up from the train platform.

"Come on, old man. The train is about to leave."

***

"You can use this room to prepare," the giant leering bodyguard said.

He stood in the narrow hallway by the open door to the stateroom. There were no windows in the hall, but Dubois could sense that the train had already started to move. She felt the first lurch as it began to leave the platform, and now there was the feeling of smooth acceleration.

The man stared down at her. He was tall, probably 190 centimeters, at a guess. And he was broad, with a chest like a brick wall. He wore a plain, black t-shirt and jeans, with work boots on his feet that might have given him a little more height. His hair was buzz cut to his head. His face and eyes were hard. He reminded her of a movie version of a fascist storm trooper, or maybe the Russian boxer in one of the old *Rocky* movies from America.

And yet, he smiled at her. She didn't trust that smile. It didn't reach his eyes.

He reached out and grabbed the bag with #7 on the tag. The bag had breezed through security. Now, she was holding it, and he was also holding it. They were practically holding hands. The bag had the cocaine in it. He must know that. But the bag also had the guns inside. Dubois hadn't had time, or anywhere safe, to remove them.

"The boss said you need a little nap," he said. "He told me on the telephone."

Dubois nodded. "I'm tired. I feel a little sick."

The smile was as if a shark could smile. "I hope you will not give me a disease."

She went to pass him. "I don't think you're one of the guests."

He grabbed her by the arm. He was fast. His free hand snaked out and had her bicep in an instant. And he was strong. She could feel the squeeze through her coat. His hand was big enough to circle her entire arm.

"You work for who I say. You make me happy, and then I assign you."

Normally, she would shrug off someone who did this. But the man was just too big and strong. A burst of *something* went through her entire body—adrenaline, fear, excitement—she didn't know what to call it. This was a very dangerous man, and she was trapped on this train with him.

And he thought she was a prostitute.

Then Gallo was there. He pushed his way past the other two girls, who were more than happy to let him pass.

"That's not for you, Boris."

Gallo barely came up to the man's chin. Also, he was probably two decades older. But his eyes were calm. They might have even seen some humor in the situation. One thing was clear. Gallo was not afraid of this man at all. But then again, the man wasn't interested in him.

The big man's shark eyes fell on Gallo. "The name is Stan."

Now, Gallo did smile. "Well, Stan, thanks for opening the door. We'll see you a little later, all right?"

Stan's big hand snaked away from Dubois's bicep. He shrugged, but he did not let go of the bag.

"This is for me," he said.

"It's ours until we hand it over," Dubois said.

"We already paid for the bag," Stan said. "Istvan demands that I receive it right away."

They could have a tug of war over the bag, but it wouldn't make sense. The man's eyes were fire. He had backed down from harassing Dubois, but he wouldn't let go of the bag nearly so easily. His job probably depended on it.

But the guns ...

Gallo shrugged. "Of course. It's your bag."

Dubois released it.

Stan pulled it way and smiled. "Nice and heavy." He waved his free arm into the open doorway. "Enjoy."

He looked at Dubois and winked. "We will meet again."

She shook her head. "Only if I have a nightmare."

The smile came back, sharper and more shark-like than ever. Clearly, the big man enjoyed this witty back and forth.

"I can't wait. But I promise it will be your dream come true."

Dubois stepped into the room first, if only to get away from that guy. But then her perspective changed. This was instantly the best train compartment she had ever seen. There was a big, king-sized bed against the wall to the corridor, and she put her bags on it. The entire far wall was a long window, nearly floor to ceiling.

Outside, the astonishing white-capped mountains of Innsbruck were passing in the distance. Closer by, there was a quiet snowy village, still asleep in the early morning, firewood smoke coming from chimneys.

"That's some view," Gallo said as he came in.

"What are we going to do about that bag?" Dubois said.

Gallo raised both hands in a "Don't Shoot" gesture. "We're not going to worry about it. We couldn't fight him over the bag. If they look inside and find the other things, we'll tell them to call Casimir. We don't know anything about it."

The whole thing gave her a sinking feeling.

"Yes," Dubois said. "But now we don't have …"

The two other women came in and Dubois stopped talking. They were both blondes, but at least one of them got the blonde from a bottle—she had dark roots. Dubois understood the urge to color her hair—the customers probably preferred blondes. Dubois herself had never understood that desire in men.

"My God," one of the women, the true blonde, said. "It's amazing."

"I wonder if the people out there can see in here," Gallo said.

The girl shook her head. "Oh, I don't think so."

"Anyway, it's a little tight in here," Gallo said. "But we'll make do."

The girls looked at him blankly. It probably hadn't occurred to them that the room was tight. Personal space was probably not a luxury they got a lot of, and in any event, they probably weren't going to spend much time in here.

They were already stripping out of their heavy coats and down to their party clothes.

"That big man is going to be a problem for me," Dubois said.

Gallo smiled and shook his head. He was shrugging out of his coat too. "Don't worry. If it comes to that, I'll just kill him. We'll call it self-defense."

Now, the girls were ignoring him. They probably heard men make idle threats of murder all the time, and nothing ever happened.

The bottle blonde was wearing a purple bodysuit that seemed painted on. She sat on the bed now, removing her boots and switching into high heels. The true blonde was wearing a red mini dress.

The way Gallo spoke was so nonchalant, and Dubois didn't doubt that he meant it. "Are you Stark's dad?" she said.

Gallo shrugged and smiled. "I don't remember. Do you have a picture of his mom?"

The true blonde was touching up her makeup in a tiny compact mirror. The bottle blonde was staring at Gallo again.

Gallo didn't seem to like having them around.

"Okay, you ladies get to work," he said. He raised a finger at them. "Don't say a word about anything to anybody. Understood?"

They both nodded without enthusiasm.

"I work for Casimir. And Casimir would be here with you if he could. So, if you have any trouble, any problem at all, let me know, and I'll take care of it."

He looked at Dubois. "That goes double for you."

CHAPTER TWENTY

6:20 am Central European Time
A guesthouse
Flusspromenade (north bank of the Inn River)
Innsbruck, Austria

"You did a good job, Casimir," Troy said.

The entire conversation had been on speaker phone. Casimir and whoever was on the other end, one of Gajdos's goons probably, had spoken English, a language they had in common. It sounded like Dubois got on easily, as Troy suspected would happen. And the guard let Gallo on too. It just took a little cajoling.

"I'm proud of you. The entire continent owes you a debt of gratitude."

Troy still didn't like it, but at least there were two of them on board, and the operation was moving forward. If Gallo couldn't get on, they would have had to abort the mission. Though knowing those two, they probably would have just had Dubois soldier on by herself.

"You gonna let me go now?" Casimir said.

Troy shook his head. "No."

Casimir lay in the bed with the girlfriend, who Troy had learned was named Emona, and who was not one of the working girls. Casimir and Emona were tied up together and incapacitated in a manner of Troy's own design.

"I'm not gonna talk to anybody," Casimir said.

Troy nodded. "No. You're not. And we're going to make sure of that."

Casimir and Emona lay side by side on their backs, their arms stretched above them, wrists clasped to the headboard of the bed. At the bottom of the bed, Casimir's right ankle was zip-tied to Emona's left ankle. Casimir's left ankle and Emona's right ankle were both cuffed to the bed frame. Troy had long ago taken the gag out of Emona's mouth. She wouldn't need it anymore.

After they were secured, Troy covered them with blankets, including their feet. It was still chilly in here, and Troy was sympathetic to their plight.

He had found some sleeping pills in the bathroom. Earlier, he had given two to Emona, who had taken them right away. She was already out and snoring gently. Smart girl. She knew the best course of action was to sleep through whatever trouble Casimir had gotten them into.

"This is uncomfortable," Casimir said.

"It'll be okay for a few hours," Troy said. "As soon as we know the story with that train, someone will be by to let you go."

"I'll be dead by then," Casimir said. "I have a bad heart."

"I know," Troy said, glancing over at the various adult toys these two had on the dresser. Casimir had the kind of bad heart that would still be racing decades from now while he pursued his naughty fun and pimped out women half or even one-third of his age. "Try to survive a little longer, okay?"

Now, Troy pulled the blankets all the way up to their chins. He had two more sleeping pills. He popped them into Casimir's mouth.

"Swallow those."

"I need water to swallow," Casimir said.

The pills were tiny. "Swallow them or I will push them down your throat with my fingers."

Casimir gulped the pills down.

"Can I get you anything before I go?" Troy said.

"I need to go to the bathroom," Casimir said.

Troy shook his head. Talk about an obvious ploy. The whole thing was set up. Troy undoes the binds so that Casimir can go to the bathroom. Then Casimir tries to extend the bathroom visit in some way. Maybe he locks himself in there, and Troy has to break the door down. Maybe he slips and falls and cracks his skull. Maybe he has a heart attack. Then Troy has to deal with Casimir the heart patient on the floor of the bathroom. Then Casimir needs a trip to the hospital. Only a cold-hearted animal would ignore an older man's dangerous heart fluctuations.

"No."

If Casimir needed to go to the bathroom, he should have said it before now.

"What am I supposed to do? I have to go."

Troy shrugged. "Piss in the bed. Anything else?"

"Why are you doing this?" Casimir said.

Troy's shoulders slumped. It should be obvious why he was doing this. But everybody was the hero of their own story. Everybody was the good guy.

"I don't trust you, Casimir. You're a criminal in case you didn't know that. I need to keep you wrapped up for a while. Otherwise, you're going to call your friends on that train. Or you're going to start moving around town, seeing people you know, and someone will ask you what happened, and you'll tell them. You're going to compromise my operation in other words. I can't allow you to do that. So, you're going to stay right here until the operation is over."

"You don't know me very well," Casimir said.

"You're right. I don't. All the more reason to keep you here."

"I'll get out of this. I'll scream the minute you leave."

Troy nodded. "I know. I figured that."

Troy went back to the dresser and took the red ball gag from Casimir's pile of goodies, the same one Emona had been wearing earlier. He came over, popped the plastic ball in Casimir's half-open mouth, and pulled it hard into place. Then he fastened the leather strap around Casimir's head.

"Hmmmm!" Casimir said. "Hey!"

There was a TV set across the room from them. Troy went over and turned it on. He put the sound on low, but loud enough to compete with Casimir's grunts and exhalations. He took the remote control from the top of the TV and clicked around until he found a movie channel. It was still early in the morning. The channel was showing the original *Blue Lagoon,* dubbed into German.

"Enjoy," Troy said. "Have a good sleep."

He went out of the bedroom and left them in there. The door to the flat had a door hanger on it. Troy glanced at it. It said something in large letters, probably in German, and beneath that it had what must be the translation in several languages.

Sure enough, one of them was *Do Not Disturb.*

Troy went out into the hallway and pulled the door shut behind him. The locking mechanism fell into place. He hung the door hanger with the *Do Not Disturb* side outward. Now all he had to do was figure out a way to get himself on that train. Either that or find a way back to Madrid.

He passed through the lobby of the building and went outside onto the boulevard. It was a cold morning. Winter started early around here. Across the street, the ice flowing downriver made loud cracking sounds.

A man was standing near the door to the building, also watching the river. He was smaller than Troy, wearing a heavy coat and smoking a cigarette. He had on winter pants made of wool. His hair was dark.

He turned to Troy. It was the man who called himself Alex.

"Hey buddy," he said. "Here for the skiing?"

Troy smiled. "Why am I not surprised to see you?"

Alex shrugged. "I'm everywhere at once. I wouldn't be surprised, either."

"Why are you here?" Troy said. "Metal Shop?"

Alex shook his head. "Nah. Way outside my bailiwick. Missing Persons thinks they're going to haul you into a committee or tribunal sooner or later. He says to mind your neck in the meantime."

"You mean Stu?" Troy said.

Alex stared at him.

"You here to protect me?" Troy said.

"Nope."

"Kill me, in that case?"

"Ha!" Alex said. "Could I kill you?"

"Nobody's been able to so far. But you're pretty sneaky."

"Persons is interested in why you guys came this way. There are two hundred other trains in motion, but you picked Istvan Gajdos. Persons said to get close in case you need anything, but then I come here and find out your team infiltrated, and you're not even on the train."

"I was a game day scratch. Our contact said I wouldn't be believable."

Alex nodded. "I buy that. But what about Istvan caught your eye?"

"I don't know. He was all over the news, this inaugural train ride of his, so he popped out at me. It seemed to have clear similarities to Scotland."

"Right," Alex said. "I can see the similarities. Not exactly the same, but similar. But there are at least a dozen luxury trains in motion at this moment. And the interesting thing is Gajdos wasn't all over the news. The coverage was minor at best, as least in Western Europe. The guy is a blip. He's beneath most people's contempt. No one believes his wealth is anything more than a house of cards. One of these years, some people we know are going to pull the plug on his friend Racz, and Gajdos is going to go straight where he belongs, the dustbin of history."

Troy raised an eyebrow. It was one thing for Alex to know what was happening now, it was quite another to know what was going to happen. "Is that a fact?"

"I can't guarantee the timing," Alex said. "Otherwise, I'd put a bet on it."

Alex reached into his coat pocket and came out with a slim aluminum can. It was silver. Rock Star Zero. Two cups of coffee in one small can, plus various unregulated substances to keep the high going. At one time, Troy lived on these things.

"Here. You look tired."

"To be honest, I haven't gotten much sleep," Troy said.

"No one can tell," Alex said.

Troy took the can and popped it open. He took a long gulp and watched Alex over the rim. A dark-haired guy with coffee-colored skin. Alex was a little out of his element in winter clothes. He could be a Middle easterner. Troy thought back to the time when Alex insisted that he was a Sikh from Kansas. He didn't bring up any of that anymore.

"In any case, Gajdos was all over the news feed on my computer," Troy said. "There was no way I could miss it."

Alex eyed him closely. "How's the cyber security at your shop?"

Troy shrugged. "As far as I know, it's tip top. Why, you think someone fed me the Gajdos thing?"

The truth was, he had no idea how the security was. He had assumed Jan Bakker was in charge of it, but that might not be right. Bakker was an analyst. Cyber security could well be handled by the Interpol main office.

"I'm the paranoid type," Alex said.

"It pays to be that way."

Alex stared out at the icy river flowing slowly along. "I like to work. It's hard to work when you're not alive."

A thought occurred to Troy. "You have wheels with you?"

"Range Rover. Four-wheel drive. Pretty sure-footed, so far."

"I need a ride," Troy said.

Alex nodded. "I know. That's why I'm here."

CHAPTER TWENTY ONE

6:45 am Central European Time
Aboard the *East Meets West*
The Austrian Alps, Austria

"Grigori, are you awake?"

Helena of Troy stood at the open doorway of a tiny cabin near the back of the train. The cabin was the security command center. Inside, there was a desk and chair facing a bank of sixteen video monitors showing scenes from cameras mounted in various places throughout the train.

Each video monitor cycled through four different camera views every ten seconds, meaning there were sixty-four cameras in total. With the touch of a button, the guard tasked with watching the monitors could choose to extend the amount of time a monitor displayed a particular camera. He might do this if something unusual or suspicious was taking place in one scene, or in the event of an emergency.

There was an extensive intercom system here, which could communicate with staff members in the kitchen, in the staterooms, as well as with the train driver, and with Istvan's personal train car. There was a radio the guard could use to call outside the train-to-train stations along their path and the train line control room.

Helena knew all this because she had befriended the guard who was watching the monitors. He told her all about his work. He even showed her how several of the cameras were secretly mounted in staterooms. Istvan had done this so that when the train became popular among the European elites, he could blackmail public figures and wealthy individuals with footage of their bedroom activities.

"Grigori?"

Helena had brought Grigori a strong mug of coffee soon after they left Innsbruck. It had been a long night, and he was growing tired. She'd been more than happy to bring him the coffee. She had also crushed and stirred two powerful opiate pills into it.

Now, Grigori was in the security command room, fast asleep with his head on the desk. She squeezed into the room with him for a moment. He was a large man with a broad back. There wasn't much space in there with him.

She pushed his big head hard. His neck was so thick and strong, she could barely budge the solid block of a head.

"Grigori."

His eyes were slits. His mouth was open, pressed against the desk. A thin line of drool was spilling out onto the desk. He was out.

"Good night, Grigori."

She pulled the door shut and locked it. With Grigori out of the picture, she was free to move. She moved up the hallway toward the front of the train, a small satchel on her back. She passed through a sitting car, set up like a lounge, with several TV sets showing movies. A couple of people were asleep in here on sofas.

She didn't know how anyone would ever watch TV. The entire car was windows. The scene of jagged, snow-capped mountains going by at your fingertips was more astonishing than anything a person could ever see on TV.

She passed through another lounge, this one with a giant fish tank, and those same mountain views. The tropical fish were nice, but ...

The Swiss Bankster, the one Istvan had choked, was here. He was asleep in a plush armchair with his head cocked at an uncomfortable angle. Lars was his name. He had claimed that he needed to get off at Innsbruck, but it seemed like he had missed his stop. He was going to have a serious neck ache when he woke up.

She passed through the dining car next. Half a dozen well-dressed and tired people were in here, eating breakfast and chatting quietly while the mountains streamed by them, unnoticed. One of the diners was an Istvan bodyguard. Helena could tell by his size. She didn't fully understand the schedule they were on.

A couple of servers hovered nearby. These people were all awake. Helena wasn't sure if any of them got sleeping pills or not. She didn't think so.

She passed through the empty bar car, her normal station. No one was in here. It was silent, and the lights were dimmed. She stood for a moment at the bar, letting the train rock her. She was doing good.

Some people had already been taken out, not as many as she might have hoped. But it would save Sokolov some trouble and might save those sleeping people's lives.

Here was where things got interesting. Just because the cameras were no longer being monitored didn't mean the footage wasn't being recorded. She had no idea how to stop the filming. Her next moves would make it clear to some future watcher that she, Helena, was involved in the hijacking of the train.

No, her name was not Helena. No, her hair was not normally black. No, she did not normally dress this conservatively. No, she was not married, and the wedding ring wasn't even a real diamond. But this was her real face. She could be recognized. The new computers had facial recognition software that could match her against a database of known criminals.

The next steps were written in stone. They had to be taken.

They might mean she would be on the run the rest of her life. They might mean she would go to prison, possibly for the rest of her life. Whatever happened, these were the steps that were also making her rich. She could not turn her back on this now.

Let's go.

She took a deep breath and nodded. There was no decision to be made. She opened the door to the foyer between cars and passed into the disco car. She heard the bass thump of the music before she even went in.

The French singer Calment was in here with a small group of his hangers on. They were still dancing. The laser lights were still flashing. The car had a trick of engineering in which it could shut out the light of day and create a sense of eternal night. The young DJ was in a corner of the room, still spinning records. He was soaked in sweat, probably some reaction to the drugs he was on.

Helena wended her way through the dancers. A few of them, including Calment himself, had accepted drinks from her spiked with sleeping pills. The pills weren't enough to put these people to sleep. Whatever else they had put into their bodies, whatever uppers they had taken, were stronger than the downers she had given them.

They were like zombies now, cursed by a powerful shaman to dance in here forever. They were up and moving, but their eyes were blank, and their jaws were slack. Calment, a bit overweight, with graying hair and dressed all in black, looked like a candidate for a sudden heart attack. His face and fat neck were splotched unevenly with red. If anything, he was sweatier than the DJ.

Helena passed through the car, along a narrow hallway, and into the next car. She was now in the stateroom cars near the front of the train. Each car would have three or four staterooms, except for Istvan's personal car near the front of the train.

She hadn't seen Istvan at all this morning, which suggested he was in his car. That probably meant he had at least two bodyguards with him. Grigori was asleep. One guard was at breakfast. Perhaps one was at the very front with the driver. That would account for five and leave an extra one floating around somewhere.

They're with the prostitutes.

She smiled and nodded to herself. Of course. Any missing bodyguards were sampling the women.

As if on cue, as she moved along this car, up ahead a young woman popped out of a stateroom, wearing nothing but a towel. Her hair was wet. She disappeared into the next stateroom as fast as she had emerged from the first.

Helena kept moving.

The next stateroom car was even quieter than the first. The only sounds here were the rumble and clatter of the train itself. Beneath her feet was a hatch that led to a maintenance crawlspace below the train car.

There was a key device mounted in a glass box on the wall. She opened the box and took the metal device out. It was long and narrow, and when inserted into the lock on the hatch, it would turn a tumbler and open the hatch. She slid the end of the device into the lock and turned. It took a little bit of strength to get it to turn, but then it did.

A metal ring was embedded in the hatch. She reached down and grabbed the ring with two fingers. She pulled, but the hatch was heavy.

As if by magic, the hatch then opened by itself.

Anatoly Sokolov appeared, pushing the hatch upwards with his shoulder. He was on a small ladder, and after a moment, he emerged in the hallway, carrying his large bag on his back. He was followed closely by the thin, bald-headed man calling himself Ivan the Terrible. Ivan resembled an eagle or some other sharp-lined bird of prey.

Sokolov looked like a movie star. Thin, but broad shouldered with a square jaw and eyes that could cut you open like a knife. His hair was salt and pepper, as were the whiskers that had grown on his face while he was hiding under this train car.

Dear Sokolov, the best man she had ever known. He looked tired, a little drawn. They hugged, and she wanted to melt into his arms and against his chest. But the hug only lasted a moment. There was no time for that now.

"Helena, it's good to see you."

"It's good to see you both," she said.

"The camera watcher?" Sokolov said.

"Asleep," she said. "He'll probably sleep for days. He was tired and a little drunk, and I gave him two pills."

"Very nice," Ivan said.

"We'll need coffee," Sokolov said. "Strong. Black. With a shot of vodka."

She nodded. "I have it here. In my bag. Coffee and breakfast sandwiches."

"Good girl," Ivan the Terrible said. "Very good girl."

Sokolov shook his head and smiled. Did Ivan embarrass him a little? Maybe. Ivan's chatter was a little bit sexist. She wasn't the office girl. She was a team member. Sokolov never spoke like that to her. Except in the bedroom, he treated her the same as he would treat any man on his crew.

And he should. She was a pro. She had infiltrated this train. She had already put a bunch of people to sleep, including the guard who watched the video monitors. Those people were not a worry anymore. Then she had snaked her way up here and let them out of purgatory.

Sokolov valued her and what she could do. She knew that.

Ivan? He was a typical man from the old days. Secretly, he probably thought it was too dangerous for her to be here, or that she didn't know what she was doing. She didn't feel the need to prove him wrong. She already had. He should do his job half as well.

As if to prove this, Sokolov held out a gun to her. It was small. You might even say it was tiny. She took it in her hand. It fit the hand perfectly. She had grown up learning to shoot. She was no stranger to guns.

"Four shots," Sokolov said. "No safety, so be careful. Very easy. Very little recoil. If you see something you don't like, just point, and shoot."

Helena smiled. "Thank you. I'll be careful."

She slipped the gun into the front pocket of her black pants and turned to the stateroom nearest them. She listened at the door, but she couldn't hear anything. This was the tricky part.

She took her staff key, unlocked the door, and stepped away from it.

Sokolov already had his gun out. He left his big bag on the floor in the hallway and stepped into the stateroom. A man and a woman were asleep on the bed. Helena could see them clearly from her vantage point.

On the far side of them, the blinds covering the giant windows were all the way down, and the heavy drapes were pulled across. They did a good job keeping the room in a state of twilight.

The man stirred at Sokolov's entry. "Hey!"

But Sokolov was upon him. Sokolov hit the man in the head with the butt of his gun, once, twice, three times. The man, still half asleep, raised his hands to ward off the blows, but it did nothing. After the fourth hit, Sokolov turned the gun around and stuck the muzzle in the man's open mouth.

"Sshhhhhh."

Ivan the Terrible was in the room now, and as the girl in the bed woke up, he placed the muzzle of his gun to the side of her head.

"You speak English?" Sokolov said.

The man in the bed nodded.

"Don't say a word to me. Just roll over onto your stomachs. Both of you."

The man complied instantly. The girl followed a second later.

Ivan the Terrible had his bag with him. He worked quickly, handing Sokolov a plastic zip tie and a black, leather hood. Sokolov pulled the man's arms behind his back and zip-tied the man's wrists together. Then he yanked the leather hood down over the man's head and zippered it closed.

Ivan did the same to the woman.

"Can you breathe?" Sokolov said.

They both nodded.

"Be completely quiet and you'll live through this. Do you understand?"

The two hostages nodded again.

Helena had watched the whole thing. Sokolov and Ivan had worked together like an efficient and well-maintained machine. If they could take control of everyone like that, then perhaps this job would be easy. Of course, they had the element of surprise here. But they still did.

Sokolov looked at her and winked.

Helena smiled, despite everything—the violence, the uncertainty, the sheer danger and seriousness of the situation. Sokolov could inspire you to rise up above everything.

"Leave the food, Lapochka," Sokolov said, calling her the Russian term of endearment *sweetie pie.* "And the coffee. Go let the other two out."

Helena nodded and did exactly what he said.

132

The door closed after Helena left.

Sokolov opened his thermos and took a sip of his coffee. It was still hot, and there was the bite of the vodka. This was good. He remained standing, swaying with the movement of the train, and looked around the stateroom. The bed was wide, maybe not king-size, but the compartment was somewhat small. Gajdos almost certainly had a king-size in his stateroom. Gajdos probably had two naked people tied up face-down in his stateroom too. Sokolov smiled at the thought.

There was a chest of drawers built into one wall. There was that long window with the blinds drawn. After spending so much time in the dark below the train, Sokolov had no urge to open the blinds and flood this room with bright light. There would be snow out there. He could tell by slivers along the edges of the window that he would practically blind himself.

Ivan was sitting in an easy chair across from the bed. He had already unwrapped and was eating his sandwich. They had been down in that tomb a long time. Ivan stuffed a big chunk of the sandwich into his mouth and unzipped one of his bags. He had Sokolov's gun in his hand. He pulled out a compact hard case and opened it. Embedded in the case were two silencers. Sokolov watched as Ivan expertly mounted the silencer onto the muzzle of the gun. Ivan handed the gun back to Sokolov and then pulled out the next silencer.

Sokolov felt the reassuring weight of the gun in his hand again. He took a deep breath. It was real now. Things were underway. Lying in that cubby hole under the train … he had been daydreaming down there or sleeping and dreaming. He had drifted into some kind of fugue state. If Helena had never come, he could have almost ridden the train to Switzerland, then broken out of there, more of a stowaway than a hijacker.

This was better.

"We have to move fast," he said to Ivan, though of course Ivan already knew that. "The driver can't know what hit him. Once you take control of the train, you cut off all communications with the outside world."

Ivan nodded. He had another gun ready. "The bodyguards and passengers have mobile phones, of course."

"Peter, Vlad, and I will take care of the bodyguards. Hopefully, we'll be finished with them before they get any calls out. Helena will collect the phones from the passengers as we go through and count them. Many of them should already be asleep now. Either way, that's not your worry."

"I'm the driver," Ivan said. "Just the driver."

"I don't mean it like that," Sokolov said.

He considered the futility of the situation, which was why he had considered this a suicide mission from the beginning. For him, dying on this mission or any other was not a worry. He had been suicidal for years. He was a man out of time and out of place. He had been born in the Soviet Union. His formative memories were of that time, now long gone. In his mind, his memories of childhood and his teen years were like black and white photographs.

He had come of age in the violence and chaos of the Wild 1990s. The oligarchs had succeeded in stealing everything of value. The society was decrepit. The people lived in poverty. And Sokolov had spent much of his adult life languishing behind bars.

He glanced around the room, looking for a smoke detector. He had no idea if this train was nonsmoking or not. He longed for a cigarette, but he couldn't risk setting off an alarm. It was a minor issue but frustrating. What else had he not thought of?

The people on his crew wanted to live. That was safe to assume. So safe, in fact, that he didn't even bother to ask them.

Peter the Great and Vlad the Impaler were young. They still dreamed of growing rich, leading their own gangs and maybe even becoming bosses one day.

Ivan the Terrible was older and was hoping for the payday that meant he could finally walk away from everything.

Helena was a mystery. Sometimes, she seemed like she was hoping for a future with Sokolov. Sometimes, she seemed like a leopard, moving fast, enjoying the hunt, closing in on an antelope. Maybe what she was after, and all she really wanted, was to be rich.

And Anatoly Sokolov? A walking dead man. A wraith. A leftover from a previous time, waiting to be put out with the other trash. It would be enough to live long enough to bleed the mini-oligarch Gajdos, then take him out, as a warning to others like him, and perhaps as an inspiration to others like Sokolov, if any still existed out there.

But the others wanted more, and he had to respect that.

"I imagine a few calls will go through," Ivan said.

Sokolov nodded. "I imagine so, yes. But we will do everything we can to stop it from happening."

On the bed, one of the two prisoners mumbled something. Sokolov assumed it was the man. The voice was deep, and anyway, the girl appeared to be weeping abjectly. She was in no position to say anything.

"Mmmm, hmmm!" the man said, more emphatically this time.

His entire upper body wrenched up and away from the bed, to give his face enough room to make the noises. Sokolov looked at his back. He was a strong guy, with a muscular back and broad shoulders. For a brief instant, Sokolov wondered who he was. Some guy in the Gajdos orbit, he supposed, living a life of luxury on the backs of ordinary workers.

"I told you to shut up," Sokolov said. "This is the last time I'll tell you."

He looked at Ivan again. Ivan was putting together the parts of a semiautomatic rifle, a version of an American AR-15. It was the perfect weapon for a project like this. High-powered, high-capacity, fast shooting but not automatic. You didn't want to race through all your bullets too quickly. You want to shoot at a rapid pace but also judiciously.

Ivan was a smart man. A capable man. He was a good friend and partner. Sokolov would spare Ivan if he could. He would spare them all if he could.

"I imagine they have already begun to block outgoing radio calls. An encrypted text will go out to them on the satellite phone as soon as we take the cockpit, and you are in control. They should commandeer the train remotely soon afterwards. It will speed up gradually, so as not to set off any alarms. But it should start right away. Don't allow it to worry you. Let it happen."

"As we discussed," Ivan said. He was drinking his coffee now and eating a bag of chips. Where had those chips come from? It didn't matter. Sokolov still hadn't even touched his sandwich.

"Keep it on the rails as best you can. When the time comes, we'll decouple and let the front cars crash. After that, we abandon. The devastation of the crash may be enough to let us escape."

"Then it'll be in God's hands," Ivan said.

It was a quaint idea and a little troubling. Sokolov had never known God to have an especially sure grasp on things.

The man on the bed started making very loud noises, groans, booming guttural grunts like a seal lion, derailing whatever Sokolov might say next. Of course, the man was overhearing this conversation. Maybe the idea of God deciding whether he lived or died was unappealing to him. Maybe he had committed such crimes in his life that the very prospect of meeting God was the problem.

"Mother of God!" Sokolov said. The last thing he needed right now was this mewling from a bit player. Maybe that was the real problem. The man had been the centerpiece of his own stage drama for so long that he failed to recognize when he had been relegated to a non-speaking role.

The man's muscular back and broad shoulders made an impression on Sokolov now, more than before. In Sokolov's world, back in the bad old days of Moscow gangsters, bodyguards were always on high alert. A bomb could go off, or a maniac with a rifle could turn up any second. But now …

"Are you one of Istvan's bodyguards?" he said. "Answer truthfully."

The man nodded without hesitation.

"You idiot," Sokolov said. "What are you doing asleep with one of these girls?"

The man mumbled something. "Mmmmm. Hmmmm."

Sokolov grabbed the man by the seam at the back of the leather mask. He yanked the man to his feet. Blood had seeped from under the mask down onto the man's neck and shoulders. There was blood all over the white linen of the bed. Sokolov had given him a few hard hits, he supposed.

The man was an inch or two taller, and certainly broader, than Sokolov. He guided the man into the bathroom. The bathroom was bigger than he expected, with mirrors along the wall above the wide sink, a toilet, and a stone tiled shower stall. It was a better bathroom than many ordinary people in the former Eastern Bloc had in their homes. These people, Gajdos and his ilk, were thieves.

"I told you to shut up," Sokolov said.

He shoved the man onto his knees on the white tile of the bathroom. He didn't hesitate at all. Killing had long ago become meaningless to him. He placed the muzzle of the gun to the back of the man's head and shot him. A spray of blood came out the front, and the man's heavy body sank to the floor.

Sokolov came back into the stateroom and shut the bathroom door behind him. The mess in there didn't really matter. They weren't going to be in here very long. There were other bathrooms on board.

The silencer was not exceptional. The shot made a bit of noise. If someone overheard it, they might think of a gunshot, but probably not. No one on the train was expecting gunshots. Of course, the suppression would deteriorate with each shot, but it wouldn't be important. Silence meant secrecy. Soon enough, the secret would be out.

Now, the girl on the bed was acting up. She was making a whine high in her throat. Sokolov felt some pity for her. He was a little calmer than before. The first kill was out of the way. It was good. The ice was broken. There were more to come. And one of the bodyguards had already been eliminated. The man had given himself as a small gift.

Ivan took a sip from his thermos. He poured the last of his chips into his mouth.

Sokolov touched the woman's bare back. "Did you know that man? Did you ever meet him before last night?"

She shook her head.

"Then don't mourn him. He was trash. He wasn't worth your tears. Just learn the lesson he taught you and keep quiet. Can you do that?"

She nodded. Her body shook with silent sobs.

"Good. Tomorrow will be another day for you."

Across the stateroom, a mobile phone on the arm of Ivan's chair began to buzz. He picked it up and put it to his ear.

"Da."

Ivan listened, his eyes on Sokolov. "Okay," he said. "We're ready." He hung up.

"Peter and Vlad are out. They've eaten and are ready to begin."

Sokolov smiled. After all these years, when the game finally started, he was happiest. He loved the action. He loved the excitement. He loved the engagement.

"Let's   go,"   he   said.

CHAPTER TWENTY TWO

7:10 am Central European Time
A mountain road
The Austrian Alps
Driving west of Innsbruck

"How far back am I?" Troy said.

He sat in the passenger seat of Alex's blue Range Rover as they traversed a narrow road, winding its way through the mountains. The road was well-plowed, with snow humped high on either side. But it moved through the mountains like a snake, circling around the peaks in large S-curves, with only the occasional pass through a tunnel.

It was slow going. Cars and trucks coming the other way made it even slower. Sometimes, the Range Rover was hugging the side of the mountains. Sometimes, it was on the outside, practically skimming the guardrail. Either way, the drop-offs were staggering.

Troy was on the phone with El Grupo headquarters in Madrid. The call had already dropped twice.

"I have your mobile phone pinged," Jan Bakker said.

"I know," Troy said. "But don't go to too much trouble."

The last thing Troy needed was Bakker homing in on the car with a satellite camera. *"Oh, who is your friend there in the car with you?"*

"Friend? I don't have friends."

He looked over at Alex, who was driving. Alex seemed completely relaxed as he expertly handled the turns. He had a lit cigarette in one hand, and the window cracked just a bit. He held the cigarette near the window, between his pointer and middle fingers, letting the smoke curl out into the cold air. He rarely seemed to take an actual drag of the thing. Alex was just a guy who preferred to have a lit cigarette in his hand, Troy decided. He could choose to smoke it or choose not to, but he wanted it there.

"The train took some time climbing to its current altitude," Jan said. "By my calculation, you are about thirty kilometers to the east and north of it at the moment. This is just a little less than twenty of your miles."

Jan Bakker, always helpfully translating kilometers into miles, not that Troy needed that help. It was funny to Troy how Bakker often referred to miles and feet and yards and gallons with the word "your," as if Troy owned these concepts and he was the only person on Earth who still used them.

"The climb has evened out now, and the rail line, while curvy, is straighter than the roads. So, the train will begin to leave you behind from now on."

Troy wondered if there might be some way to get out ahead of it. Maybe what he should have done was simply fly to St. Moritz and meet it there.

"Thanks Jan," he said. "I'm going to see if I can raise them on the phone before I lose coverage altogether."

"We received a message via text from them a little while ago," Jan said. *On board, all is well,* was all they said. After that, they went dark, as agreed."

"All right," Troy said. "I'll speak with you soon."

He hung up and looked at Alex.

"We're twenty miles behind, and we're going to start falling further back."

Alex nodded. "Yeah. I kind of figured that."

"What do you think?" Troy said.

"I don't know," Alex said. "Does it matter? If nothing happens, then who cares how far behind we are?"

Troy shrugged. "It's a nice drive."

"The views are incredible," Alex said.

Troy dialed the number for Dubois. There was a delay as the call bounced around, looking for a signal, but she answered on the first ring.

"Stark?" she said in a low voice.

"Yeah."

"Where are you?"

"I'm following you by car. I might have to find a better way to do this, though. How's it going?"

"We're in a stateroom, hiding. Everything is quiet so far."

There was a deeper male voice in the room with her. Probably Gallo, saying something to her.

"Wait a minute," Dubois said. "What?"

Gallo spoke again.

"Gallo just opened the door a crack. We're near the front of the train. He said he heard something out in the hall. A group of men just passed by, on their way to the front. He's saying they were carrying guns."

Troy's heart skipped a beat.

"What is he seeing now?"

It would be a perfect storm of Murphy's Law if this really was the next train to get hijacked, with Troy not on board. Not only not on board, but following behind by car on slow mountain roads, with no way to catch up. He thought back to how arrogant Gallo was about the whole thing.

Towel boy. Bench warmer.

It was going to take a while to get over that.

"Wait …" Dubois said. "Wait, wait, wait."

"Dubois, what the …?"

"Is that shouting?" she said.

Behind her, Gallo said something.

"Dubois …"

"Shot fired," she said. "Was that really a shot fired? Or something else."

"Shots fired?" Troy said.

"Trains make noises," Dubois said.

Was this a game? Had Dubois and Gallo not only happily left him in the lurch, but were they now playing some kind of practical joke on him?

"Dubois, if you're trying to punk me …"

"Punk? What does that mean?"

"Never mind," Troy said.

"We're not sure," Dubois said. "It might have been a shot fired up towards the front. This could be it. Or it could be nothing, a misunderstanding."

Troy doubted that. What kind of misunderstanding sounded like gunshots? On rare occasions, a car misfiring. But they were on a train.

"Stark, I have to call you back."

"Dubois!"

"Five minutes," she said.

"Dubois, don't you …"

The line went dead.

Troy looked at Alex. Alex was intently focused on the road. Through his window, behind his head, a jagged, icy peak reached up towards the blue sky.

"We have to ditch this car," Troy said. "She thinks maybe a shot was fired on board. Maybe it happened, maybe it didn't, but I need to get on the train."

"I have an idea," Alex said.

"Good," Troy said. "I'm looking for ideas."

Alex nodded. "You'll like this one." He glanced over at Troy and smiled. "It matches your personality."

CHAPTER TWENTY THREE

7:15 am Central European Time
Aboard the *East Meets West*
The Austrian Alps, Austria

"Grigori, do you see this?" Big Stan said into his hand-held radio. "Grigori! Are you even awake?"

Big Stan was at the eastern end of Istvan's big stateroom car. The entire train car was basically a bedroom for Istvan, and whoever joined him in that bedroom, along with a narrow hall running alongside of it.

Big Stan had seen the inside of Istvan's room. It was more of an entire mini-flat than a room. There was a bedroom with a larger than king-size bed. There was a hardened glass observatory for a roof, so that Istvan could lie on his back and look at the stars or the sun. There were the large windows for watching the landscape pass, typical of most staterooms on this train. There was a giant, flatscreen TV, which a few of the other staterooms had, which could only show satellite TV depending on the weather, along with pre-loaded programs or DVDs.

There was a master bathroom, better than any of the bathrooms in the rest of the train. This one had a two-meter marble sink and vanity, and a stone tile shower that could accommodate two or maybe three people.

The room also had a sitting room with easy chairs, a sofa, another flatscreen TV, along with a refrigerator, a wet bar, some pantry cabinets, and a microwave oven. There was an entry door to this stateroom here where Big Stan stood, and another at the other end, near the entryway to the driver cockpit. It was a flat for very special people, and Istvan hoped to loan it to the important friends he planned to make in Western Europe. So far, those friends hadn't fully materialized, so he used the place for himself.

If Big Stan had Istvan's money, along with a stateroom like that, he would never come out of it. He would just load it up with girls, booze, and drugs and ride it back and forth from Hungary to Switzerland non-stop.

He was losing it. A moment ago, he had been standing here, daydreaming about these things. He had also been musing about the black girl with a cold or a little flu who Casimir had sent, and how he was going to find her again before this day was over. He had a simmering excitement for that girl.

But now four men were marching up through the next train car, coming this way. They wore the coveralls and jeans and yellow striped jackets and boots that suggested they were train yard workers. Why were regular workers on this train now?

It didn't make sense.

The two men in the front were big, nearly as large as Stan himself. And Grigori, who was supposed to be watching everything on video, wasn't answering his radio.

"I don't like it," a voice said.

Big Stan didn't turn. He knew it was Vadim, another bodyguard who had been stationed at the far western end of this car at the threshold to the cockpit. Vadim was coming up behind him. That was good. Vadim had a clear head on his shoulders. He was older, in his mid-thirties, and Istvan's closest bodyguard.

Those other men were going to be here in seconds. Big Stan watched them come through the window to the foyer between cars.

"Grigori!" he shouted into his radio.

The opposite door to the foyer opened.

Suddenly, the two big men dropped down and away, one to each side. The next man up was smaller, thinner, and older, much older, with a bald head and the black, intelligent eyes of a crow. He cradled a semiautomatic rifle in his hands. It had just appeared there as if by magic.

You're thinking too much.

The rifle had a long silencer attachment.

Big Stan dropped his radio and reached for the gun tucked behind his waistband. The gun would not be enough. The other man had too many rounds.

The man with the rifle aimed at Big Stan's window.

DOONK! DOONK! DOONK!

The bullets hit the window. The window cracked but did not break.

"Get down!" Big Stan shouted.

He dropped to the floor as the window shattered above him. Thick glass rained down in tiny cubes.

DOONK! DOONK!

Big Stan's gun was in his hand now. He glanced back at Vadim. Vadim was on the floor perhaps three meters back, bleeding from the throat. His eyes were wide, and his hands were grabbing there, trying to push the blood back in.

Vadim was done. He would be dead seconds from now. Big Stan had seen these things before.

"Ah, God."

Big Stan aimed his gun up at the gaping hole where the window had been.

A head appeared there, the head of one of the big men.

BANG!

Big Stan fired and hit the head right in the middle. From this angle, the shot must have pushed the face up through the brain. The head snapped back and disappeared.

He waited for the next target.

One down.

A hand appeared through the window. It held a pistol, also with a silencer. The hand was reaching over from behind the door. It pointed the gun down, right at Big Stan. Big Stan changed his aim to shoot for the hand, or to hit the gun.

CLACK! CLACK! CLACK!

The pistol fired three times. Big Stan felt the shots hit his body. He bucked involuntarily as each shot penetrated him.

"Unh."

The hand with the pistol snaked back before he even got a shot off at it.

He lay on his back and began to push himself backwards with his feet, away from the door. He was mindful that he was moving through shattered glass. Istvan must have heard that. Maybe Big Stan could crawl like this all the way to the other door, and Istvan would open it to let him in.

Over Vadim, you'll have to climb over Vadim.

He could make a stand against these men if he could get behind a locked door. It didn't matter if he was injured.

He moved backwards and backwards. He had to reach Vadim soon.

At the end of the hall, the door slid open by itself. Someone in the foyer had hit the large silver button that was the automatic door opener.

No one was there.

The smaller, bald-headed man appeared in the opening with the rifle.

DOONK! DOONK!

He fired downwards, then disappeared again.

BANG!

Missed.

But the bald man had hit his target. One of his shots had pierced Big Stan's chest. Another had shot through his foot and maybe embedded itself in his leg.

"Oh," he said, the sound a combination of a word and a groan.

He wasn't going to make it. He'd been shot five times now, he thought. Five was a lot. There was nowhere to hide in this hall. Behind him, there was a heavy lump. Vadim. Big Stan tried to push Vadim's body along, but it was dead weight. It wouldn't move at all.

Another man, one of the big men, appeared at the doorway. He stood in a two-handed shooter's crouch. He aimed a pistol.

CLACK! CLACK! CLACK!

"Ah!" Big Stan said as the bullets hit him.

He tried to fire back, but he no longer had the gun. He looked for it. It was back down the hall the way he had come, just a meter or two. He must have dropped it. It wasn't far, but he would never make it back there now. Big Stan was propped up on Vadim's body, as though smart, well-ordered Vadim was a pillow.

The man at the door wasn't even trying to cover now. He came walking into the hallway toward Big Stan. The bald man with the rifle was behind him, and another man was behind that.

There were four when they first came. At least he had taken one of them out.

After a moment, the first man was here. He hovered over Big Stan. He was a young guy. His eyes were hard.

"I killed your friend?" Big Stan said.

The guy pointed his gun at Big Stan's head. "Yes."

Big Stan nodded. An image of the black girl flitted through his mind for an instant, and how he was going to …

"Why are you doing this?"

The guy shrugged. "Why do you think? Money."

"It's always money," Big Stan said.

"Yes," the guy said. "But not for you. Not anymore."

***

CRACK.

145

Sokolov watched as Vlad the Impaler shot Istvan's bodyguard in the head. The hallway outside what must be Istvan's stateroom was a bloody mess. Two corpses now, one with several gunshot wounds and a final kill shot to the skull, and one other shot through the throat and bled out. And Vlad's sound suppressor was already beginning to deteriorate.

"What a mess," Sokolov said.

Peter the Great was dead out in the foyer between cars. It was his own fault. No one asked him to stick his head in the window like that. Even so, it was hard to lose him. He was a good kid, maybe not the brightest, but good.

Now, he was dead, just a few minutes into the operation.

"Peter's dead," Ivan said behind him.

"Tell me something I don't know."

"We better act quickly."

Sokolov nodded. "Yes."

He stepped forward, carrying an equipment bag with him. It dangled from his left hand. His gun was in his right. He moved toward Vlad, who was standing over the two bodies. Vlad was a bad kid, in the way Peter was good. He was smarter than Peter, cunning and cruel. He was a tall blond with blank eyes that made you think he had probably tortured stray cats when he was a boy.

"Vlad, this is Gajdos's train compartment. Do not let him, or anyone else, in or out of the doors on this hallway. I think we have him trapped in there. I want him to stay that way."

Vlad nodded. "Aye aye, captain," he said.

He was also a little too sarcastic sometimes. Almost certainly, he was upset that his friend Peter was dead, but sarcasm could get him killed too.

"Ivan, let's go."

Sokolov squeezed past Vlad, with Ivan the Terrible just behind him. They moved up the long hallway, to the door to the next foyer. Sokolov looked through the window. It wasn't so much a foyer as a sort of anteroom or lounge. The cockpit and Istvan's stateroom were part of the same long, train car. In the anteroom was a table with a couple of chairs, a closet of some kind, a counter with a coffee maker and a microwave oven, and a mini refrigerator. It was an area where the train driver could relax.

The driver was nowhere in sight. The door to the cockpit was closed. The driver had probably shut it the moment trouble started. It was probably sealed with some new technology. The driver was probably inside there, frantically calling for help, and wondering why he couldn't raise anyone on the radio.

Sokolov opened the door to the anteroom and passed inside. Ivan was with him. Sokolov went right to the cockpit door. He put down his equipment bag and opened it. First, he came out with a metal crowbar, which was thick along its length, but tapered to a very thin front edge.

Sokolov tried the cockpit door, but of course it was locked against him. He found the narrow crack along the seam of the door and wedged the crowbar in there. He bent back on the bar, then pushed it forward. Bent it back, pushed it forward. Bent it back … He put all his weight into it.

The bar wrenched open the door nears its hinges the smallest amount. Sokolov went back into his equipment bag and came out with a small amount of the American-made plastic explosive C4. It was very malleable, like clay that children would play with. He molded a piece and worked it into the bent seam of the cockpit door. Then he took out the tiny blasting cap and stuck it into the C4. Finally, he snaked a long fuse into the top of the blasting cap. He lit the fuse with his cigarette lighter.

"Big bang coming!" he said. He rolled into a corner of the foyer and ducked into a ball, away from where the explosion would direct energy.

Ivan was here with him, rolled into a ball as well.

Sokolov waited. It seemed like a long wait. He resisted the urge to get up and go see what was wrong with the explosive. That's how people's lives ended.

BOOM!

The explosion came, more powerful than Sokolov expected. It felt from like the whole train shook with the force of it.

Smoke rose within the anteroom. The door was hanging off the wall. One thick, iron hinge was completely severed. One had held up, leaving the door akimbo.

Sokolov pushed the door sideways. It seemed like the remnants of a space capsule that had crashed to Earth. The door shrieked as Sokolov wrenched it away from the wall. Finally, he pushed it completely aside.

He stepped through the ruined doorway and into the cockpit. The cockpit was hyper-modern, more like Sokolov's idea of what a spaceship would be like than what a train was like.

The driver had a tall leather seat, like a captain's chair, in the center of the cockpit. It faced the three computerized control boards. There was a joystick of some kind to the right side. Sokolov didn't know what to make of these controls, but Ivan would.

The most eye-catching thing about the cockpit was the 180-degree wrap around view of the tracks ahead. This ride was going across the Alps. The view through the front windscreen was incredible.

The train driver stood there by his chair, in the midst of the smoke from the door blowing off. His face and hands were bloody. His mouth hung open. He was a small man with a mustache and wearing a blue uniform. The uniform came with a hat, but the hat sat on the control counter behind him.

"What are you doing here?" the driver said to Sokolov. "Get out of here."

The man's eyes were large, round, and almost as blank as Vlad's. But this man was in shock. A shootout had just taken place in the car behind him, and then an explosion had blown his door off its hinges. The man coughed as some of the smoke reached his throat and lungs.

"I'm going to kill you," Sokolov said. "Or you can just leave the cockpit."

"You don't have to kill me," the train driver said. "I haven't harmed anyone. There's no reason to kill me."

Sokolov made a gesture with his arm and hand, as if clearing a path for the man.

"Please step out of there."

The man folded his arms.

"You cannot do this."

"One last time," Sokolov said.

"Don't bother," said the train driver.

Sokolov went up to the man and placed the gun to the side of his head. Once again, he didn't hesitate for a moment. He didn't understand this driver's stubbornness. He wasn't protecting anything of value. He was offering himself up as a sacrifice to Istvan Gajdos. It made no sense.

Sokolov aimed the gun through the man's head and down toward the floor.

"You don't have to do this!" the man shouted at the top of his lungs, just before a coughing fit bent him over forward. The bend was helpful. Sokolov pointed the gun down from behind the man, so the bullet wouldn't damage the controls or front window.

148

"Get out," Sokolov said.

"I won't," said the driver.

Sokolov pulled the trigger. BANG.

Now there was another corpse on the floor, bleeding from the head.

"Ivan!" Sokolov shouted. "Come on. You're up."

Ivan appeared behind him, still with the AR-15 in hand. His face seemed as placid and calm as ever.

"I know. I heard you." He looked down at the corpse. "I can't drive the train with this body here."

It was a fair point. Sokolov slid the gun into his pocket, bent, and dragged the dead man out of the cockpit by the arms. He pulled him to the spot in the anteroom where he and Ivan had taken cover. Then he came back.

"Satisfied?"

Ivan was already in the driver's seat, assuming the controls. He raised a hand.

"Keep an eye out behind you," Sokolov said. "Vlad and I will go deal with Gajdos and the rest, but we're down a man."

Ivan had placed the rifle against the wall beside him. He patted it with one hand, while gazing down the tracks and working the controls with the other.

"I'll   be   careful."

CHAPTER TWENTY FOUR

7:30 am Central European Time
Headquarters of the European Rapid Response Investigation Unit (ERRIU)
aka El Grupo Especial
Outskirts of Madrid, Spain

"Miquel?" a deep voice said.

There was a brief pause, during which Miquel hoped it was just the voice in a dream.

"Miquel. Wake up, please."

It wasn't a dream. It was the voice of Jan Bakker. Miquel reached up and pulled the airplane eyeshades off his face. Across the darkened office, Bakker was standing in the doorway, creating a hulking shadow from the low light in the hallway.

Miquel was lying on a fold-out cot, which he had moved into his office for nights like this one. The cot was not comfortable, but Miquel had lain in worse places.

"Yes," he said.

"The Gajdos train," Agent Bakker said.

Now, Miquel sat up. He swung his legs onto the floor. "Hijacked?"

"It appears so, yes. A large denial-of-service attack began in the past few minutes. It seems to come from that office in Sofia I described last night, among a dozen other places. I received a text from Agent Dubois some time ago that she and Gallo were on the train, but not Stark. He couldn't board. I called Agent Dubois a few moments ago, but her telephone went to voicemail."

"Okay," Miquel said. "Try her again. I'll be there in a moment."

"All right."

"Where is Agent Stark?" Miquel said.

"I spoke with him. He's in a car traveling along mountain roads, perhaps thirty or thirty-five kilometers behind the train. His calls keep dropping."

Miquel nodded. "Wonderful. What are his chances of catching up?"

"At the current pace? Zero."

"Okay."

Then Jan was gone. Miquel bent and pulled his loafers on. It was good, he supposed. They had guessed right again. That's what they were supposed to do. But it felt different this time. The last train hijacking had ended in disaster. His agents had been eager to board this train, but without Stark, their ability to stop a hijacking was limited. And the hacking?

Some cyber attacks could be very sophisticated and planned months in advance. Entire teams often couldn't take them down, after long investigations. Could one man stop a concerted effort to take control of that train?

Miquel walked down the dark hall to Jan's office. His office was flooded with light. He had three laptops in a row on a table. His phone was at his elbow. As Miquel came in, Jan sensed his presence.

"Look at these readouts," he said.

Each of the laptops was showing a stream of data. The data seemed to flow downwards from the top of the screens to the bottom like waterfalls.

"They're bombarding Gajdos's system with requests. I can't even get through it to see the train's information. I assume that means they've taken it over."

"Did you speak to your friend in Bulgaria?"

Jan nodded. "Yes. He's ordering a raid on that location in Sofia."

"When will the raid happen?" Miquel said.

Jan shrugged. "This morning. As soon as he can put it together."

Miquel stared at the streaming data on the screens.

"Call the Austrian Federal Police," he said.

"The *Bundespolizei*," Jan said. "Ya." His German language skills were the best of anyone at El Grupo. Miquel thought about what to say to them. This was all going to seem very sudden. *Hi. You have a runaway train in your mountains.*

"Inform them a train in the Alps has been hijacked. Give them the coordinates. Tell them it's the famous Gajdos train. Remind them of the Scotland crash."

"That Orange Notice has not gone out yet," Jan said. "Most police forces aren't going to be aware that the Scottish train was a cyber attack. They might not even know a hijacking took place. As of yesterday, the details still hadn't been made public."

Miquel noticed his hands balling into fists. That was going to make the situation even more sudden.

151

"Call them anyway," Miquel said. "This is their territory. They need to know."

"We don't know one hundred percent that the train is hijacked," Jan said.

Miquel just looked at the back of his head. "I don't understand."

"We know there's a cyber attack targeting the Gajdos train system internal network. But we don't know the result of the attack. We haven't spoken to Agent Dubois or Gallo, so we don't know if there are actual hijackers on board or not. This is part of how they succeed. They mask their activities and shut down communications until it's too late for anyone to intervene."

Miquel shrugged. "Let's pretend we know for a fact, okay? There's a hijacking. If it turns out there isn't one, I take full responsibility for the false alarm."

Jan nodded. "Okay." He picked up the phone. "I will tell them."

"Good," Miquel said. "Do you want coffee?"

Jan held the phone to his ear. "Yes, please."

Miquel padded down the hallway to the office kitchen. The overhead fluorescents flickered for a second as he entered. There was half an urn of good coffee remaining from last night. It wouldn't take but a few moments to heat it up.

He wasn't fully awake, and that meant his decisions were not the best they could be. It was too late to second guess the choice to send the agents in the first place. They were good agents, and they wanted to go. They wanted to be on the front line. Now, the important thing was to either stop the attack, or failing that, get those agents and as many civilians as possible out of there safely.

Miquel sighed. He was going to have to tell his superiors at Interpol that this was happening. He was going to have to let them know that his own agents, Interpol agents, were on that train. They would say the same thing they always said. Miquel Castro-Ruiz was too far out in front. He didn't operate through proper channels. All of this should have been cleared through headquarters beforehand.

There hadn't been time for that. And on second thought, there was no sense telling his bosses now. What were they going to do? What help could they be?

He moved back up the hall with the two cups of coffee, his own, black with sugar, and Jan's, completely black.

He reached the doorway. Jan was speaking in German. After a moment, he hung up, and turned around. Behind his glasses, his eyes were bloodshot and tired. He had been up all night. At least Miquel had gotten some sleep.

Jan handed him the coffee. "What did they say?"

"They're going to try to confirm what I'm telling them. Once they have some confirmation, they will scramble police and rescue units to intercept the train. All of this might take them anywhere between forty-five minutes and a full hour. Maybe longer."

Miquel shook his head. "Not fast enough."

Jan nodded. "I know."

"Let's see if we can Dubois on the phone," Miquel said. "Or Gallo. Or Stark. Someone. And let's hope the raid in Bulgaria amounts to something."

Jan took a sip of his coffee. His eyes watched Miquel over the rim.

"I'm beginning to believe this operation is more complex than I gave it credit for," he said. "I think there's a real chance that everyone on that train is going to die."

CHAPTER TWENTY FIVE

7:40 am Central European Time
Aboard the *East Meets West*
The Austrian Alps, Austria

"I need to go up there. My things, my belongings, are in my room."

Helena stood at the doorway to the first of the stateroom cars. A small knot of people stood at the door, hoping to push past her.

The first in line was a slight man with black-framed glasses. His jet-black hair stood up in tufts. Everything hung loosely on him—his pants, his oversized, black sweater, even the gold watch around his wrist. The man looked weak and did everything he could to accentuate that fact. He had deep bags under his eyes from exhaustion. It was a style, Helena supposed.

"I have valuables in my room," he said. "More than that, I don't want to say."

"I understand," Helena said. "But right now, you just have to wait."

"It felt like an explosion," a young woman said. "Was there an explosion?"

The woman was dressed in a skintight, electric blue mini dress. If she was a prostitute, she wasn't doing her job correctly. Prostitutes weren't supposed to spend the whole night dancing.

Helena shook her head. "There was no explosion. But for your own safety, I need you to stay towards the back of the train. There may be a security …"

Looming behind the group was the bodyguard she had seen eating breakfast in the dining car. Helena knew him only by sight. He was large, with blond hair, blue eyes, and massive shoulders. And like all the bodyguards, his eyes had the blank look of murder and mayhem. These were dangerous men.

He firmly moved a couple of the people out of his way.

"Excuse me. I need to come through."

He was just behind the man with glasses now.

"What happened?" he said.

"I don't know," Helena said. "I think there's a security issue."

He nodded. "Okay."

He pushed the man with glasses out of his way. The shove was not hard, it seemed almost effortless, but it moved the smaller man a full meter to the left.

"I said excuse me." He turned and faced the group. "Everyone go back to the dining car or the lounge. Go dance if you like. There is no problem. But you cannot access the staterooms for a little while."

They stared at him.

He shooed them with a wave of his hands. "Go! Out!"

The man was good in an emergency. He treated wealthy guests like small children. And they complied.

The man in black glasses tried one more time. "I need to get something in my room."

The bodyguard raised a giant finger at him. "Go to the lounge. Have a drink and enjoy yourself. Come back here in one hour."

The man in glasses nodded and turned to follow the others.

"I'm locking this door," the bodyguard said to them. "I don't want to find you trying to enter."

He looked down at Helena and sighed. "Come with me."

She nodded and followed him as he headed down the first hallway. This car had the smallest of the staterooms. If your room was here, you didn't rate as a special friend of the oligarch. You should be happy you were even on the train.

"You didn't lock the door," Helena said.

The man shrugged. "I don't even know if it does lock. I just said that."

This hallway had twists and turns, with rooms on either side. Now, they were out of sight of the doorway they had left behind. The big man had long legs and walked quickly. Helena took double steps to keep up.

She slipped the small pistol Sokolov had given her out of her pants pocket. It was a tiny thing, "a lady gun," Sokolov's friend Ivan would probably call it. But it was a perfect size for Helena. It had four shots and fit comfortably in her small hand.

She raised it and pointed at the bodyguard's wide back. But she didn't shoot for some reason. Now was the time when he least expected it. This man was a terrible threat to Sokolov and the rest of the crew.

"Have you heard from Grigori?" the man said.

"I tried to raise him on the intercom," Helena said. "But he didn't answer."

"Typical."

She couldn't do it. That was the problem. She couldn't shoot a man in the back.

"Hey!" she shouted. "Wait a second. I can't keep up. Turn around."

The man turned, exactly as he was told. He was two meters ahead, gigantic, the size of a large storm. His eyes went WIDE at the sight of the gun in her hand. A whole system of thought crashed and burned right in front of her. He had made all kinds of assumptions about the situation, and they had proven wrong, all at once.

His gun was not out. He had two choices—run or attack.

He chose attack.

He came for her, his bulk filling the entire hallway.

She fired.

BANG!

And again.

BANG!

All the shots. Empty it.

BANG! BANG!

Click, click, click …

The man was on top of her. They crashed to the floor, his height and weight driving her downwards. She landed, the back of her head connecting with the flooring. She could not get him off. She struggled against him, but he held her down.

"Aaah! Ah!"

She writhed like a snake, wasting her energy against his superior strength. She stopped because it was no use. He had her. Only then did she realize he wasn't moving at all. She was just pinned underneath him.

His limp body pressed down on her. It was so heavy. There was something terrifying about the sheer weight of it. It was like being trapped under an elephant.

She pushed and writhed and squeezed and kicked.

"Oh. Oh my God."

Finally, she slithered away from him. She crouched in a corner. His eyes were blank, really blank now, like a doll's eyes. His mouth was open. Sounds were coming out of his mouth, an exhalation of air or gasses, she didn't know. Maybe he was still alive, technically speaking, but there was no one home.

Blood was spreading in a lake around him. She had fired straight into his massive chest, into the center mass, like she had been taught. She must have pierced his heart with one of the shots.

Her little gun was under there somewhere. She didn't want it back.

"Okay," she breathed. "Okay."

She had killed a bodyguard. And she had put the video watcher, Grigori, to sleep. Two guards down, by her hand. She was doing her job.

She was doing good.

***

"Oh man. Oh, bloody hell."

Istvan stood beside the bed. He had just pulled some shorts on. There was a t-shirt here somewhere and some pants. Beside him, bright light streamed in from the wall of windows. There were mountains out there, snow-capped peaks, and jagged cliffs. He could barely take it all in, the light was so bright. Above his head, the sky roof showed the pale blue as far as the eye could see.

"When did it become daytime?" he said.

He found the white shirt and pulled it on over his head. He did not feel well. He was groggy, his sinuses were clogged, and his heart was thumping in his chest, galloping along like a herd of wild horses. All this partying was becoming too much. He recognized that. Racz had been telling him so for months, but Istvan hadn't listened. It was only in times like this when he saw the wisdom in it.

He looked at the girls. They were both standing nearby, eyes wide and worried. The blonde had wrapped herself in a comforter from the bed. The sultry brunette was trying to dress quickly, just as Istvan was.

"What is going on?" he said. He would ask them by name, but he couldn't remember their names.

Everything was happening suddenly, but he didn't know what everything was. He didn't know any of it. He only knew he was awake in this moment, and not long ago he had been asleep.

He shook his head. He could barely keep his eyes open.

"We woke you," the blonde said. "There's been yelling and shooting, right out in the corridor. There was glass breaking. Then there was an explosion."

"Did you go to see what it was?" he said.

They just stared at him. Of course, they didn't. They were tiny, and he was large. They were his little ones, and he was the big man, the protector. He was the rich one, the sultan, and they were his slaves, or maybe just his serfs. Did a sultan even have serfs? They were here to do his bidding, in any event.

He raised a hand to them. "Okay, okay. It's okay. I'll look."

"Don't open the door," the brunette said. "Please. Don't do it."

He turned and met her eyes again. He hadn't grasped the extent of her fear until now. Each second he was awake, he was becoming slightly more alert than before. He saw it now. She was very afraid.

"My dear, what's the problem?"

"People have been murdered out there," she said.

He shook his head. "No. It's not possible. I have guards everywhere. There are cameras in all the hallways. There's a man who …"

BAM! BAM! BAM! BAM!

Sudden hammering came on the door closest to the front of the train. It was on the other side of his sitting room from here. Istvan stared at it. The door rattled and shook from the force of each blow.

BAM! BAM! BAM!

Someone or something was trying to knock the door down. It was almost as if a ghost or some unholy presence, a poltergeist, was trying to break through.

"What in the …"

BAM!

The door crashed inward, folding, and breaking as it fell to the ground. A man blasted in behind it. He was a big, strapping young man, and he had taken down the door with his shoulder. He shoved it and kicked at it, disintegrating it further.

Then he was fully in the room. He turned and looked at Istvan, his head cocked to the side like a dog who is trying to understand its owner. His hand went behind his back and came out with a pistol.

Now, a second man came in. He was smaller and older, thin and sinewy. His hair was black but shot through with gray and white. He was wearing the coveralls of a working man. But he was no worker. The man was wearing a black t-shirt under his coveralls, and the zipper of the outer shell of the coveralls was pulled down.

Istvan could see that the prison and gang tattoos came all the way up to his neck. He looked at the man's face. The eyes were hard, but also had a complacency about them. This was a man who had lived with death a long time. He was a Mafioso of some kind.

The man walked further into the room. He had a pistol in his right hand.

"Russian?" Istvan said.

The man nodded. "Hello, Istvan."

"Ah. What can I do for you?"

Istvan was instantly aware of how he looked. He was large and imposing, yes, but the young Russian gangster who had knocked down the door was almost as large and much stronger. He had crushed a security door into fragments with nothing but brute force. And they were both armed.

Moreover, the gang leader was handsome. He was about as handsome as a Russian could get, which ... it wasn't much, but Istvan had never been handsome, not even clothes. And now he was here in his underwear, with his sagging gut and skinny legs that he had meant to work on soon with a personal trainer, but he had never quite ...

Forget it.

"Your men are dead," the smaller, older man said.

Istvan nodded. "I know. My men are dead, and now you want to stick me, yes? What am I going to give you, the train? My hotels? Do you want the cash I'm carrying with me? Because I'll tell you, you can have it. It isn't much, a hundred thousand euros maybe. Quite a bit for you lot, but not much in the grand scheme. Anyway, you won't get far with it. Do you think you'll just step off the train and walk away?"

The smaller man gestured to the bigger one. It was a subtle gesture, just a slight head move.

The big man approached Istvan. Istvan noticed that he had probably been a mere boy not that long ago. As he came, he switched his gun from right hand to left.

"Oh yes, by all means. Send your enforcer after me. Is he supposed to hit me? Have I not been hit before? The two of you are pathetic."

The boy stepped up to him and ...

BOOM.

He drove a punch across his body, which connected with Istvan's jaw. Istvan's head spun around sideways, sending the room itself into a spin all around him. He saw the girls, big gaping Os for mouths as they watched him in horror now—more than fear, more than terror, real horror.

Istvan's face collided with the wall. He fell backwards. He thought he would land on the bed, but no.

BOOM!

The boy must have punched him in the back of the neck. His head snapped backwards, and he sank to his knees. He paused there for a moment, waiting for the next blow, but then dropped forward onto his face.

"Oh. Oh you …"

He felt like he was going to vomit. He had been in fights as a boy and a young man, but he had never been hit that hard in his life.

His guts were full of vodka, and food, and the pills he had been taking last night and all day the day before, uppers to keep him awake and partying, because Istvan Gajdos was superhuman in every way. He hoped he wasn't going to evacuate all of it onto the floor. He was also drifting now. In another moment, he would probably be out cold. One more hit would do it. He hoped he didn't puke while he was unconscious.

The older man was crouched next to him. He turned Istvan's head so that their eyes met. The man's gun was pointed at Istvan's head. Istvan found he felt nothing about that. He had never been fearful of much. He still wasn't.

"You're a common thief," the man said. "A bicycle mechanic turned thief."

"Envy," Istvan said. "It poisons the mind."

The man turned and looked upward, probably at the younger man again. Then he stood and disappeared from Istvan's sight.

"What do you want?" Istvan said. Even he could tell his speech was slurring.

Rough, strong hands grabbed his wrists and pulled them tight behind his back. Something narrow and sharp bit into his thick wrists, pressing the flesh and obstructing the circulation there. They were tying him up.

"Oh, don't do that," he said. "Look, I do have money with me. You can have it. Just take it. I have a small bag of diamonds. What else?"

He searched his mind, trying to think of what else he might have here that was portable, and that these cretins could take with them. But his mind was too slow. Jewelry. He had some gold jewelry on the train. They could rob the passengers, maybe. Some of them must have brought …

Then everything went dark. The boy's strong hands had yanked some kind of black mask or bag over his head, like something the CIA or the Russian SVR would do.

His mouth was still outside the bottom of the mask. "You're not SVR, are you? Tell me that much."

The hands pulled the mask all the way down now. The darkness, which had been black before, reached a new level of black. He felt the mask tighten as the boy zipped it down the back. The black became even blacker.

"I can't …" he tried to say, but he could no longer open his mouth. The mask was too snug. It kept his jaw shut. He opened his lips and gasped for air through clenched teeth. He found he could breathe, the smallest amount, though his mouth in this way. But he had to force it. His sinuses were blocked from histamines and breathing through his nose was out of the question.

He was forcing it hard now, the oxygen coming in tiny increments, not enough, not nearly enough. His face turned numb in seconds. His heart was racing in his chest.

He wanted to scream at them, "You're going to suffocate me!"

He had no idea what these maggots were doing with the girls. He didn't know, and he didn't care. They could have the girls if they would just take this mask off his head.

"We'll be back," a voice said.

***

"Stark?" Dubois said.

"Yeah."

His voice sounded tinny and far away. She had the phone on the lowest volume and pressed to the side of her head. She was lying under the bed in the stateroom they had taken. She had no idea where the girls they had brought aboard with them were. They hadn't come back.

There had been shooting, and then there had been an explosion. *This stateroom wasn't far from there,* she thought. Maybe three cars. It was clear that someone had set off a charge near the front of the train. The whole train shook when it blew.

It had been Gallo's idea for her to crawl under the bed. It was tight, and most people probably couldn't manage to squeeze themselves in here. The sheets were hanging down so someone would have to bend down and lift them to find her.

The terrorists, or hijackers, or whoever they were, were moving through the train cars, kicking in doors to the staterooms. Gallo felt, and Dubois agreed, that they weren't in position to engage the hijackers until they knew more about them. How were they supposed to find out more? That was the question.

Also, they had no guns. She had handed the bag with the guns in it to the big jerk who let them in here. She groaned.

Jan Bakker had tried to reach her three times, but she was ignoring those calls for the moment. It seemed more important to get Stark on board this train, than to give Jan an update. She could call Jan back in a moment.

"We have problems, Agent Stark."

"Dubois? Can you speak up? It's noisy here."

"No!" Her voice was a fierce whisper. "The train is being hijacked. It's started."

"All right," he said. "I'm on my way. Sit tight if you can."

She sighed. That was the last thing she needed, to feed Stark's ego a little more. He had been angry that they left him behind, and now they needed him. Gallo could fight, certainly, and so could she, but neither of them were the war machine that was Troy Stark. Few people were.

"Okay?" he shouted. "I'm coming."

"Listen," she said. "We're locked in a stateroom. There was an explosion. But they don't want us. We know that. They don't even know we're here. We may be able to get the element of ..."

BOOM!

She heard but didn't see the door to the stateroom cave in without warning. She couldn't see anything from under here. She heard Gallo grunt as the door broke apart.

"What was that?" Stark said.

She hung up the phone. Then she turned it off entirely in case Stark tried to call back. The phone went through its little shut down display. She had long ago disabled the sound for that. She took a sharp breath and held it.

"Hello?" Gallo said. "What's happening here?"

"Who are you?" a voice said. The voice had an accent, Eastern European.

"I work for Casimir."

"Who is Casimir?" the voice said. The voice was calm, but there was an edge to it. It could lose its patience very quickly. "I don't have time for guessing games."

"Casimir sends the girls," Gallo said. "The girls for Gajdos."

"He's the pimp, then?"

"Yes, if you like. I work for him."

"What do you do?"

Gallo cleared his throat, as if he had some phlegm deep down. "I mind the investment. Clear up any problems. Make sure no one harms the merchandise."

"They're human beings, you idiot. Don't speak of them as if they are products. Not everything and everyone in this world is a product to be bought and sold. Not yet."

"Okay," Gallo said.

"You're a prisoner now. This can be hard or easy."

"Easy," Gallo said. "I don't want trouble."

"Turn around."

A sound came, like a THUD. There might have been two or three thuds in rapid succession. The bedsprings bounced above Dubois, pressing against her. It was very tight down here.

"Anh. Oh." It was Gallo's deep voice, right above her. The voice was deeper than normal. They had hit him and knocked him onto the bed.

"Okay, okay," Gallo said. "No trouble here."

"Shut up and give me your hands."

"Yes."

Something was going on. They were tying him up, maybe. Dubois heard a zipper close. She should rescue him. She should *do something*. But from this position, it was impossible. They should have stood and fought. Maybe they wouldn't have been overwhelmed by them. Maybe they would have gotten lucky.

She should never have handed those guns away. They should have revealed themselves then. If these men killed Gallo now, Dubois could not live with herself.

"Stay silent, and we won't bother with you again. Count yourself lucky."

Gallo said nothing in response to that.

Dubois lay there under the bed, waiting. The sound of the voice or voices was gone. Now, there was just the sound of Gallo's heavy breathing above her. He wasn't speaking, and she took that to mean the danger hadn't passed.

She waited another minute. Down the hall, she heard them breaking another door apart. Above her, Gallo mumbled something. Then he went silent.

"Gallo?" she said quietly.

"Gallo?"

CHAPTER TWENTY SIX

7:50 am Central European Time
The Austrian Alps
West of Innsbruck, Austria

"So, I looked into this place ahead of time," Alex said. "Just in case we might need to come here and borrow something."

He handed Troy the binoculars. They were pulled off the road and onto a scenic lookout. Down a steep, switchbacked hill from them was a station of sorts. It sat on a cleared plateau, surrounded by the snowy mountains. There was a high fence around the station, and a couple of small buildings on the property.

"They work out of the low-slung, one-story building," Alex said. "The two-story building is a dormitory. They stay here, pulling three- and four-day shifts."

There was a white sign with a red cross on it and some words, Troy would guess in German. There were three or four cars, all four-wheel drive, in the parking lot. There were two small helicopters, one sitting on a helipad, and one sitting on a wheeled deck that could be pushed out to the helipad.

"What does the sign say?" Troy said.

"Alpine Search and Rescue. The chopper on the pad is supposed to be ready to go at all times. The extra one is in case of a real emergency."

Troy noticed the windsocks on the helipad. They were straight out, left to right.

"How's the wind look?" he said.

Alex shrugged. "Windy. These are the Alps. You don't get a lot of non-wind days."

Troy nodded. "Yeah."

"We'll get knocked around a bit," Alex said.

"Looks like it."

"If it's blowing in one direction, that's the best we can ask for."

Troy sat and thought about it for a moment. The wind was one thing. Alex could probably fly in wind. Moreover, this place probably picked choppers that could handle mountain winds. There were other problems to worry about.

"They're not going to just give us the chopper," he said.

Alex shook his head. "Afraid not. The red tape would be unspeakable. Weeks, months, years. We could walk in the office and stand at the counter for the rest of our lives. Who knows how long? We don't have that kind of time."

"No."

"We're going to have to borrow the chopper," Alex said. "And people are there. So, it might be a forcible borrowing."

"Hmmm," Troy said.

"There are some goodies in a bag in the back seat that I brought with me," Alex said. "They might make the thing go a bit smoother."

Troy turned and looked in the back seat. There was a large gym bag back there, the kind of bag in which a hockey player would carry equipment. He reached back, dragged it between the seats, and onto his lap. It was reassuringly heavy. Troy liked heavy equipment bags. Things that were useful often had some weight to them.

He unzipped it and looked inside. The first thing he saw was a gun box. He pulled it out and opened it. There was an Uzi submachine gun inside. There were three long magazines in the box, each fitting snug into a molded compartment. Troy picked one out. It was loaded.

"Standard Israeli-made submachine gun," Alex said. "Three box magazines, each one holding thirty-two rounds."

Troy nodded. "Very nice."

Alex powered down his window about three inches. He lit a cigarette, inhaled deeply, and then held it near the opening. Then he exhaled out the opening as well. The blue smoke was caught on the icy breeze and swirled out into the sky.

"What else?" Troy said.

"Glock 27," Alex said. "Probably good for taking the chopper. We don't want to look like a couple of nuts out here. Another three magazines, ten rounds a piece. A large electric cutting tool, with a curved and serrated knife. Very sharp. Heavy duty."

Troy looked at him.

"You're going to be coming down on top of the train. You'll need to get inside somehow."

That was true. Troy didn't like the sound of that. "I'm supposed to cut my way through steel, yeah?"

Alex shook his head. "Have you studied this train at all? Between cars, it has those thick rubber accordion things that create an indoor environment in the foyers. They create a lot of flexibility. It's a very bendy train, because the tracks that cross the mountains make a lot of turns."

"What are you going to do, land on the roof of the train?"

Troy was mindful of wasting time with this conversation. Alex had made several assumptions here, and one of the assumptions was that Troy could read his mind.

Alex looked at him. "It's a rescue chopper. It has a basket that can be lowered, for going down and taking injured or trapped people off the mountains. Kind of like the baskets the Coast Guard uses for storm rescues back in the United States.

Troy nodded. "Ah."

"I'm going to lower you down. You're going to climb out on top of the train, and then cut your way through the flexible accordion-like material."

"All of this while both the train and the chopper are in motion," Troy said.

Alex nodded. "Now, you get it."

Troy was silent for a long moment, the feeling of a clock ticking and racing out ahead of him stronger than ever.

"What do you think?"

"We steal a helicopter, possibly at gunpoint."

Alex nodded. "Yeah. From a government rescue installation."

"Then we fly through the Alps at high speed, and I drop down in a basket to a train, also moving at high speed, then cut my way into it. Then, and only then, I battle some unknown number and quality of hijackers to the death."

"Mmmm," Alex said.

Troy felt the adrenaline begin to race through his veins at the mere thought of it all. He rooted in the bag again and found what he knew would be there, a can of Rock Star Zero. He opened it and took a long slug.

"I love it. What are we waiting for?"

"That's what I was thinking," Alex said. He put the car in gear.

"You think I should call my boss?" Troy said.

"Who, Missing Persons?"

"No," Troy said. "My real boss. My boss at Interpol."

Alex shook his head. "Why worry him unnecessarily? We don't even have the chopper yet."

Troy nodded. "Good point. Hit it."

The Range Rover's wheels spun as it tore out from the icy overlook. The car entered the roadway and headed downhill. Alex made the first turn and then the second. He began to speed up into the third.

Troy glanced out at the drop-off on that one. It was on his side and a long way down. This was going to be fun.

They came out of the turn, and there was a downhill straightaway. The car accelerated into it. Troy could see why. The gate at the entryway to the rescue station was closed.

"Is the gate locked?"

"I don't know," Alex said. "I think we shouldn't park there and find out."

Troy nodded. "Good point."

The car was going very fast now. Wisps of snow were blowing across the roadway. The station was on their left. The gate was coming up. It was going to be a bit of a sharp turn to break through that gate.

"There's a hammer in the bag," Alex said. "I'm going to need it."

Troy looked in the bag, found the small hammer, and pulled it out. The hammer was purple, with a sort of swirling paisley design on it. There were even a couple of yellow sunflowers.

He glanced at Alex.

"It's a hammer," Alex said.

Troy nodded. "Yes."

He quickly took the Glock out of its box. He checked a magazine, saw it was full, and slid it home. He tossed the box back into the bag.

The engine raced now as they sped toward the bottom of the hill. At the last second, Alex turned sharply left, bounced over a curb, crunched across some snow, then down over another curb. The Range Rover hit the gate at an angle, blasting it open.

The fencing collapsed as the heavy car burst through it. The Range Rover's windshield cracked into a spider web pattern but didn't shatter. It fishtailed and skidded, then slid to a stop, maybe thirty feet from the chopper.

Steam rose from the front grill of the car.

"We better go," Alex said.

Troy got out on his side with the heavy bag, the Glock in his right hand. He moved toward the buildings, not going to the helicopter right away. Behind him, Alex went straight to the chopper.

167

Almost instantly, two men came running out of the low-slung office building, pulling on heavy blue coats as they ran.

Troy put the gun on them.

"Stop!" he shouted. "Don't come out here."

They saw him there and slowed but did not stop.

Troy pointed the gun at the sky.

BANG!

The sound of it carried off toward the surrounding mountains, then echoed back. The sonic impact of that one shot was amazing.

Both of the men flinched and stopped. It got their attention.

So, he did it again.

BANG!

Incredible.

Troy could picture the shots causing avalanches across the region. It was a fun thought.

"Don't come out here!" he shouted, then realized the men were already out. Behind them, two more men were coming down the low front steps of the building.

"Go back inside!" Troy shouted.

He had the drop on them. None of them seemed to have a gun. That was good. If they did, he'd have to surrender. He wasn't here to shoot anybody.

"GO!"

One of the men, the one farthest out of the building, said something in German. He raised his hands in the air.

Troy gestured with the gun. "GO!"

He sighed. This was being lost in translation. "Go." How hard a word was that to understand? German and English had a lot of the same words.

Behind him, there was a repetitive banging noise, as Alex must have been hitting something with the hammer.

Troy and the Austrian rescue team were frozen in place, like a group of boys playing Red Light, Green Light.

Now came the whine of the engine starting and the rotors on the helicopter beginning to turn. Troy didn't dare turn around to look.

"Stark!" Alex shouted. "Ready when you are."

"We're just playing a little game over here."

"I'm leaving!"

Troy backed away from the men, then turned and ran low to the chopper. The door on his side was open. He slipped into the seat and pulled the door shut behind him. He shoved the equipment back into the back. The cockpit of the chopper was basically a glass bubble. The back was wide and open.

He glanced back. The rescue basket was there. It was a solid frame, large and orange, and looked like a cage. It was made of some kind of steel mesh. Four chains were clipped to each corner, coming together above the basket at a heavy, black fastener. A heavier chain came out the top of the fastener and was attached to a winch system mounted inside the chopper, which must be controlled from the cockpit.

The basket sat on what was basically a trap door. The door must just drop open, allowing the basket to hang free.

"Oh, man." Troy did not like the looks of that set up.

The men outside were standing around, watching the helicopter. They weren't running. They weren't getting guns. Troy imagined people stopped by and stole helicopters from time to time.

Troy was barely settled in before Alex was off the ground.

The men outside were waving now. It looked like they were indicating that Alex should land. It was too late for that. Troy just waved back, saying goodbye.

The chopper rose quickly into the air. Thirty feet up, fifty, one hundred. The crosswinds hit them, and the chopper was knocked sideways, out over a deep drop.

One hundred fifty feet, two hundred. Alex banked it hard left, and they took off over a frozen white canyon. Troy looked back. The rescue station, with the men standing outside, looked like a child's model now.

He gazed out at the majestic, jagged mountains all around them.

It was a very clear day. Many miles in the distance, behind and to his right, he fancied he could see a cluster of buildings that was the city of Innsbruck.

He let out a breath. He looked at Alex.

The chop of the rotors was incredibly loud.

"That went well!" Troy shouted.

Alex was manipulating the controls with one hand, while pulling a white helmet on with the other. He shook his head. Then he tapped the helmet and gestured in the back.

Troy looked back there again. There was another helmet. He took it and pulled it onto his head. It was a bit small for him, but he jerked it into place.

There was a small computer readout on the dashboard. It was a touch screen. Alex's fingers moved across it, pressing various buttons, and scrolling through screens. After a moment, there was a crackle of static inside Troy's helmet, and then the rotors were canceled out a bit.

Troy pulled the mic in front of his lips. "That went well."

Alex nodded. "Easier than I thought. But they're going to start calling us any second. Air traffic control. The Austrian government. Somebody."

"What are you going to tell them?"

Alex shrugged. "I'm not going to tell them anything."

Troy nodded. He looked down at all the snow.

"Why worry them unnecessarily?"

CHAPTER TWENTY SEVEN

7:55 am Central European Time
Aboard the *East Meets West*
The Austrian Alps, Austria

It is beautiful.

The pop star Calment was dancing.

His dance was slow and snakelike, as befit the music that was on. He was older now, and heavier, but he had always been an excellent dancer, and still was. The DJ was playing a slow mash-up of part of an old disco song from the 1970s, wedded to the music of Calment's 1999 hit, "Too Much is Not Enough."

The woman's voice was incredibly sultry. It was the living embodiment of female sensuality. There was a promise in this song and an invitation. She was like a feline, crying out again and again to the tomcat in the alley. Her voice and Calment's own beats brought the song near the level of the divine.

"Aaaaahhhhhh. Love to love you, baby."

Calment was in a form of ecstasy. His stage name, Calment, suggested a drug that calmed you down, a sedative, a tranquilizer. That was what he had always tried to deliver with his music—a high that put you softly in the clouds. Whoever this young DJ was, he had achieved a thing of genius with this mash-up. Who knew if he would ever reach this height again?

Calment moved with the people in the crowd, down to six or eight now. It was still dark in the club car, the laser lights were still firing, and the DJ was still up there spinning. Istvan had apparently spared no expense when building the sound system. Great sound, great music, and the lingering effects of last night's high.

It was enough.

Yes, Calment knew there was some problem or other with the train. Yes, he could feel that the train was going faster now than before. He could feel it jerking and rattling on the turns in a way that it had not done during the night. Something was indeed different.

Yes, he had heard the anxious whisperings and questionings of some of the people, and he had tried to allay their fears. After more than twenty-five years in the music business, he had seen every possible crazy thing under the sun and some impossible ones.

A disturbed man had taken Calment's entire entourage at gunpoint in a hotel suite one night (and that was when he had a *big entourage*), and then proceeded to kill himself in front of them all. The mess left over was impossible to describe, and Calment didn't like to think about that. But later, he did write a song about the experience—"Don't Die Here." The song was a hit in several countries.

Another time, his bus had been hit by a random missile one afternoon during an ill-advised, but well-intentioned four-night tour of Lebanon. He had been asleep in the back, and the impact woke him up. Later, he wrote a song about that experience—"My Dreams Are Shattered."

The missile passed right through one side of the bus and out the other side. The windows were smashed, one of the walls was essentially ripped out, and some audio gear was destroyed. Most important, no one was hurt.

The Lebanese driver surveyed the damage, found the engine would start up fine, and declared the bus roadworthy. Calment had a one-night only gig in Tripoli, Lebanon's second city, and it was a relatively short drive up the coast. He didn't want to miss it.

So, that's how they went there—in a tour bus that was nearly shredded in half. A warm but stiff breeze blew through the bus as they drove. A few papers went out through the holes. The driver obeyed the speed limit, but that appeared to be the only accommodation he made to the damage.

A police cruiser pulled them over at one point. The young policemen were astonished to see Calment there, took selfie photos with him, got his autograph, and then accompanied the bus to the concert venue. By the time they arrived, there was a phalanx of at least a dozen police vehicles surrounding the bus on all sides, including three armored cars.

This train incident … he couldn't even bring himself to think about it. Maybe he would write a song about it, maybe he wouldn't. The awful truth was his career was mostly over. He was forty-seven years old. No one was waiting to hear a new song from him.

They didn't sell records these days. All the money was in online streaming. The kids didn't know or care about Calment, and they didn't stream his songs. These children listened to music *on their telephones.*

It was too horrible. The loss of sound fidelity was something Calment hated to know existed. The loss of album tracks. The loss of album covers, and the artwork, and all of the information and the messages presented there.

If he could turn back the clock to a time before Steve Jobs was born, he would do it right this moment. And then he would take benign measures, without harming anyone, to keep Steve's biological parents separated and make sure Steve never came to be.

Destroy the music in some parallel reality, Steve, not this one.

Oh, these disrupters and their mindless disruptions. They would erase entire ways of being, and they would boil entire cultures in a pot if they could just squeeze a few extra euros from it.

Suddenly, the train jerked again, harder than before. That was the worst one yet. The music skipped, the lights flickered, and one or two people made sounds that were almost screams. Poor over-alerted mice. Calment didn't want that for them.

He sighed. This party was coming to an end.

The train jerked again as if to put the finishing touch on it.

A woman nearby shrieked.

Yeah. That was a bad one.

Calment felt no fear at all. But he recognized that something unpleasant, potentially bad, was happening.

It figured. This train ride, and other events like it, was what he had been reduced to. Istvan Gajdos, rich but widely ignored, and desperate to make some sort of impression on the world, had offered Calment half a million euros to ride on the train overnight, and be present during the partying that went on. Half the money was paid up front, so even if Istvan reneged on the second half, it was still good money for maybe twenty-four hours of work.

Calment was getting old. He was getting fat. He had three ex-wives that he was still supporting to varying degrees. He had five kids, including three young adults, none of whom had worked an honest day in their lives. The record sales had dried up. The streams weren't happening. The concerts on offer were club dates.

This was it. The only paydays out here were parties thrown by rich narcissists. Calment would do these until they dried up too. Then he supposed he would appear on reality TV shows where he was forced to live in group housing and share towels and toothbrushes with other people who had once been serious artists, or maybe world-class athletes, but who now had syphilis or some other hard to manage bacterial infection.

It was a grim future facing him. And yet, if the music was right, and with a little help from the designer drugs, he could still reach these ecstatic states of mind like he always had.

Now, the lights in the car went on.

All around them, the screens that were giving the illusion of nighttime began to go up, revealing a daytime world outside the windows.

The sudden light streaming in was nearly blinding.

A group of three people had entered the car from the front side of the train. There were two men and a woman. One of the men was big, broad, and young. The other man was older and thin. The woman was of indeterminate age, with dark hair, and dressed in the white shirt and black pants of one of the train workers.

Calment saw them all in almost exquisite detail. The older man had a long gun in his hand, a pistol with an attachment on the front. He went over to the DJ and said something to him. Now the music stopped, putting an official end to the party. An instant later, the lasers went off. They had barely been visible with the overhead lights on anyway.

Everyone stood and stared at the intruders.

"The train is hijacked," the older man said, without preamble. "It is under our control."

Calment studied his face. It was lined with the deep experience of long years. There was struggle, violence, and disappointment written there. The eyes were hard but also tired. The face had perhaps a day's worth of beard growth.

Perhaps this man was older than Calment. Perhaps they were contemporaries. It was hard to say.

"You will surrender your mobile phones. Then we will subdue you with plastic ties. If you cooperate, you will not be harmed. When the hijacking is over, you will be released. It's that simple for you."

He turned and said something under his breath to the larger man. The larger man was quite young. He nodded and continued through the disco car toward the back of the train. He left through the rear door.

"This woman is coming around with a bag. Place your phones inside of it. Do this silently. Do not ask questions. Do not give even a word of resistance or complaint."

The woman moved from person to person. Each in turn dropped their telephone into the bag. Calment watched them silently. These were good party people, mostly in their thirties, a few of them legitimate freaks. They were the counterculture, and yet, here they were, surrendering easily to an act of … what?

Violence, certainly.

Fascism, maybe.

Some holdover of Piscean Age domination and dead end winner-take-all philosophy. No, it was more a policy than a philosophy. It was too empty to be considered a philosophy. There was no thought to it. It was the barbaric, ape-like savagery that would destroy every living thing on this planet if we allowed it. A man with a gun seized a train that did not belong to him and told everyone the party must stop.

The germ of an idea occurred to Calment.

A hero stood up.

That was the whole idea, but it contained worlds within it. Someone said no. This aggression will not stand. This harm will not continue.

Yes, he was high, but the sentiment was real, and he felt it in every part of his body. There was perfect alignment. And also, he could see himself doing the rounds of the morning talk shows and the nighttime interview and variety shows, across the continent and on others as well, answering questions in the dozen languages he was comfortable speaking, if even just a bit.

"Someone needed to say no to this. We all need to say no. We can still usher in the New Age we were expecting."

Calment was relevant again. The online streams ticked up, yes. But he didn't care so much about that. His newfound platform gave him the opportunity to lament the lost art of the complete album. *His physical album sales went way up.*

He went on tour again, a hundred lucrative dates all over the world.

A new album appeared.

"A Hero Stood Up."

The woman stood in front of him now. She held out the bag to him. He looked inside of it. There was a pile of telephones at the bottom, mostly sleek and black modern smartphones. There were a couple of older flip phones in there too.

Calment wasn't even sure if he had his telephone on him. It didn't matter.

He looked into the woman's eyes.

"I won't comply."

Around them, the screens were now all the way up, revealing the daytime mountain landscape. The views were incredible. Peaks scraping the blue sky, bright early sunlight reflecting off the snow.

But it was moving too fast. That was clear. Things close to the train, electrical poles, outbuildings, whatever they were, flew by in flashes, barely seen. They cast shadows like bats and then were gone.

The train swayed from side to side, as if it was having a hard time staying on the tracks.

"Put the phone in the bag," the woman said. "Please."

"No," Calment said. "I will not comply."

The woman's shoulders slumped. Her eyes widened in something like irritation but also something else. It might be fear.

"Do you know who I am?" Calment said.

"Of course I know who you are. It's an honor to meet you. Do you not recall me serving you drinks last night? I drugged you. You were supposed to fall asleep. But your resistance to drugs is too strong. Put your phone in the bag before he kills you."

Calment looked across at the man with the gun. The man was staring back at him.

"He's an animal. And you and I are here, trying to be angels."

"He's a good man," the woman said. "But he's not going to have patience for this. We are pressed for time."

"How can you be with him?" Calment said. And, of course, now that fact was there too. It was as clear as the stark mountains outside the windows. She was with the man. He was the ringleader, but she was more to him than a mere follower.

"He's a good man," she said again.

It would be ridiculous to argue with her. He was not a good man. If she hadn't come to terms with that by now, no amount of evidence was going to change her mind. The man could beat her with a wooden club, and she would say, "He only does it because he loves me."

"You're a lost cause," Calment told her.

She shook her head. "You don't know him."

Okay. Never mind.

"I refuse," Calment called out, louder this time, so the man could hear him.

"Oh God," the woman said.

Now, the man was walking toward them. The woman turned to the man as he approached. She spoke in rapid fire Russian, which Calment well understood. "He doesn't have a phone! He doesn't have a phone!"

176

"A hero stood up!" Calment shouted. The people, people who were here to dance the night with him, now stared at him wide-eyed.

"Stand with me now! It's time to say no!"

The man walked up to him, pointed the gun, and shot him once in the chest. It was surprising how quiet it was. It made a sound like someone punching a single key on an old manual typewriter.

CLACK!

Of course. The gun had a long silencer on it. Calment had seen that without really taking it in. He hadn't grasped the full implications of it. The gun was quiet, though not completely silenced.

It was interesting that people called them "silencers."

Calment lay on his back, staring upwards. Incredibly, the roof was open to the sky as well. Istvan was a terrible braggart, but his train really was an amazing feat of engineering.

Calment didn't remember falling here. One instant, he was standing, facing the hijacker. The next instant, he was down here. He was impaled by pain. The drugs put some distance between he and it, but pain was now the central fact of his existence. PAIN. A bullet had gone in through his chest and seemed to have gone out through his back. The pain went straight through his body like that long ago missile went straight through his bus.

More people had screamed when Calment was shot. He heard them. But no one had done anything.

The hijacker man stood over him now and looked down.

"You don't want to become like this piece of trash," he said to the gathered crowd. "So, do everything I ask. Immediately. Without question."

The woman was looking down at him now too. Her eyes were softer than the man's eyes. Even so, Calment half expected her to say, "See? I told you."

"Tie them up," the man said to her. She nodded and then she was gone.

Now, it was only Calment and the man who had murdered him.

"I shot you near the heart," the man said. "You're bleeding out. Do you feel cold? It's from loss of blood. You'll be dead soon."

Calment noticed that he did feel cold. But maybe it was the power of suggestion. Maybe if the man hadn't said it, then Calment wouldn't be feeling it.

Maybe he could reject the man's suggestions, even the part about death.

He was fading, though. He could feel that too.

"A Hero Stood Up."

Someone else would have to make that album.

But Calment might well be relevant again. Sales would increase, of course. They always did when you died. And there would be career retrospectives. Interviews with all the old band mates, and ex-wives, and the many ex-lovers. And if these witnesses to his death survived this coming train wreck, then they would be interviewed too.

His songs would get another listen. One more time, at least.

"Are you satisfied?" the man said.

He meant the question as a criticism, that if only Calment had obeyed, he wouldn't be dying now. But that's not how Calment chose to take it. He looked away from the man and up at the blue sky, with white clouds skidding by high above the train.

"Yes," he said. "I think so."

***

"What am I looking at?"

Grigori Kovacs stared at the monitor screens in front of him. Something had happened to him. He had been asleep. He wasn't sure how long he'd been asleep, and he wasn't even sure when he had awakened.

He didn't know how long he'd been staring at these screens without really seeing them. He was security personnel. There were cameras placed throughout the train, and his job was to watch these screens for any suspicious activity.

There was suspicious activity all over them, and he hadn't noticed it until now. There were two men lying in a lake of blood in the corridor outside of Istvan's stateroom. He knew both men, although at the moment he couldn't remember their names. Neither one appeared to be moving.

Something is wrong with my head.

Another man was lying in the foyer between cars, also near Istvan's stateroom. A man was lying in the foyer at the entry to the cockpit. He was wearing the blue uniform that the train driver wore. Grigori would guess that he was also dead.

A completely different man was now driving the train.

To top it off, the disco car was wide open to daylight, which was not supposed to happen on this trip, and a man had just shot what appeared to be the old pop star Calment. Grigori clocked through the secret cameras placed inside staterooms. People were tied up on the beds with black hoods on their heads.

Grigori pressed in the code that unlocked the cameras in Istvan's personal stateroom. There were two cameras—one in the bathroom, facing the shower, and one facing the bed. The bathroom camera showed an empty shower. The bed camera showed three people tied down and masked, lying across the big bed. Two were the whores Istvan was with last night. The other was Istvan himself. None of them seemed to be moving, but they were not bloodied in any obvious way.

Whatever was going on here had been happening for a while. Things were completely out of control. Grigori felt his heart skip and race inside his chest. He had been drinking coffee all night to stay awake, and yet he felt like he had a hangover.

He found another body on the floor in one of the cars with smaller staterooms. He felt like he knew this man too. The man was face down on the carpeting, a dark stain around his upper body like a halo. Grigori's fingers worked the control board in front of him. On the screen, the footage raced backwards, demonstrating how the man came to be in this state.

The camera picked up the man walking, the bartender named Helena walking behind him. Helena—at least Grigori could remember her name. He should remember everyone's name. These were his coworkers, but his mind seemed to have been blanked.

Suddenly, Helena had a gun in her hand. She allowed the man to get several steps in front of her, then seemed to call out, because the man turned around. He dashed toward her, probably trying to get the gun. He reached her and crashed to the floor on top of her. They lay without moving for a few seconds. Then Helena squirmed out from under him like a snake.

Helena. Helena was killing people. Helena and partners.

Helena had brought Grigori a large cup of coffee from the kitchen. He had been dragging a bit as the morning came in, getting tired, and she had kindly brought him the coffee to revive him.

Then he had fallen asleep.

And now, people were dead all over the train.

Grigori looked at the live footage of the disco car. Calment was lying in a pool of blood, staring up at the ceiling. He was no longer moving. A thin man with a gun, the man who had just shot Calment, was standing by. Helena was tying the hands of people behind their backs, pushing them to their knees, then knocking them over sideways. The people were not resisting her at all.

As Grigori watched, she tied the hands of the young DJ.

Call someone. You're supposed to call and alert them.

Grigori looked on the counter for his mobile phone, but of course it was gone. He flicked on the radio transmitter. Nothing. He flicked it on and off several times. That didn't change anything. Of course. They were hijacking the train. They had disabled the radio. No one could call out. No one could call in.

Helena had drugged him. He still felt drugged. He wasn't thinking clearly, he understood that. There were answers here that he wasn't seeing. There had to be another way to contact the outside world. But he couldn't think of it.

There was the urge to go back to sleep, yes. If he slept again, maybe they would just leave him alone. But that wasn't the way he was. Grigori was hired on here to do a job. He was supposed to protect Istvan Gajdos, and he was supposed to protect the train.

He took his key ring out of his pocket and pulled the key to the desk in front of him. On the lower left was a big drawer. He unlocked and opened it. Inside was a small flask of whisky and a Czech-made pistol. He picked up the pistol and opened the magazine. It was loaded. Eight rounds.

Eight chances to take this train back.

He stood, gun in hand, and swayed with the violent motion of the train. It seemed to be moving quite fast. Grigori was woozy, not good on his feet. In fact, he felt like he might throw up.

Well, it was all right if he did. He had thrown up before.

He turned and opened the door to the monitor room and stumbled out into the narrow hallway. He could get lucky. He had also gotten lucky before.

He began to make his way up the hall toward the front of the train.

CHAPTER TWENTY EIGHT

8:59 am Eastern European Time (7:59 am Central European Time)
An office building
Outskirts of Sofia, Bulgaria

"Ready now," the team leader said. "Ready."

Gavril Petrov stood along a concrete wall about a dozen men back, in a stack of sixteen commandos who were going to storm the office on the second floor of this utterly nondescript building. The building was low to the ground, made of cinderblock, and had no identifying markings on it of any kind, which was always a bad sign. It meant there were no legitimate businesses inside.

The police had parked their trucks a block away in order to maintain the element of surprise. They also wore black hoods, helmets, black jumpsuits, and vests with the word "Police" in English across the front. A few of the men carried shotguns, and the rest carried short clubs. Gavril himself had a club in his hand. They had been standing out here for five minutes now, waiting for the order to go in.

Cars drove by on the street, and at least three or four had already honked their horns. Maybe ten pedestrians had walked by, looked in alarm at them standing here, and quickly moved on. A couple of them had taken out their mobile phones as they walked away and immediately made calls.

The element of surprise was long gone if it had ever existed. Gavril wasn't sure if the element of surprise could exist in Sofia, or anywhere in Bulgaria. Half the reason he even kept this job, besides the monthly salary, was to tell his cousin Dimitar what the police were going to do before they did it.

Dimitar was a low-level Mafioso, and he was trying to curry favor with his superiors by passing the information up the line.

"One day, it can be good for both of us," Dimitar always said.

Gavril didn't know if that day would ever come, but he hoped so. That's why he hated raids like this one. Apparently, there was some kind of cyber crime taking place here. A team of Bulgarian hackers was causing trouble in other countries, and Interpol had requested that the National Police put a stop to it.

This morning, less than an hour ago, was the first Gavril heard of all this. Raids that loomed out of nowhere, without warning, were the worst kind of raids. There was no time to inform Dimitar about them.

That was also why Gavril had positioned himself toward the back of the line. God forbid he should end up arresting someone in Dimitar's organization.

"GO!" the team leader shouted.

The door facing the street was glass. The first two men in line simply smashed the glass with a battering ram. It made a very loud noise. Then the men kicked at the remaining glass in the door with their thick, heavy, black boots.

It was almost as if all this waiting and noise making was to alert anyone inside that now was a good time to leave.

The line of men surged through the shattered door and up the stairs. At the top, the first two men bludgeoned the office door with the ram. This was a heavy, wooden door, and it took several hits to break the lock.

Now the line surged through the door, shouting, "Hands up! Hands up!"

It felt like a police academy exercise. It was going fine so far, but everything about it was easy, trite, and slow. By the time Gavril pushed through the door, the shouting was over. The entire event was over as it turned out.

The office was a generic place, with brown carpeting. The walls were a shade of pale yellow. There was a desk against the far wall, with a tower CPU beneath it, and a desktop screen. The computer was plugged into a black routing device on the floor. It was also plugged into an electricity socket in the wall.

The computer was on. Gavril knew this because the screen was showing swirling, colorful lines against a black background. The overhead fluorescent lights in the drop ceiling were not on. Moreover, no one was here. The place had an unused feeling to it. There was a metal folding chair in front of the computer, but no mysterious hacker was sitting in it.

A few cops were poking through the office, opening doors, and looking inside. The rest were simply standing around. From where Gavril stood, there looked to be a kitchen across the way, with a refrigerator, a few cabinets, and a round table and chairs. A few cops were in there, opening the cabinet doors, probably looking for snacks.

Gavril went to the desk with the lone computer on it. He removed the black glove on his left hand. He stuck out his index finger and ran it along the top of the desk. A light film of gray dust appeared on his finger.

Yeah. No one had been here for a while.

The team leader drifted by. "Don't touch that computer," he said. "It's evidence."

"Evidence of what?" Gavril said.

The leader shrugged. "I don't know."

Gavril reflected that this was not a bad raid, after all. No one was here to be arrested, and judging by the dust, there was never any danger of arresting anyone. There was a single computer. It was on, and maybe it was even doing something. Maybe there was some damning information on there.

But if there was information on that computer, there was also a good chance it would be wiped clean between here and the evidence locker at the police station.

Let's face it—there was a better than zero chance the computer would never reach the evidence locker and would instead wind up at the team leader's house.

That was fine with Gavril. He preferred police raids that amounted to nothing. Not that he would ever demonstrate this preference, however. The trick was to seem enthusiastic for a real police raid, one where criminals were taken down and sent away.

"Why do they send us on these pointless missions?" he said out loud.

CHAPTER TWENTY NINE

8:05 am Central European Time
Aboard the *East Meets West*
The Austrian Alps, Austria

Pistol-whipped. I got pistol-whipped.

Carl Gallo sat on the bed, trying to make sense of his situation. He remembered nearly everything. He had convinced Dubois to hide under the bed, and it had turned out to be the right move.

A couple of Russians had blown in through the door moments later. They were armed and had the drop on him. They pistol-whipped him, then bagged and tagged him. After that, things got fuzzy. He was in the dark for what seemed like a long time but could have been five minutes.

The next thing he knew, Dubois was there, looking at him, eyes wide with concern. She was speaking to him, but he wasn't hearing her. Or maybe he was hearing her, but he just couldn't follow what she was saying.

Those guys had given him the business pretty good.

The black bag was off his head. His hands were free. After the guys were gone, she must have crawled out from under the bed and released him. That might not be a very good move. What if they came back? Carl was in no shape to do anything. He couldn't fight. He couldn't even stand up. His thinking was shattered.

He turned his head to the right. Dubois was over there, near the wrecked door to the suite, speaking into a telephone. She poked her head out into the hallway, then darted back inside.

She was probably talking to the headquarters of El Grupo. Miquel Castro was in charge, Carl's old friend from his younger days. Miquel had a sixth sense about things. He was always close to something.

Money. It was money.

Carl wanted money, and Miquel was close to it. But Miquel was too honest to want money. His unique sensitivity brought him right next to it, but he didn't want it. Last month, it brought him to CERN.

There were military secrets at CERN, weapons research being conducted independently, and which appeared to have been up for grabs. A group tried to infiltrate and steal the information. Carl was *right there*, in the hallway with the last surviving thief, and she shot him.

He wasn't expecting that. He thought he could talk her into dropping her gun or handing it to him. No dice. She shot him without hesitation and then walked right past him. Later, Troy Stark killed her. The files she had, whatever they were, went up in flames when Stark shot down her helicopter. CERN was in total lockdown these days. Whatever secrets they had would remain with them.

Now this train. Istvan Gajdos, Hungarian oligarch and international comedy relief, was suspect #1 in a gigantic crypto theft. He was here on the train. The train was being hijacked. That money was hanging in the balance. Carl Gallo was also here. But the first thing that happened was he got savagely pistol-whipped by the Russian hijackers.

At this point, he was useless. He should be up, sneaking through the train, looking to thwart the hijackers, but also to find Istvan. Find him and make him see that his only way out of here alive was with Carl Gallo.

But Carl couldn't stand up. His balance was gone. He just wanted to go back to sleep. He was getting too old for this.

The train was racing along. He could feel it. It was all true, everything they said. The hijackers were here, probably to get Istvan to hand over the crypto to them. What else could they want? Meanwhile, the train had been hacked from somewhere and was speeding out of control.

All of it. All of it was real and exactly as advertised.

And Carl couldn't do a thing.

***

"I don't know," Dubois said. "He doesn't seem well."

She glanced over at Gallo. He was sitting on the bed, his head cradled in his hands. She had tried to talk to him before, but he didn't seem to understand a word she was saying.

"I suggest both of you escape from there," Miquel said over the phone. "It may be too late to stop the hijacking. Jan is working on it, but he says it's a blizzard of an attack, coming from what seems to be dozens of locations at once. It almost certainly isn't, but the hackers have masked their location effectively enough that it appears that way. We've just learned that the place the attack first seemed to come from was a decoy. Jan's trying to stop the attack himself, with no success so far. The train will continue to accelerate, at least for the moment. If the hijackers are armed, there's very little you can do there by yourself. The Austrian police are coming, but they cannot stop the train."

Dubois looked out the window. The landscape zipped by. She didn't know if she had ever been on a train moving this fast before. It was hard to focus her eyes on anything out there, except the mountains in the far distance.

"I don't see how we're going to get off the train," she said.

The phone cut out for a moment. She waited.

"What was that, Dubois?" Miquel said. "I didn't hear you."

"I don't think we can escape the train."

"You can't jump off?"

Dubois thought back to the idea of jumping off the train. Even if they could somehow open a door while the train was moving, jumping out there would be a form of insanity. They would just as likely get sucked into the train's draft and crushed. If not, they were likely to crash at two hundred kilometers an hour, or faster—instant death at those speeds if you were lucky. A shattered body if you were unlucky.

"Dubois?"

"Yes, I don't think jumping out is viable at this time. We're moving fast, and I'd have to almost push Gallo out the door."

"What else is available to you?"

"I talked to Stark some moments ago. He said he's coming."

"Stark is?"

She shrugged. "That's what he said."

She popped her head into the corridor and looked both ways. She had done this several times now. No one was out there. Just a narrow, brown-paneled hall with no one in it. She didn't know if she expected to see Troy Stark come up the hallway. She knew it was silly. The most likely people to arrive would be the hijackers, but so far, they hadn't come back.

"We're unable to reach him."

"I can't reach him anymore, either," Dubois said. "I only spoke with him briefly."

"Who's driving the train?" Miquel said.

From here, she couldn't see to the front of the train, so she had no idea who was driving this thing, or if anyone was. She supposed she should go up and there and find out. In the meantime …

"I don't know."

"Do you have a weapon?"

"No," Dubois said. "We lost the weapons when we boarded."

"Do not engage with the hijackers," Miquel said now. "You're likely to get yourselves killed. My advice is to continue to evade them and look for any method of escape available."

"What about the passengers?" Dubois said.

"It's a difficult call," Miquel said. "But I'm making it. You will be fortunate to save yourselves. There's nothing you can do for the passengers. We will continue to try to stop the hack from here. We've alerted the Austrian authorities, and in a little while, we will alert Interpol. These things are the best we can do for the passengers."

Dubois felt a tickle of fear deep in her belly. They were well and truly trapped on here. They had blundered on here with a blindly optimistic plan, and now the holes in it were abundantly clear.

"Your job is first to save your own lives," Miquel said.

Then the phone call died. Dubois stared at the phone for a long moment. The phone calls kept dropping. There was no sense calling Miquel back.

None of this felt right. They didn't come here to witness a hijacking, then escape from it. They came here to stop it.

She glanced at Gallo. He was lying on his side now, eyes closed.

She went over to him. "Gallo?" She shook him gently. "Agent Gallo?"

His eyes opened, saw her there, and then fluttered closed again.

"I'm tired, Dubois. That guy really tagged me."

Dubois put her fingers to his neck and took his pulse. She checked it against her watch, timing for fifteen seconds, and then multiplying by four. Gallo's heart was beating normally, if a little fast, about 100 beats per minute.

He seemed okay. He probably had a concussion. There was nothing she could do for him here. He was out of the game.

Whatever Dubois was going to do, she was going to have to do it herself.

***

"Vlad, get rid of that thing, will you?"

Sokolov watched out the train window at a helicopter that had just begun to accompany them. It was off to the north of the train, far enough away that he couldn't make out what the words were on the helicopter's body.

They were in a lounge car to the rear of the train. A handful of people were in here, passed out in easy chairs and on sofas. Helena had drugged them last night. She was going from person to person, determining who they were.

After subduing the people in the kitchen, Sokolov's team had run out of zip ties. There were more people on the train than Ivan the Terrible had anticipated. They had run out of black masks some time ago.

That was all right. There were very few people left, and they all seemed to be asleep. Things were going according to plan. They were a man down, but casualties were to be expected in a job like this. There were just a couple more train cars to clear at the back and then Sokolov could go deal with Gajdos.

But now that helicopter was here. Maybe it was the police. Maybe it was a news station. Maybe he should simply ignore it, but it was an annoyance, like a buzzing mosquito in the room. He looked out at it again. It was closer now, coming ever closer. He still couldn't read the markings on it.

"Get rid of it?" Vlad said.

Sokolov nodded. "Yes."

"How do I do that?"

Sokolov questioned the intelligence of the youngest generations, he really did. How were they going to survive? Moreover, how were they going to inherit the world and run it? Everything had to be spoon-fed to them. Sokolov had been under the impression that Vlad was the sharper of the two young people on this team.

He still suspected it was true. Which led him to wonder a little bit about Peter the Great. Because if Vlad was like this …

"Go back to the cockpit and get the AR-15. Don't talk to anyone on your way. Just go get the gun. And then get rid of the helicopter. Smash a window if you need to."

"If I shoot at a helicopter," Vlad said, "won't that call attention to us? I thought we were trying to hide our presence here."

"If a helicopter is following us, we can guess that our presence has been detected."

Vlad shrugged. "All right, Uncle Joe. You're the boss."

Sokolov nodded. "Yes. I am."

"Of course, you are," Vlad said. He turned and went back the way they had just come.

Sokolov looked at Helena. She had checked the last of the sleeping passengers. She stared back at Sokolov. Her eyes had hardened against him. It was the pop star, naturally. Women had some unexplainable fascination with celebrity. The throw-away magazines in England that covered the so-called "royals" were purchased by women. The corresponding magazines in the United States that covered the Hollywood stars were sold to women as well.

Sokolov had killed the pop star. The man wasn't listening. He had been given several opportunities to do so. He had pursued the path he was on for his own reasons. It was possible that he wanted to be martyred. In that case, he got his wish. He was no better than anyone else. He was also probably no worse. Good and bad, they all died alike.

"Who are they?" Sokolov said.

He was just going to move on like this pop star thing was not an issue. Helena would have to do the same. She could be angry about it some other time.

She shrugged. "A banker from Switzerland. He had been planning to get off in Innsbruck, but I guess he passed out instead. A prostitute. A couple of hangers on of Istvan's, here for the party. No one dangerous. They are all in a deep sleep."

"Are you sure?"

Trust was breaking down. He recognized that. He had killed a pop star, and now he was concerned she would lie to him to protect other people.

She stared at him blankly. Her opinion of him had changed. She was looking at him like he was a cold-blooded killer. He was that, of course, but this was the first time he saw it reflected in Helena's eyes.

"Helena?"

"Yes, I'm sure."

He nodded. "Good. Let's go."

She moved ahead of him toward the doorway to the next car in line. She walked quickly, showing him her back, as if she no longer wanted him to read her face. The train rocked, side to side, and she nearly lost her balance. He would have steadied her, but she was too far ahead.

"Helena!"

She ignored him. Instead, she pressed the large square button that opened the door to the next foyer between cars.

A large man was there, looming just to the side of the doorway.

Sokolov saw it unfold as though it was happening in slow motion. The man had a gun. He raised it.

Sokolov began to run, raising his own gun toward the man.

"No!"

BANG!

The man shot Helena in the head. She barely had time to flinch. A spray of blood went out the exit wound on the left side of her skull. She collapsed to the floor like a rag doll. The door began to slide shut again, but her body was in the way.

The large man turned toward the open doorway. He raised his gun.

Sokolov fired wildly, his sound suppressor deteriorated completely.

BANG! BANG! BANG! BANG! BANG!

The gun bucked in his hand.

The big man jittered and danced as the bullets pierced him. His gun flew away. His head snapped back, and he slipped to the floor. He was large enough that his falling was a surprising sight, like a cliff face on a mountain falling.

Sokolov went to Helena and dropped to his knees. He cradled her head, but it was too late. Blood was all over the floor and now all over his hands. Her eyes were lifeless, like a doll's eyes. They accused him silently. Her mouth hung slightly open, her tongue poking out a tiny mount.

He kissed her. Her mouth was warm, as if she were alive.

There was blood everywhere. It was getting on him, on his clothes, on his face.

"Oh God. So much blood."

He hugged her and held her close to him. She was heavy, like dead things were heavy.

"Oh no."

How did he do this? How did he bring her here?

He, Sokolov, had done this. One last job. One giant payday, to leave a legacy for his son and his ex-wife. He had been focused only on himself. He was the walking dead, but he had brought the living with him.

He would weep now if weeping was in him. But it wasn't.

Helena was dead. She knew the risks. She had come of her own accord.

Not true. She had come to please you.

He let her go gently to the floor. The door to the foyer tried to close automatically again but hit the dead weight of her body and reversed course. It slid back into the wall.

He stepped over her.

The big man, the man who killed her, was alive. He squirmed on the floor of the foyer, trying to reach his gun. It seemed he couldn't find it. He looked up at Sokolov. His eyes were afraid. He was gasping for air. There was blood all over his chest.

"I probably hit your lungs but missed your heart," Sokolov said.

The man tried to say something, but it came out as a rasping shriek, almost like a train whistle.

"Who are you?" Sokolov said.

"Grigori," the man said. He said it almost with a sense of despair, his face a mask of pain. He grimaced, as if he would start crying.

The word Grigori meant nothing to Sokolov. Just another dead man on a train full of dead people, in a world full of marching zombies.

"She drugged me."

Sokolov felt cold, empty, like the snowy wastes outside the windows.

"So, you killed her," he said.

The man's eyes were insane. He looked like an animal trapped in a corner.

"I acted without …"

Sokolov shook his head. "I wish I had the time to kill you properly," he told the man.

He aimed and …

The man raised a large hand, itself dripping with his own blood.

"No."

BANG!

Sokolov turned away from the man. The door had tried to shut again, getting caught on Helena's body one more time. It was gruesome to look at it. He needed to pull her out of there.

There was no reason to keep anyone on this train alive. There was nothing left, no longer anything to live for. Not for him, not for them. He had been right all along.

No, there was one more thing left to do.

He must go deal with Istvan Gajdos.

CHAPTER THIRTY

8:10 am Central European Time
The skies above the Austrian Alps
Austria

"How are you doing?" Alex said inside Troy's helmet.

His voice was quiet and calm.

Troy crouched inside the rescue basket. His gear bag was on the bottom. He was going through his stuff. He took a sip from the water bottle. He placed the Uzi on the floor, with one magazine loaded. The other two mags were in the deep leg pockets of his cargo pants. He strapped the Glock in a holster under his arm.

The Glock felt unwieldy under his heavy coat, so he shrugged out of the coat and tossed it aside. Without the coat, he was wearing a fur-lined jumpsuit and a tight windbreaker. He was going to be cold. So be it. He needed freedom of movement. He had been cold before. A large part of his training was about overcoming cold. Being cold adapted. Shrugging off the cold like you would a warm jacket.

Inside the bag at his feet was the cutting tool. He had tried it out a few moments ago. It was heavy. It ran on electric battery power—the battery was large and was mounted on the back. There was a sharp-toothed saw, like a chain saw, but with a curved beak like a bird, that folded out from the main body of the thing. It had a little bit of kick when it was running. It was going to be fun trying to control that thing while clinging to the top of a speeding train.

He noticed he was breathing high in his chest. Shallow breathing was evidence of, and often caused, a panic attack. He stood tall, his head near the winch, and took several slow deep breaths.

"Stark?"

He nodded. "Yeah."

Outside the chopper, white mountains rose on either side, scraping the pale blue sky. They were in a gorge between ranges. The tracks were below and to the left, cutting a dark path through an endless sea of frigid white. The train was just up ahead. It must be going fast because the helicopter was ripping.

"You okay?" Alex said.

"Yeah. I'm fine. How fast is that train going?"

"I don't know. Fast. We'll catch it though as soon as we're ready. I'm hanging back a little bit."

Down on the ground, maybe three or four hundred feet below, Troy watched as the train entered a black tunnel carved into the side of a mountain. The chopper stayed to the right, curving around the steep slope. In a moment, they passed the mountain and the train appeared again, zipping out of the tunnel on the far side.

"How's the clearance on those tunnels?"

"I'd say good," Alex said. "Several feet. But I'd keep my head down. Hell, I'd get down and crawl like a worm if I was you."

Troy shook his head. "Thanks."

"I think we're going to lose the helmet radios when you're down there," Alex said.

"How soon?"

"I don't know," Alex said. "These rescue guys often use satellite phones, hand signals, rope-pull signals, flares, the works. And they're not usually going that fast, yeah?"

"Just hovering, I'd imagine," Troy said.

He caught himself sighing. He took another deep breath.

"Do you want to come up with some quick hand signals?" Alex said. He turned his head all the way around in the cockpit and looked back at Troy. Troy would prefer he pay attention to where he was going.

Troy held up his black-gloved right hand an extended the middle finger.

"How's that hand signal? Do you get it?"

Alex smiled and turned back around. "Let me know when you're ready," he said.

Troy shrugged. He was about as ready as he was ever going to be. He had his weapons, and he had his cutting tool. He was geared up. He felt okay—well-fed, alert, and reasonably hydrated. No amount of waiting here was going to make this situation better or change what he had to do. He might as well get to it.

He took another deep breath. He stared at nothing for a moment. He found that he was calm. He was more than calm. He felt nothing at all, just a small amount of fear or terror or maybe excitement in his belly. But it seemed far away, not part of him.

He was in that place he went to. He might die in the next few minutes, maybe even the next several seconds. He might not. Either one was okay.

"Now. I'm ready now."

"Good luck," Alex said.

"I'll need it."

A buzzer sounded, and a red light came on, mounted overhead to his right. The sound was harsh, like the buzzer at the end of a basketball game. Beneath the basket, the trapdoor dropped away, two doors actually, swinging down from the middle. The basket was suspended out over nothing, just hanging from the winch system. Everything was wide open around him now.

The wind howled and the helicopter rotors were louder than before. The helmet was not nearly as good at canceling the noise as it was a moment ago.

Alex said something, but Troy couldn't make it out. Lose the helmet radio? It might as well already be gone.

Suddenly, the chopper banked hard left and down. They dropped a hundred feet in a few seconds. They were coming in fast. Three hundred feet. Two hundred.

Troy felt his stomach try to come out through his throat. He crouched low in the basket again, his hands on the top railings of it.

He scanned the railroad bed below them. The chopper was flying fast, just to the right of the tracks. The train was up ahead. They were coming in behind it.

The chopper came down further. Soon, it was fifty feet in the air, zooming now. The train was coming to them, almost like it was going in reverse.

Suddenly, the chopper pulled up and to the right, hard.

Ahead, the front of the train disappeared into another dark tunnel.

The helicopter banked, nearly rolling onto its side. Sparse trees climbed the snowy side of the mountain. The chopper was close enough for Troy to see each individual tree. He was nearly close enough to see wisps of snow falling from the branches.

He nearly screamed as the chopper buzzed close to the treetops. Then they were up and over the hillside and blue sky filled the windscreen and windows again.

"Alex!" Troy shouted. "I need you to anticipate that!"

Alex said something in response. Troy couldn't hear a word of it.

Below them, to the left, there was the train, moving like a burst of lightning. The sun glinted off the metal, enhancing the effect. The train was all the way out of the tunnel.

They didn't need to communicate. They both knew what came next. The helicopter began to drop towards the train. It was time to try again.

They fell in above and behind the train.

Troy felt the basket lurch and then drop out of the helicopter. He watched the chopper seem to fall away above him. He crouched low.

The screaming wind whipped around him.

The sky was wide open. They were moving so fast that the basket did not hang straight down. It hung backwards in an arc at the end of its tether.

Ahead and below, and to his left again, the train was zipping along, like a red, white, and green blur. The chopper was pulling even with it. Everything was happening in a flash. For several seconds, his eyes couldn't make sense of it all.

Along the right side of the train, near the front, a series of windows suddenly shattered, the glass spraying backwards like icicles.

A man appeared there. For a second, Troy thought the man would start waving for help, a passenger trying to escape. But that was wrong.

The man pulled out a gun. It was a rifle. Troy saw the muzzle flash. Once, twice, three times. The man was shooting at the helicopter, or maybe the basket. Semiautomatic, one shot at a time. Troy couldn't hear the shots. The gun was too far away, and there was too much wind.

Troy looked up. The basket was hanging way below the helicopter now. The open trap doors were a dark square, getting smaller and smaller.

Alex was letting the basket down and increasing the altitude of the chopper. Smart. For him. He might as well not take any fire from that shooter. The guy had a rifle, and it was pretty far, but there was no reason to take chances.

That left the shooter nothing to shoot at except the basket.

Troy poked his head up. The odds of getting hit by one of that guy's …

CLANG!

A shot ricocheted off the metal frame. Troy shook his head.

"All right, then."

He picked up the Uzi. He popped up and fired a burst toward the front of the train.

DUH-DUH-DUH-DUH. The sound was swallowed almost out of the gun.

He fired another burst, the gun jumping in his hands. The shots sprayed toward the train. He fancied he saw sparks fly as the shots hit. He wasn't sure if that was true at all. With the wind and the speed, he had no idea where the shots were going.

But the man in the window jumped back.

Troy got a bead on where the man had been …

The man appeared, and Troy sprayed again. DUH-DUH-DUH-DUH. He fired the last of the magazine and ejected the mag to the floor of the basket.

The man in the window was gone again.

The basket fell in behind the train. The bottom of the basket was just feet above the track. For a second, Troy thought Alex was just going to drop him onto the tracks and let him bounce along after the train.

The basket rose above the last car, a backward facing front car. The helicopter sped up, the basket skimming across the top of the second train car. Far up ahead, Troy spotted what looked like the entrance to another tunnel.

Did Alex see that? Troy looked up, but all he could see was the belly of the chopper and the black square of the trapdoor. It was quite far ahead. The basket was trailing behind.

The bottom of the basket scraped and bounced on top of the train. The jolt of the landing was like a powerful jolt of electricity up Troy's arms and legs and then throughout his entire body.

He guessed that was his cue to leave. He dropped the Uzi on the floor next to its spent magazine. He picked up the bag with the cutting tool and heaved it over the side. It landed on the roof of the train, slid toward the edge, but then stayed.

He glanced at the Uzi but decided against it. He was going to lose it anyway. He had nowhere to strap it but around his shoulder or neck. It was liable to get hooked on something and drag him along with it.

All right, there was nothing left to take. He got ready to hop over the railing of the basket, but then …

He was ten feet above the train again. He looked up and that tunnel was coming. The big gaping maw of the entrance would be here in seconds.

"Alex!"

Alex was pulling up. He couldn't let the chopper get hooked on that opening. Troy flipped over the side of the basket and dropped to the train. He landed on his feet and rolled onto his back.

The train was flying. It shuddered as it crossed some rough patch, tossing Troy into the air. He bounced over the top, rolling backwards. His hands frantically grabbed for anything. They caught a horizontal metal pole or thick pipe, and he clutched it as hard as he could.

He was extended out straight behind it, face down. He tried to pull himself up, but the tunnel was RIGHT THERE.

He turned his head. In the corner of his visor, far above him and ahead, he caught a glimpse of the basket. Jettisoned from the helicopter, it smashed into a sheer cliff face. Above that, he saw the chopper, tilted nearly sideways, veering sharply off to the right.

Troy ducked, shutting his eyes as the train roared into the dark tunnel. He lay in the dark, hands gripping the metal. He didn't want to move. He just wanted to stay here for a moment and get his wind back. He wanted to relax and just hold this pole. Adrenaline was exploding through his bloodstream.

He was trembling. He could feel that. It was good.

He was here. He was on top of the train. It was dark. It was freezing cold. The wind was whipping, and sharp pieces of ice and snow and rock showered down from the tunnel ceiling and pelted him. But his clothes and his helmet gave him some protection.

And he was here. Just like he said he would be.

Now, all he needed was to get inside.

CHAPTER THIRTY ONE

"A man is on top of the train."

Sokolov turned from what he was doing and looked at the doorway. Vlad the Impaler stood there, cradling the AR-15 in his thick hands. Vlad didn't look the least bit afraid. The train was barreling along, shrieking and gnashing. It bumped, it jerked, it lurched. At these speeds, it could derail any moment.

Meanwhile, a helicopter had been pursuing them and might still be. And now a man was on the roof, certainly a commando of some kind. Vlad's eyes showed not even a hint of concern. If anything, they were without emotion.

Blank. The boy is blank. How did I not see that before?

"So kill him," Sokolov said.

"He has a machine gun."

Sokolov didn't care. He didn't want to hear it.

"For the love of God, Vlad. Kill him anyway."

Vlad nodded and went out.

At some point, you'll look up, and he'll be killing YOU.

It didn't matter. There was very little time left. If the boy tried to kill Sokolov, he would find out the hard way, as others had, that it wasn't an easy thing to do. Sokolov put Vlad out of his mind and turned back to the problem at hand.

Istvan Gajdos.

Gajdos lay face down on the bed, right where they had left him, his epic bulk like the deadest of all dead weights. He was lying sandwiched between his two whores, who were also face down, bagged, wrists tied, but who were probably fine. They were young and not overweight like Gajdos.

Gajdos didn't seem to be moving, and he hadn't answered when Sokolov called him. Sokolov looked at his chest and stomach. They were rising and falling, taking shallow breaths. At least he was alive.

Sokolov would try to fulfill the obligation that seemed to bring him here—to seize Gajdos and force him to make an anonymous transfer of the cryptocurrency funds he had stolen. But once that was done, then he would complete his true mission, what he now realized was why he was on this train.

He would kill Istvan Gajdos and strike a blow for ordinary people everywhere against the thieves who had stolen the industries and the futures of the former Eastern Bloc. Men like Gajdos hadn't caused the disaster. But they were parasites, like blood ticks, who had swooped in and gorged themselves on the disaster before most others even understood what was happening.

Gajdos was late to the looting game, but he proved as adept at it as any of the Russian oligarchs. Sokolov couldn't kill the Russians—they were too rich, too powerful, too far off, too well-protected. But he could kill this fat lump of meat. Gajdos's entire security apparatus had been annihilated by four men and one woman.

An image of Helena lying dead, with the automatic door trying to close on her, flashed through his mind. He shook that away.

He unzipped the mask from the back of Gajdos's head and pulled it off.

"Gajdos. Are you awake?"

The man grunted.

On either side of him, the two girls stirred. A spasm of rage went through Sokolov. Who was Gajdos to have these two young women at his side while Helena lay dead at the back of the train?

Sokolov took a deep breath and waited a moment until the feeling passed. He didn't want to kill these girls. None of this was their fault. The punishment meted out to Gajdos should have nothing to do with them.

Unless they were very, very lucky, they would die with everyone else aboard this train. But he may as well give them that chance. Working quickly, he cut their zip ties and unzipped their masks.

Within several seconds, they were both rolled over and staring up at him with wide eyes. They were young, but their lifestyles were sapping whatever loveliness they once might have had. Sokolov valued this, even if they didn't. One of the girls was nude. The other was wearing only underwear.

"Get out," he said to them. He gestured toward the door. "Go to the back of the train. Forget about Gajdos. He can't help you. Do you understand?"

They both nodded and said nothing.

"Go! NOW!"

When they were gone, Sokolov turned back to the lump of whale meat in front of him. "Gajdos."

"Yeah," Gajdos said, his face against the bed. "Still here."

"You have one chance to live. One and only one."

"Tell me," Gajdos said.

"A crypto called SafeCoin. You've stolen it. I'm going to make a call, and you are going to receive instructions to transfer all of the stolen coin anonymously to a different account holder. You will do whatever you need to do to make that happen. Once the transaction goes through, the train will stop. If it doesn't go through, or if you refuse to do it, the train will continue speeding up until it crashes. Then you, and all of your friends, who you probably don't care about anyway, will die."

"I don't have the crypto," Gajdos said. "I told the banker ..."

Sokolov punched him in the back of the neck.

"Annhh!"

"I'm sorry," Sokolov said. "I don't think I heard you correctly."

"I said I don't have the crypto."

Sokolov punched him again in the exact same spot. Then he wound up and did it again. There was a lump of flesh at the back of Gajdos's neck, which padded the impact on Sokolov's fist somewhat. But Sokolov's blows were connecting well enough with Gajdos's spine. Sokolov could punch him there comfortably until his neck broke.

Gajdos grunted. The sound wasn't even a word. It was pre-verbal, the sound of a caveman terrified of lightning. He gasped for air.

"Don't say that again," Sokolov said. "Say something else."

"Why would I have it?" Gajdos said.

"I'm going to hit you again," Sokolov said. "I will gladly hit you there until you die. Please understand this. It will be a gruesome finish for you."

Gajdos croaked out his next words. "Everybody thinks I have the crypto. I don't. I don't know anything about it."

"You paid to establish the trading platform. You are an owner."

"Yes, and why would I steal from myself?"

"It wasn't your money," Sokolov said.

"It's my customers," Gajdos said. "Trust is everything in crypto. Once that's gone, so are your customers. I funded that platform so people in Eastern Europe would have their own platform, one they could trust. There's no other reason. I don't care about cryptocurrencies. I make money from the transactions, but it will take me a decade to earn back my investment if even then."

"All the more reason to steal," Sokolov said.

Gingerly, Gajdos shook his head. "Look at the other things I own. Cars. Hotels. TV and radio stations. Trains. I like real things that have real value. Crypto is just a game people play."

Sokolov stared down at Gajdos's wide back. The man was a professional liar. And yet, in this one case, he might be telling the truth.

"All of your men are dead. No one is coming to help you. I can blow your brains out at any moment I choose."

Gajdos nodded. "Yes, and I don't want you to do that. I'm not afraid to die, but I do want to live. A bunch of collapsed crypto coin is nothing to die for. If I had it, I would give it to you without argument. I don't have it. I do have a little bit of crypto, but it isn't the stolen crypto, and it's not nearly as much as was stolen. You can have that, but you probably don't want it."

Sokolov shook his head. "No. It won't be enough."

"There's nothing else," Gajdos said.

Sokolov turned away from Gajdos. As if for the first time, Sokolov noticed the giant windows that made up this room and the wide-open mountain vistas outside. The view was stark, enormous, breathtaking.

They had fought and died today over nothing. Helena was gone. Peter the Great was gone. The silly pop star was dead. The train driver. Gajdos's security detail. What did they all die for? Fake, invented money that someone stole. The man who was supposed to have stolen it claimed he didn't even have it. And Sokolov believed him.

He caught a movement in the corner of his eye.

At the furthest door to the stateroom, Ivan the Terrible was standing. He stared across at Sokolov.

"The train is out of my control," Ivan said. "It's going too fast for conditions. We'll derail in another few moments. If I don't decouple the engine from the rest of the train, we're all going to die."

Sokolov shook his head. "I'll decouple it. I'm not done here yet."

"There isn't much time," Ivan said.

"I understand. Right now, I need you to go to the back and help Vlad. A man, some commando or secret police, is on top of the train, trying to get in. We need to stop him. And there will be more where he came from. Our only hope of escape is if there are no secret policemen on board to watch us leave."

"You have no hope of escape," Gajdos said.

Sokolov glanced down at him. He could kill him right now, Gajdos knew that, and yet he didn't keep his mouth closed. He couldn't help himself.

Sokolov looked back at Ivan. "Go."

"Where is Helena?" Ivan said.

Sokolov shook his head. He gestured at Gajdos. It was better not to speak of these things in front of him.

"Oh no," Ivan said. He sighed heavily.

"What happened?" Gajdos said. "Did your friend die, like my friends died?"

Sokolov's shoulders slumped. Gajdos was becoming confident again. It was a horrible thing to witness. The man was truly a monster.

"You'll decouple the cars?" Ivan said.

"Yes."

"You know the process?"

Sokolov shrugged. "I know it as well as you."

"Okay. I'll go kill the cop."

Ivan the Terrible disappeared out the door as suddenly as he had appeared.

Sokolov turned back to Istvan Gajdos. "Where were we?"

***

Another man went by.

Dubois stood pressed to the wall of the room, in the corner, behind the ruined door. She wasn't completely out of sight, but the man had been moving too fast to notice her. He was a smaller man than the first, head totally bald. He was carrying a pistol in his right hand.

Both men, the big one with the rifle, who had shattered some windows in the hallway right outside this room and who had tried to take down a helicopter, and this man, were headed in the same direction—toward the back of the train.

Something is happening back there.

It was Stark. What else could it be?

The helicopter was still in the sky. Dubois could see it from here, out the broken windows, in the far distance now, too far away to shoot at but still close enough to follow the train.

Someone had been suspended from that helicopter not long ago. If Dubois hadn't seen it with her own eyes, she wouldn't have believed it.

Whoever it was had returned fire with an automatic weapon and sent the big guy sprawling to the floor.

Stark. Who else but Stark would be so crazy?

And where was he now? He wasn't hanging from the helicopter anymore. He had to be somewhere on the train. Somewhere …

On top of the train.

Those men were going to try to shoot him off.

Dubois's heart skipped in her chest. Gallo was out of commission. She had no partner. She had no gun. She had no weapon of any kind.

All she had were her fists and her feet.

She slipped into the hallway and looked toward the front. There was nothing but a closed foyer door that way. No one was in the far hall. No one was coming.

She turned and moved quickly but carefully down the narrow corridor toward the back of the train.

Like a cat. Move like a cat.

***

Troy groped his way to his feet. He needed to work fast.

The train was flying, rocking from side to side. He stayed in a crouch, stumble-stepping forward along the top of the train car, dragging the big equipment bag behind him. Shards of ice were pelting him like tiny daggers. The wind tore at him. The only saving grace was his helmet, with the visor pulled down, protecting his face.

He staggered toward the nearest foyer between cars. It was just a few feet away. He fell to his knees in front of it. He reached down and felt the flexible material with his gloved hands. It was a sort of thick, black rubber, corrugated like an accordion. At each bend, it had some sort of hard spine inside of it, giving it a skeleton, shape, and form.

He would have to cut a slice in the rubber between each spine, and then squeeze through the gap. There was enough space. The train was going so fast, the accordion was elongated.

He looked up.

Everything was dizzying. Everything was moving too fast. His eyes had trouble focusing.

Another dark tunnel was coming. He slid onto his stomach, like a worm, his helmet and hands pressed against the top of the train. His hands reached for anything to grip and found a shallow metal lip at the edge of the train car. He had one arm looped through the strap of the equipment bag.

These gloves were no good. He couldn't feel anything with his hands inside of them.

The train zoomed into the tunnel. The dark descended. It was pitch black inside. The tunnel could have been two hundred meters long. It could have been a mile. He had no way of telling. It went by in what seemed like a few seconds. Suddenly, a round bright light was approaching, far away, and then an instant later, it filled his entire vision. Then he was outside in the daylight again.

He lifted the visor of his helmet. Immediately, the wind and ice tore at his face. He put the finger of his right hand in his mouth and pulled the glove off. Then he spit the glove out. Instantly, it flew away behind him.

The glove was gone, just like that. It made him reluctant to remove the other one. His right hand was cold immediately. He was probably going to get frostbite out here. Maybe he'd keep the left glove on. One cold hand, one warm hand, neither one of which could feel anything. He was going to lose the feeling in his ungloved hand within a couple of minutes.

He pushed himself to his knees again, staying low, swaying with the side-to-side rocking of the train. He was getting the hang of it a little bit.

He reached into the bag and pulled out the saw. It was heavy. The instant he had the saw in his hands, the equipment bag blew away, just as the glove had done.

The saw was a touch button start. It was device meant to be held with two hands, dominant hand in back on a handgrip like a gun stock and non-dominant hand forward, holding a horizontal bar and guiding the thing. He was going to have to lean out over the foyer, knees on the back car, and force the teeth through the heavy rubber.

Is this even possible?

He had no idea. He pressed and held the starter button. He could feel the saw come alive in his hands. The blade had sharp, serrated teeth, moved by a chain. The saw probably made a noise, but he couldn't hear it. It was too loud out here. He was being hit by a wall of sound.

He leaned forward and plunged the blade into the rubber. It dug deep, better than he expected. He yanked it back towards himself, ripping a line in the rubber. He pulled it all the way back, too far, until it hit the metal spine embedded inside the rubber. The saw bucked in his hands, the jolt of the impact went all the way to his shoulders, and he nearly dropped it into the hole he had made.

He grunted and pulled it free. That wasn't bad. He needed to cut sideways at the top and bottom of the gash and then he might have a little doorway he could plunge or force his way through.

He gasped, making exhalations that he couldn't hear.

He reached all the way out, dug the blade into the rubber again, and cut sideways. He managed to move the blade about a meter across, like a capital T at the top of the earlier cut. He was opening a sort of flap door. Now all he had to do was cut another one closest to him. It was going to be a …

Something ripped another hole through the rubber, coming from below, inside the train. It tore a chunk of the flap out.

"What the …?"

Another one ripped through. Bullets. Someone was shooting down there.

Another one. This one hit the saw. A piece of the saw's black casing splintered, breaking apart. The whole thing was knocked out his hands. He dove back, ducking the flying saw. The blade came backwards and narrowly missed hitting him.

Troy sensed, but didn't quite see, the saw bounce away and disappear.

Troy slid sideways on his stomach along the icy roof. He tried to stop the slide, but there was no way to do it. He slid to the right edge of the train car, going … going … trying to hold on. He slid off, his hands grabbing madly for anything.

He screamed as he went over the side.

His right hand found a thin, metal rail along the top edge of the car. His fingers wedged under it, barely gripping. He tried to grip it with his gloved hand, but the fingers were too thick. He brought the fingers to his mouth, pulled that glove off, and spit it out too. It flew away somewhere.

He held on with two hands, his fingers wedged in behind the rail. He was hanging from the side of the car, the wind trying to tear him off.

His feet slid along the outside, looking for purchase.

There was nothing.

He was hanging by his fingers.

He turned to his right, looking forward. The train snaked along the track, jerking and lurching, going terribly fast. It was almost impossible to see. Ice and snow were kicked up from the rail bed, spraying along the side of the train.

He was trapped in a whiteout. He could not feel his hands. In another minute, he was going to fall off of here.

There was no time. He had to pull himself up by his fingers and nothing else. He steeled himself for the effort. One, two, three, and he yanked himself up, bending his elbows and pulling with his hands.

The wind blew, and his legs slipped out sideways. He lost it and fell, his arms extended, still hanging by his fingers.

"OHhhhhh."

He wasn't going to get too many more chances. Try again.

One ... two ... three ...

He pulled with everything he had.

***

Dubois watched the men shooting at the ceiling in the foyer.

She crept up behind them. They hadn't noticed her yet. The larger of the two men, the one with the rifle, had wedged himself in the doorway, crouched in there, holding the door from sliding closed with his right leg. The other man, the smaller man, was inside the foyer, shooting nearly directly upwards with a handgun.

They're shooting at Stark.

Of course they were. This train was a killing field.

She had passed through the disco car. One man was dead there, and an entire group of people were tied up, masked, and lying on the floor. Staff were tied up in the kitchen. A large man was dead in a hallway, lying face down in a shallow lake of blood. A woman and another large man were dead in the foyer she had passed through just a moment ago.

Without another thought, Dubois began to run toward the men. The big man was turned away from her, and he was crouched low, shooting upward at an angle.

BANG! BANG! BANG!

The men were firing continuously, randomly, as if they couldn't see what they were shooting at.

The man was just ahead now, his broad body braced in the doorway, the gun gripped in his two hands, the stock steadied against his chest.

Ten meters ahead, then five meters.

She accelerated toward him.

Three meters. She leapt, her legs extending straight out horizontally in a flying dropkick.

BOOM. Her boots connected with the back of the man's head. The man was heavy. It was a thick head and neck. She felt the impact all the way up through her body.

The man fell forward, crashed into his partner, and sprawled to the ground.

Dubois dropped to the floor but bounced up instantly. The big man still had his gun. Both men did. The big man pressed himself to his feet, turned and …

Dubois kicked him in the chin.

"Ha!" she screamed at him.

His head snapped back, but it wasn't good enough. The head came back to center, and he shook it, as if to clear out the cobwebs. He stared at her, his mouth open a tiny bit. He seemed irritated to see her there.

"Woman, what are you doing?"

She threw a punch, a hard one that cut across his jaw. He barely moved.

Both men were looking at her. "Get out of here before we kill you."

She glanced up where they had been shooting. There was a hole in the roof, like a large T. A pair of legs dangled through the opening above their heads. The legs squirmed from the waist and then …

A man fell through the hole. He landed on the smaller of the two gunmen, crashing down on top of him.

The big man turned to look.

Dubois leapt at him again.

She punched him, left, right, left, his head snapping this way and that. The head came back to center again, but this time the eyes were surprised. They said she had hurt him. She brought a looping fist around and clubbed him in the side of the neck.

He winced, but then grabbed her by the waist, a hand on either side. His hands were strong, immensely so. He lifted her and squeezed her midsection, nearly crushing the breath out of her. Her feet were off the ground.

Desperate now, she scratched at him like a tiger. Her hands ripped into his face. She slashed him with her fingers, her nails not very long, but still good weapons, still like claws. She drew blood across his cheeks. She reached for his eyes.

The man hurled her against the wall.

Her back slammed into it, followed by the back of her head. She fell to the ground, her legs bent under her. That hurt.

She shook her head and tried to stand, but she didn't seem able.

Now, the man came to her. He pulled her up by the hair.

"Bitch, I'll teach you respect."

He slapped her. The impact was incredible. He followed through all the way. Her head rocked around to the side. Now, she came back to center, trying to focus on this guy. She saw his eyes. They hovered above the bloody mask of his face. They were hard eyes, empty of human feeling. He was holding her up by the hair.

WHAP!

He hit her with the back of his hand this time. Her head rolled around the other way. The back of his hand was hard like a rock. He could break the bones of her face like that. She had to do … something.

BAM! BAM! BAM!

The attacker's head rocketed off the wall.

The man who had fallen through the roof was behind him. The man was wearing a helmet. It made him seem like an astronaut or a space alien. He had the big man by both sides of the head and hammered the wall with his face again.

BAM! BAM! BAM!

The big man released Dubois, and she slid to the floor again. He put both his hands against the wall and shoved backwards, crashing into the man who had his head. They both fell to the floor and rolled over backwards.

The big man fought his way to his feet. The astronaut grasped the rifle from the man's shoulder and ripped the strap away. He pulled the gun down. It dropped to the floor and slid toward Dubois.

The big man didn't seem to care. He just wanted to get away. He wrenched open the door to the train car behind them, stumbled in there, and was gone a second later.

The astronaut crawled to the rifle, picked it up, and pointed it toward the other door, the one leading to the front of the train.

Dubois turned that way. The door had just shut. The smaller gunman was gone. He had run toward the front. One went forward, one went backward.

The astronaut kneeled in front of her. The helmet framed Troy Stark's face. His cheeks and nose were red from windburn and cold.

"How you doing, Dubois?"

"Agent Stark," Dubois said. Her voice sounded strange to her own ears. It was as though she was listening to someone talk in their sleep. "Nice of   you   to   drop   in."

CHAPTER THIRTY TWO

9:25 am Eastern European Time (8:25 Central European Time)
Foinikion, Island of Carpathos
The Greek Islands
The Aegean Sea

"He's a liar," Lucien Mebarak said into the telephone. "If his mouth is moving, it means that he's lying."

Lucien was sitting on his patio, looking out at the sea. He wore a light jacket and blue jeans. It was an overcast morning and cool. The water, normally a sparkling blue, was gunmetal gray.

His girls were not in their customary place, lying out next to the pool. It was too chilly for that. They had mentioned taking the car into town and going shopping. That was fine with Lucien. It was better that they weren't here for this conversation.

There was a breakfast of eggs and sausage in front of him, going cold. The only thing he had touched was the coffee. This was the morning. He supposed he was nervous. He had no appetite.

"I know that," Sokolov said. "He insists he doesn't have it and knows nothing about it. He is willing to die insisting this. He only steals physical things, according to him, like hotels and entire railroads."

Lucien stared out across the cliffs. Buzzards were circling in the sky. Something dead or perhaps dying was nearby.

He had spent more than twenty million American dollars on this project. The payments to Sokolov and his team had been made. Sokolov's payment had gone to Royal Heritage Bank in the Cayman Islands. Royal Heritage did not tolerate attempts at clawbacks.

The project had always been risky. Lucien understood that. But this was the first moment that he had considered the possibility of utter failure.

Istvan Gajdos did not have the crypto. Who the hell else could have it in that case?

"Everything points at him."

There was a delay of several seconds as Lucien's voice bounced around the world, into outer space, and back down again.

"I understand," Sokolov said. "He denies it."

The train must be moving very fast by now, practically beyond anyone's control. Sokolov's voice was incredibly calm, given the circumstances. He was the right choice of man for a project like this. He didn't let little things like violent death approaching distract him. If Gajdos didn't have the money, that was hardly Sokolov's fault.

"Have you ... hurt him at all?" Lucien said.

"I have. But I can do more. I was waiting to talk to you. The more treatment I give, the more likely I lose the patient."

Lucien nodded. "Understood. Please proceed."

BANG!

The gunshot was perfectly clear over the phone. Lucien's entire body jerked at the sound and then the sound of Gajdos screaming in response. It was like Lucien had been stuck with an electric cattle prod.

"I shot him in the left kneecap," Sokolov said.

"Very good," Lucien said, keeping his voice flat and calm, just like Sokolov's. "May I speak with him, please?"

"Of course."

Another delay of several seconds passed.

"Who is this?" a husky voice said. Lucien mused that there was a great deal of pain in that voice.

"Istvan Gajdos?"

"Yes. Who is this?"

"This is your worst nightmare. I want the SafeCoin that you stole. It doesn't belong to you. As such, it may as well belong to me."

The voice was breaking now. Lucien had studied Istvan a great deal. It was definitely him, but the arrogance he normally displayed was on the verge of shattering.

"I don't have it. I told this Soviet pig ..."

BANG!

The call was interrupted by Gajdos screaming in agony. Lucien's body jerked again. This call was full of surprises. A moment later, Sokolov was back.

"I shot him in the right kneecap. If he lives, he will never walk normally again. Considering how fat he is, he may never walk at all and just elect to spend his days in a wheelchair."

In the background, Gajdos was screaming and shouting. There were words, but Lucien couldn't make them out.

"Will he live, do you think?" Lucien said.

"No."

"He's been shot twice. Is he still claiming he doesn't have the crypto?"

Another moment passed.

"Gajdos," Sokolov said. "Where is the crypto you stole?"

Another outburst came from Gajdos. The big baby was screaming, shouting, and possibly crying.

Lucien did not like Gajdos. The man was insufferable when he had the power of his friend the great dictator behind him. Now, he was insufferable when alone and powerless. Lucien supposed he would have paid extra to witness the last moments of this bloated failure. But he did not think these phones supported video calls.

"He says he doesn't have it."

"All right," Lucien said.

"The train is out of control," Sokolov said.

Lucien nodded. "Yes. As we discussed, there is nothing I can do to stop it. To survive, you must decouple the passenger cars from the engine. You know how?"

"I studied it."

"Good luck, Mr. Sokolov," Lucien said. "I wish you Godspeed."

Twenty million dollars. It was a disaster.

Lucien took a long, deep breath to steady himself. Sokolov. It was good to pay such people. Perhaps the man would survive, and this incident would create goodwill between them. Also, the last thing you wanted was an angry Sokolov to turn up unexpectedly. Istvan Gajdos was discovering that right now.

It occurred to Lucien, but only briefly, to ask Sokolov if Troy Stark had come aboard. But he didn't know how to approach such a question. Sokolov would smell betrayal from a mile away. In any case, the conversation was over.

"Thank you, Mr. de Klerk. And goodbye."

The phone went dead. Lucien placed it on the table at his elbow. He picked up his coffee mug and took a sip. The coffee had gone as cold as the food.

CHAPTER THIRTY THREE

"Come and see. Watch your worthless life end."

Sokolov had dragged Gajdos here to the cockpit, forcing him to walk on his ruined legs. Gajdos shrieked with every step. He had barely managed to remain upright. Sokolov gripped him under the arms at the last moment and pulled him across the threshold, Gajdos's legs dragging out behind him. Sokolov's gun was in his right hand, pressed against Gajdos's chest.

Gajdos was so far gone that he made no attempt to set the gun. Then his bulk got caught in the destroyed cockpit door, which was still hanging askew.

"You pig," Sokolov said. "You weigh a thousand kilos."

Gajdos screamed, a sound of agony so pure that there was no meaning inside of it. It was primal, a return to the caves.

Then Sokolov plopped him down in the driver's seat. He stopped to take a long breath, then spun Gajdos around to face out the windscreen.

"Do you see it? Do you see death coming for you?"

Ahead, the tracks were roaring along. The train was moving so fast that it was hard to see. Everything out there was a blur of white, so much snow and ice was being kicked up. The train was lurching and rocking nonstop. It was a miracle they were still on the tracks. It wouldn't be long now.

Gajdos was crying. "You killed the driver. I saw him on the floor in the corner."

Sokolov said nothing to that.

Gajdos's entire body shook. "I liked that man."

Sokolov pointed the gun at Gajdos's head.

"Kill me," Gajdos said. "You're going to do it anyway."

"I'll let events kill you. I'll let history kill you. You and everyone like you."

Sokolov pressed the muzzle of the gun into Gajdos's big soft shoulder.

BANG!

The suppressor was worthless now. The sound of the shot was nearly deafening in the close confines of the cockpit. The shot took out a chunk of Gajdos's shoulder. The force of it spun the man just enough that he slid off the chair and onto the floor.

Gajdos was screaming and crying. His entire body was shaking. Sokolov's ears were ringing from the gunshot. That served to lower the volume somewhat on Gajdos's sniveling.

"Can you please die like a man?" Sokolov said.

He had wanted to force Gajdos to watch the train finally derail. They could watch it together. But it would be impossible to lift him again.

The train lurched, a bad one, and Sokolov steadied himself on the control counter. He regarded Gajdos, who was now wedged under the seat, lying sideways, blood spreading on the floor behind his shoulder. There were dark red stains, so dark they were nearly black, on the man's pant legs, both right above the knee.

"The cruelty," Gajdos said. "The cruelty!"

He turned his head to look up at Sokolov.

"I did nothing to deserve this."

Sokolov was calm. He shrugged. "You were a common thief, and you had a powerful friend. So, you stole everything you could get your hands on."

It really was that simple. To Sokolov, it explained the whole disaster of post-Soviet times. Common thieves with powerful friends. There was no time to think it through now, but to a large degree, it probably explained the entire history of the human race.

"I was a businessman!" Gajdos shouted.

Sokolov shot him again. He barely heard the sound of it this time. He was basically deaf from all the noise. He felt the kick of the gun in his hand. He saw the muzzle flash. He saw the bullet tear into Gajdos's upper body, not far below his heart.

Gajdos winced in pain. He was so big, there was so much flesh, that he still wasn't dead. That last shot, though. That one was going to kill him, if not right now, then five minutes from now.

"Tell me something," Sokolov said. He almost couldn't hear his own voice. "Did you steal the cryptocurrency?"

Gajdos stared up at him, gasping for breath.

"Tell me and I'll kill you quickly. No more pain."

Gajdos nodded. Sokolov watched his mouth move. "Yes."

Sokolov shook his head and smiled. The man chose death over surrendering fake money that he stole. It wouldn't have mattered because he was going to die anyway, but that's what he chose. Money was more important to him than life itself.

"I knew it," Sokolov said.

He slid into the driver's seat. He ejected the magazine from the gun, reached into his pocket, and slipped another one in. He glanced at the magazine that had fallen to the floor. It was empty. He had always had a sixth sense about these things. It was part of what had kept him alive so long.

He gazed out through the windscreen at all the white in front of him. The speed and the blowing snow and ice were a form of violence in itself.

Oh well. It was all over. There was nothing to do but die.

***

"That big guy is dangerous," Troy said.

He crouched near where Dubois sat on the floor, getting his wind back. He extended and clenched his fingers, extended and clenched them, again and again, getting some feeling. He was still wearing his helmet. He liked it. It was his only hope of talking to Alex again. And it afforded some protection against flying fists and flying projectiles.

"He's strong. He blew right past me."

All around them, the train was rattling as though it was about to come apart.

"He nearly put me through the wall," Dubois said.

Troy nodded. "I know. Not good. How's your head? You with me?"

She nodded, too, but slowly. "I'm all right."

Troy held up two fingers in front of her face. "How many fingers?"

She smiled. "Six."

"Close enough."

He picked up the rifle where it lay on the floor, pulled the magazine, and checked it. There were about half a dozen rounds still in there. He slid the magazine back in and slammed it home. He handed the rifle to her.

215

"Take this gun. There're some bullets in there. You don't have to do anything except watch that door behind me. If the big guy tries to come back this way, don't even hesitate, okay? Just shoot him. He would have been happy to kill us both."

"Where are you going?" Dubois said.

Troy shook his head. "Don't change the subject, please. Okay? I can't have that guy coming up behind me. You're going to shoot him, right?"

Her voice was flat. "Yes, Agent Stark. I'm going to shoot the man."

He smiled. "That's my girl. I need to go to the front of the train and see if we can stop it somehow. It's going way too fast."

"There are dead bodies aboard. And many people tied up."

He nodded. "I figured. Where's Gallo?"

She shook her head. "In one of the rooms. They beat him in the head with a gun. Last I saw, he was passed out on a bed. I couldn't get him moving."

Troy winced. "Okay. Who's in control?"

"I don't know," Dubois said. "I think the bodyguards and the hijackers killed each other. I'm not certain who is who."

Troy shrugged. It didn't really matter. He would find whoever was in charge at the moment and compel them to do what he asked. That was the whole plan. He looked through the doorway, up the next hallway. The train was writhing like a deranged snake. It was going to be quite a walk up through the middle of it.

But better than walking on top.

"I have to go," he said. "Watch that door. Shoot that guy if you see him."

Dubois nodded. She still hadn't made any attempt to stand. That was fine. She could shoot from the floor.

Troy stood up and moved through the next car. It was some sort of utility car, with a hallway and doorways to his left. He moved quickly, bouncing off the walls and doors as he went. He took out the Glock from his shoulder holster, checked it, and kept moving.

The helmet created a sort of tunnel vision. That was the only downside he could see to wearing it. In fact, he might start wearing a helmet all the time.

Hey. Life was hard.

To his left, a door was open a crack. The door burst open. A man was there, the small, bald-headed man from before. The man Troy had landed on. One of the men who had been shooting at him up through the ceiling.

The man's gun pointed straight out into the hallway, right at Troy's head. Troy's left hand shot out, grabbed the shooter's arm by the wrist, and pushed the gun up and away.

BANG!

The shot clipped the edge of Troy's helmet. He felt it skim off.

That was close!

BANG! BANG! BANG!

The man kept shooting, but his gun hand was pointing straight upward. Troy brought his own gun around. The man grabbed Troy's wrist, pushing the gun away.

They were dancing now, each one holding the other's wrist.

Troy was bigger and stronger. He bulled the man backwards. It was a small space, with drawers and cabinet doors on either side, an equipment closet. Troy pushed the man up against the rear wall. He used his weight to pin the guy there. He banged the man's gun hand against the wall, once, twice …

The man brought a knee up into Troy's groin.

Troy grunted and gritted his teeth. They were eye to eye in here, body to body. They gasped for breath in each other's ears. The man tried to knee him again, but Troy twisted to his right. All the knee got was Troy's thigh. The guy lined it up and tried again. Too late. He was just kneeing Troy in the leg now. It hurt but not enough.

Troy slammed that gun hand against the wall. Again. Again.

The man dropped the gun.

Troy headbutted him, the helmet crashing into the man's forehead. No good. Troy aimed lower, crouched, and …

BAM!

The crown of the helmet connected with the guy's face.

He reared his head back and did it again.

CRUNCH. There was a lot of breakable stuff in the face. Troy pulled back, and already the guy's face was a bloody mess. His eyes were still hard though and alert. The guy was not afraid. The eyes said he had played this game before, the fight to the death game.

The man let go of Troy's wrist and went to his own jacket instead. An instant later, it came out with a knife. It was a sliding lock blade, and he knew just how to use it. One second, it was a four-inch handle, then the next second, there was a gleaming knife.

Troy leapt backwards, back into the narrow hallway.

The man was on him, a split second behind, the knife out. He lunged forward with the blade, right to Troy's belly.

Troy danced to his right and brought his gun hand around.

The knife missed. The man slashed it sideways. It grazed across the front of Troy's jumpsuit, making a slice. But the fabric was thick. Was it thick enough? Troy couldn't feel a thing there. There was too much adrenaline to feel anything.

He pointed the gun.

The man turned to him, knife ready.

BANG!

Troy pulled the trigger.

The man's head snapped back, hitting the wall behind him. His eyes were blank now, a hole in the middle of his forehead. He slid down the wall, leaving a dark red starburst on the wall behind him. A trail of blood followed him to the floor.

Troy's heart was racing, the blood beating in his ears.

Boom, boom, boom, boom ...

The train was rattling and shaking all around him. He looked down at his stomach. He couldn't see if he was bleeding or not. He felt inside the slash the man had made. He couldn't feel anything, no pain, nothing at all. He pulled his hand out. The fingers were clear. There was no blood.

Okay. Okay. There was no time. He wasn't hurt. That meant he had to keep moving.

He started forward, going faster now. He passed through a foyer, a dead guy and a dead woman piled in there. He stepped over another dead guy face down in a hallway. Gunshot wounds, plenty of blood.

He barely looked at any of them. He kept his own gun out in front of him now, his free hand steadying him on the walls.

He passed through a lounge of sorts. There was a giant fish tank, the water sloshing over the top, underneath the cover, and racing down the sides and all over the floor. A man in a suit was on the floor, sprawled out on his stomach, getting soaked by all the water. Troy couldn't tell if he was dead or alive.

People were lying in easy chairs and on couches. Asleep? Dead? Impossible to say.

Troy passed them, keeping the gun on them, keeping the gun pointing everywhere. A dining car, people tied up and masked.

Bagged and tagged. They've been bagged and tagged.

Alive though. They were moving, they were groaning, a few were making sounds of terror. They would have to wait. He passed through a bar car, bottles and glasses falling and shattering. There was no one in here.

He passed through a car with a dance floor. A man, all in black, was dead. Several others were also bagged and tagged. What the heck went on in here?

Another hallway, moving fast now, practically running. How long was this train?

He was passing by the bedrooms now, all the doors caved in. People were bagged and tagged on the beds. There was no time to look for Gallo.

He came to another bedroom car. A man was dead in the foyer between cars. Troy pulled the door open. It was a long car. Two men were dead in the hall, piled on top of each other. A lot of people died fighting over this train.

He moved through the car, gun out. There was no sound but the rapid thump and rattle of the train on the tracks. He stepped over the bodies, one big dead guy seemingly using the other's body as a pillow.

Troy breathed. Up ahead, through the window between cars, he could see the door to the cockpit, hanging off its frame. It was a heavy door, with thick, metal hinges. It looked like it had been blown off or ripped off by the hands of a giant. Someone was behind there, but he couldn't see who they were or what they were doing.

To his left, there was another caved in bedroom door. He glanced inside, looking for a shooter. He found none. The bedroom was huge. A long, floor to ceiling window extended the length of it. It looked like a blizzard out there. There was a trail of blood on the floor. It came out here to the hall and through that last door.

This was it.

He yanked open the door. It made that sound of metal sliding along a metal track.

Inside the cockpit, someone turned around. A hand snaked out from behind the broken cockpit door. It had a gun.

Troy went left. There was a body on the floor.

BANG! BANG! BANG!

Someone in there was shooting. Troy got against the wall. The ruined cockpit door was right next to him.

BANG! BANG!

The hand was shooting out into the foyer. Bullets ricocheted, but they were never gonna kill Troy like that. Only sheer luck would do it. The hand reached all the way out now, a disembodied hand, and it turned the corner, because it knew where Troy was hiding.

Troy kicked that hand as hard he could. The gun flew up and away.

Troy stepped to the door, peered through, found the target and:

BANG! BANG! BANG!

The gun bucked in his hand.

Mag dump. Might as well. He kept firing.

Kill that son of a ...

BANG! BANG! BANG!

He stopped. He was in a deep squat, both hands on the gun, pointing it past the hanging door.

Troy's mouth hung open. His breathing was loud. His chest rose and fell.

On the other side, the guy was down. Troy could just see him.

Careful now. Careful.

He went to the door and looked inside. The guy he had shot lay on his back, facing the doorway. But there was another man in here, a tall, heavy man, also on the floor. These two were practically entwined.

Troy pushed the door aside and stepped through. He recognized the heavy man from the news reports. It was Istvan Gajdos, the oligarch and train hobbyist. He was a bloody wreck. His face was white. A red stain spread across the front of his shirt. It was hard to say if he was alive or dead. He was another one who would have to wait.

Through the windshield, the train was really moving. The speed was incredible. They were rounding a shallow bend, the train jerking to stay on the tracks. Ice and snow and rocks and who knew what else was flying everywhere.

Troy looked at the other man on the floor. He gazed up at Troy, his breath coming in loud rasps. He was hit in the chest and stomach. There was blood all over him. The man was a goner. A couple more minutes, that was all.

"Are you the hijacker?"

The man nodded. He gestured with his chin at Troy.

"Police?" he said.

"Interpol."

The man blinked slowly. For a second, Troy didn't think he would open his eyes again. Troy kicked him in the foot.

"Hey! Don't die yet. How do I stop the train?"

The man smiled. A small sound escaped him, like a wheeze, but it might have been the last bit of laughter he could manage.

"You don't. We all die here. Even the policeman."

"Speak for yourself, buddy."

Troy went to the controls. He was practically standing on the hijacker now. If the guy had a knife, he could stab Troy in the legs, but it didn't seem like it was going that way. Troy looked at the various buttons, dials, readouts, and levers. None of it made any sense to him. He couldn't even find the speed. Some needle was well into the red.

Tiny cracks had appeared in the windshield. Had they been there a minute ago? He wasn't sure. But the last thing he needed was that windshield to cave in.

He looked down at the hijacker. The guy was going.

Troy put the gun on the counter and grabbed the guy up by the shirt. "I said don't die, you punk. How do I stop this train?"

There were dead people on board, yes, but there were still a lot of living people.

The man's eyes barely opened this time, before fluttering down again.

Troy shook him. "Come on!"

"I don't think you can stop it now," a voice said from behind him. Troy dropped the hijacker and turned around. It was Istvan Gajdos. He was still lying on his side. He hadn't opened his eyes. But he was alive.

"This is your train," Troy said.

"Hmmm," Gajdos said.

"How do I make it stop?"

"They did something to it. You have to decouple the train from the engine. That's the only way. The engine and its companion car will keep going. The rest will be disconnected. It will slow down and stop sometime."

"How do I decouple it?"

Gajdos's right eye opened. He saw Troy there. His body began to shake. Tears streamed out of the eye.

"I'm dying, aren't I?"

Troy shrugged. "I don't know, man. You're a mess." Then he just nodded. "Yeah. I think so. You've been gutshot, by the looks of it. Sepsis will probably kill you if internal bleeding doesn't do it first. I'm surprised you're even alive. And we're a long way from the hospital. Listen, how do I decouple the cars, okay?"

Gajdos nodded. "Behind you on the counter is a black box. If it is unlocked, open it. If it's locked, break it open."

Troy turned and looked. There was the box, welded or mounted to the control counter. Troy pulled on the lid, and it came open easily. It was unlocked. There was a key in a sort of ignition, turned to the far left. There was a shift lever below it.

"Okay," Troy said. "Got it."

There was no answer. He turned back to the oligarch. The man's body was slumped. His eyes were closed. But his chest was still heaving.

"Gajdos!"

Gajdos's left eye popped open. It roved for a second and saw Troy there. It all seemed to come back to him then.

"Turn the key to the right," Gajdos said. "All the way, until it clicks. Then pull the lever down. All the way. You might have to force it. The cars will decouple from the engine in several seconds. It's an automatic process. The companion car will stay with the engine. But it's not supposed to be done while in motion."

Gajdos was crying again, full body sobs now.

"I loved this train."

"You filthy swine," a voice said, right at Troy's feet. "Why don't you weep to your mother? Why don't you hide under her skirts?"

Troy looked down. The hijacker was awake again. Who cared what that guy thought?

Troy turned the key in the slot, all the way to the right. It clicked three times. That was as far as it would go. He grabbed the lever and stopped. He took a deep breath. He just had to do it. Maybe it would work, maybe it …

He pulled it down hard, all the way.

Behind him, something happened. The train seemed to bounce several times in a row. It was shuddering.

They were flying, and the cars were decoupling. He looked at the next car, but nothing seemed to be happening.

The companion car will stay with the engine.

"Oh … my … God."

It was going to decouple down at the far end of that bedroom car behind him. The companion car was that long bedroom. Gajdos's bedroom, the VIP suite, it stayed with the engine.

Troy reached down to Gajdos, fully seeing the miscalculation now. He was going to have to drag this big oaf down that long hallway.

Gajdos was dying, and there was probably nothing anybody could do about that. But miracles sometimes happened. Troy couldn't just leave him here while there was still a chance.

He got Gajdos under the arms and pulled.

Gajdos screamed, a piercing, high-pitched wail. He was heavy. Beyond heavy. He started coughing, and suddenly he was coughing up blood. It was dark red, almost black, a stream of it. Something deep inside was ripped or broken.

His eyes were wide in fear. They met Troy's eyes.

But then the fear faded, and the eyes became dull. He had stopped coughing. He opened his mouth and breathed. Dark blood trickled out of either side. He looked like a vampire who had just bit into someone's neck.

This guy was finished.

Troy glanced at the hijacker. His eyes were closed again.

"That's it for me, boys."

He shoved his way past the hanging door. He crossed the foyer and pulled the door to the next car back. At the far end of the hall, something was happening. The car was bouncing violently. That was the way out.

Troy started down the hall. The train car bucked and bounced. He lost his balance, fell, fought his way to his feet, and began running again. The door seemed like it was a mile away. He sprinted towards it. Then he was there. He ripped it open.

The next foyer was being torn apart. The train was decoupling, but there was more to it than just unhooking the car. The rubber accordion, its metal spine, was coming apart. Troy looked at his feet. The two cars were already five feet apart.

Above his head, a piece of metal snapped. It dropped through the gap between cars, hit the tracks and was crushed beneath the train.

The accordion was shredding. The sound was terrible. More metal bars snapped. The cars were pulling apart. The gap was bigger now. In a second, it was going to be too far to jump. The entire canopy was coming down. There was no time to breathe. There was no time to decide.

He dove across the gap, as the whole thing came down on top of him.

CHAPTER THIRTY FOUR

8:37 am Central European Time
The skies above the Austrian Alps
Austria

Alex watched from above as the front two train cars zipped around a sharp bend in the tracks, tilting, tilting … and managing to hang on and keep going.

"That thing has to fall," he said.

Now that most of the train had been decoupled, much of the weight had been left behind. The engine car and the first, long passenger car had been freed from restraint, and it showed. The two cars sped up drastically.

Alex was having trouble keeping pace with them. They hugged a mountain as the tracks ascended and curved around to the south. Alex passed the mountain to the north and entered a valley between two mountains.

Crosswinds in the gap pushed him further north. He re-oriented the chopper to the south and saw the front cars of the train take a sharp turn to the left. There was a chasm there, an abyss between the two hills. Across a long bridge was another tunnel through the next mountain.

The train cars followed the sharp left for a moment and then didn't. At the start of the bridge, the engine car derailed and pitched forward into the gap. It dragged the second car right along behind it.

They fell nose forward, diving what must be two hundred feet.

Alex fought the winds and entered the valley. The chopper was getting knocked around, turning sideways.

The engine car hit the base of the bridge, far below. The car exploded in red and yellow. The second car dove into the explosion and seemed almost instantly consumed by it. A second explosion, more powerful than the first, blew outward.

The train cars shattered into a million pieces of glass and metal. The explosions took out the lower supports of the bridge, and half the bridge came down, collapsing into the raging fire. Black smoke poured out from the flames, obscuring the snow-white lands behind it.

Anyone left inside those cars was dead.

Alex turned the helicopter and went with the wind. He turned to the east and followed the tracks back around the mountainside. The rest of the train was here, the passenger cars and the rear-facing engine car, slowing to a crawl.

The train began the ascent up the side of the mountain, but lost momentum. Like a pendulum reaching the top of its arc, the train was coming to a gradual stop. Soon it would pause at the end of its forward progress, and then begin to roll back down the hill.

In the distance, several specks appeared in the sky. Alex looked around. They were coming from every direction. Below him, there was a narrow ribbon of road that intersected the train line a few miles back. A line of vehicles was moving along that road, like a line of ants, red and blue lights spinning. It was time to leave.

Alex brought the helicopter in low, just a few stories above the train and maybe a hundred meters out from it. He watched it carefully in case any more gunmen appeared in the windows. He reached out and toggled the radio transmitter.

"Stark?" he said. "Stark?"

CHAPTER THIRTY FIVE

"Stark?" said the voice inside his helmet.

Troy lay on the lip of the first remaining train car.

His arm stretched upward from his body, his hand gripping the handle of the closed door. He was in a tangle of collapsed materials. His right leg seemed to be dangling down, pushed by the weight of the black rubber awning or whatever it was that used to form the foyer between cars.

It was dark under here. The smell of the stuff—ripped, shredded, and releasing toxic plastic dust into the air—was awful. He pushed some of the material aside. It fell off and got sucked under the train's wheels.

Bright light flooded his eyes, the sun reflected on the snow and ice. They were rolling along a slight incline, curving to the left around a steep hillside. The front of the train was just completely gone. It had raced out ahead. Troy had heard the explosions, but he couldn't see any evidence of what had happened.

"Stark?" It was Alex.

Troy sighed. "Yeah," he said. "What?"

The helmet speaker crackled. "You alive?"

"I don't know, man. Ask me later."

"I'm afraid I can't do that," Alex said. "I have to boogie. The cops are converging on this place, by air and by road. I need to lose this chopper."

"All right," Troy said. "Good luck."

"See you around."

"Not if I see you first."

Alex laughed. "Don't worry. You won't."

Troy raised a hand in goodbye in case Alex might see it. He heard the sound of a helicopter up there somewhere, but it seemed to be far away already.

It was cold out here. The train was going very slowly. It was a big, heavy thing, a train, and it could take a while to lose the last of its momentum. Maybe he should head inside, see how Gallo and Dubois were doing, untie the prisoners, and start to make some assessment of the scope of this disaster.

He dragged himself to his feet, shoving more of the ruined canopy out of his way and off the train. He yanked hard on the door, and just like that, it slid right open.

***

The train rolled slowly to a stop.

Dubois had no idea how or why. She didn't know if Stark had his mobile phone with him anymore. She wasn't even sure if she had her phone with her.

She was dizzy but on her feet. She watched through the door to the next train car, still doing the job that Stark had assigned her. If the big man came back, she was to stop him from moving to the front of the train. If that meant shooting him, so be it.

With her head the way it was, she might even say she was clinging to the assignment—anything to keep her eyes open and her thinking sharp.

The big man appeared in the window. He was standing on the other side of the door. She held the gun pointed through the window at him. He just smiled and waved. His face was red with drying blood and scratches.

As she watched, he went to the door to the outside. He pressed the large, silver button, and the door slid open. He went down the stairs, then jumped the last meter or so to the ground outside the train.

Dubois slid open the door to the car and went in there. She stepped to the open door to the outside. The day was cold and bright. An icy wind was blowing.

The man was simply walking away, trudging off across the snow. In the far distance was a line of white mountains. Closer, there was a village or small town nestled in a bowl, below the tracks and surrounded by hills on three sides.

The man was headed in that direction.

"Hey!" Dubois called. "Hey. Come back. You're wanted for questioning."

The man raised a hand and half-turned back to her. "I did nothing. I'm responsible for nothing. You can talk to my lawyer. By the way, you're a good fighter. I enjoyed tangling with you. Maybe we can go again, another time."

"What's your name?" Dubois yelled.

The man smiled. "They call me Vlad the Impaler."

He turned away again and kept going.

Dubois stared at him. The man had been shooting at Stark when she first came upon him. He would have beaten her half to death if he could. This gun she was holding originally belonged to this man. He was the one who was first holding it.

Now, he was getting away.

She didn't trust herself to chase him. She was unsteady on her legs. Her head was spinning. Also, even if she did catch him, she wouldn't be able to fight him again, not now, not in this condition.

A helicopter had been flying right nearby, but now it seemed to be gone. She had no idea who was in that thing anyway. It might not be law enforcement. It might just be the news or someone curious.

It's how Stark got here.

Right. She wasn't thinking straight. Stark must have come here in a helicopter. It was the one they were shooting at. It had disappeared.

The big man was going to disappear in another moment, just like the helicopter. He was clomping up a low hill. She would think the guy couldn't get far, that someone was going to come here and pick him up, but she couldn't know that for a fact.

She raised the gun to her eye and aimed down the barrel. She placed the stock against the crook in her shoulder.

"Hey! Don't make me shoot you."

The man raised a hand again.

"You won't shoot," he called back. He didn't even bother to turn around.

BANG!

The gun bucked in her hands. The shot echoed across the vast white lands, bouncing off distant hillsides, then doubling back to her.

The man fell to the ground, holding his left leg.

He screamed in pain.

Her father would shake his head if he saw her now. Everything he had taught her about shooting, everything she had learned in her law enforcement career, was that you aim for the center mass.

She had aimed for, and shot the man, in the calf.

"Nice shooting, Agent Dubois," a voice said behind her.

She turned and Stark was there. He must have walked back through the train. He had removed the helmet. His face was dark red from windburn.

He gestured with his chin at the man lying out in the snow.

"Did Miquel say you could do that?"

"Do what?" Dubois said.

"Just shoot a guy."

"No. You did. I haven't spoken to Miquel about it yet."

Stark stared out the door as the man attempted to crawl away across the snow. Dubois watched him too. He really wasn't going to get very far like that. Two or three new helicopters, like dark insects, had appeared in the distant sky, headed this way.

"Well, it's better to ask for forgiveness than permission," Stark said. "That's always been my philosophy."

"Did you look in on Agent Gallo?" Dubois said.

Stark nodded. "I saw him. He's still unconscious. His breathing and his heart rate are okay. He's got a sizeable welt coming up on the back of his head, but I think he's going to be fine. He's probably got a pretty bad concussion."

There was a pause between them.

"Let's face it, Agent Dubois. Gallo's a nice guy, but he's too old for this game. This is the second time in a row he's been out of the action at crunch time."

Stark smiled. He pointed at her and then he pointed at himself.

"Like it or not, you and I are the real partners here."

CHAPTER THIRTY SIX

"You are Katerina Danielova, yes?"

She eyed the short black man who had brought them into this back office. He was very dark, with a bald head and wire rimmed glasses. He was impeccably presented in a striped dress shirt, dark pants, and bow tie. His shirt sleeves were given one-quarter turn up the forearms. He had introduced himself as Mr. Johnson, the bank manager.

His office was sparsely furnished and airy, with high ceilings and an overhead fan spinning slowly. There were large windows looking out over the busy street below.

The bank would be easy to miss if a person didn't already know where to look. It was on the second floor of a small, very tidy, very well-kept, white building in the middle of George Town. The other buildings in this neighborhood were brightly painted in yellows and oranges and blues, a riot of colors, all competing to attract the eye.

The only hint that the Royal Heritage Bank was here was a black sign with silver etching on the wall downstairs and an arrow pointing up the stairs. Once inside, there was nothing bank-like about it. There were no tellers. There were no ATM machines. There was no line of people. There was merely a woman sitting at a reception desk, who told you that Mr. Johnson would be just a moment.

"I go by Katherine Daniels now," she said.

She had lived in the United States for twenty-one years. It had been an uphill struggle the entire way. She had tried very hard to erase the past, often without much luck. She had taken speech classes to change her accent from Russian to generic American Midwestern, and that had worked to some degree.

But as soon as it turned out that Sokolov had hijacked a train and killed several people as his final terrible act on this Earth, she had been dragged backwards. Reporters had turned up on her doorstep, interested to know more about him, and about her.

Where did she meet him?

How did she come to be in the United States?

Was she here legally?

Did she remember the pop star Calment? What did she think of his music?

When were she and Sokolov married?

When were they divorced?

When did she last speak with him?

Was there any indication he would do this?

"I haven't seen, or spoken to him, in eight years," she would tell them, though of course that wasn't true. "I had no idea what he was doing. And I'm an American citizen, just like you."

Mr. Johnson nodded and smiled. "Of course. In my line of work, you can imagine that people change names all the time. Names, places, nationalities, hair colors—it's immaterial to me. I care only about my customers and their well-being. And you are the person Mr. Sokolov thought of as Katerina."

He said it as a statement of fact, not a question. She figured he well knew the answer.

"Yes. I am."

"Welcome to Grand Cayman, Katerina. I think you'll be very pleased you came."

He had brought them tea, or coffee—whichever they preferred—when they had come in. The drinks came in small, white teacups, with orange, red, and yellow flowers painted on the sides. They were very pretty, very ornate. Katherine was drinking plain green tea, as was Mr. Johnson. Yuri was drinking black coffee.

Yuri was everything Mr. Johnson was not. He was large, thick, and wearing a suit that was too heavy and hot for the day. He had big, stone hands and a face as impassive as if it had been carved into a mountain. He looked uncomfortable.

When Mr. Johnson brought the coffee, he had held up a tiny bottle of vodka to Yuri. Yuri nodded. "Da," he said.

Mr. Johnson poured the entire contents of the bottle into the cup, and Yuri stirred it with a tiny spoon. Everything here was perfectly hospitable.

"And your son?" Mr. Johnson said. "Issur Sokolov, I believe?"

"We call him Kirk now," Katherine said. "Kirk Daniels."

"He is eleven years old?"

She nodded. "Yes."

Kirk was staying at her mother's flat in Brighton Beach. It was the holidays coming, so this situation did not really affect his schooling. She just took him out a day early. There were moments when she looked at Kirk, and her heart just broke. He resembled his father exactly. He was going to be just as handsome. She stayed up nights, praying that he would be different from Sokolov in every other way.

Two nights ago, Yuri had turned up at her door. It was right after news of the hijacking had come out. Yuri was a relic from the bad, old days and seeing him there did not give her a good feeling. He told her that Sokolov had left a gift for her, but they would have to travel out of the country to claim it. He wanted nothing in return for this information or for accompanying her. He had made a promise to Sokolov that he would see the thing through.

Mr. Johnson handed Katherine a single piece of paper.

"The account is numbered for your protection. We verify your identity through DNA testing. It is very simple, and if you need to make a withdrawal, the process can be completed in one business day."

"You have my DNA on file?" Katherine said.

Mr. Johnson smiled again. "Mr. Sokolov took care of everything on your behalf. Yes, we do. He provided DNA for both you and your son."

Katherine looked down at the page, and her heart nearly stopped beating. There was very little information provided. A Royal Heritage Bank logo at the top left, with the address here and a telephone number. There was a long account number, and then, several spaces down, and in the middle of the page, the balance.

The number was $9,999,250.00.

"The transfer came in some days ago. The full amount was ten million American dollars, but there was a nominal administrative fee. You understand."

She stared at the number. For a long moment, no thoughts came at all. Then a series of black and white images appeared, memories of Sokolov from when she was younger. He was dashing, she supposed, and dangerous. Older than her, a man full of mystery and adventure. She had wasted her youth, and her beauty, on him. These were wasting assets, but she didn't understand that until it was too late.

And she was always shocked by the things he did. Often enough, she refused to even believe it. He was always so tender with her. In a fantasy, he was her white knight. But it never played out that way, not in real life, not until this minute.

Mr. Johnson was saying things now, but she could hardly follow them.

"There are many options and opportunities you can pursue with us. If you desire to lock in a three percent interest rate, for example, it will mean a commitment to hold the money here for one year. Three percent of the amount you have is nearly $300,000. You may know that because of our advantageous location, it is entirely tax-free income. The American government does not know the money is here, nor will they. You could earn that amount year after year, without ever touching the principal."

She raised her eyes and stared at Mr. Johnson. He was looking right at her. He had no paperwork in his hands. He knew it all by heart.

"If you prefer not to make that commitment, you are free to remove the money at any time. There are numerous ways to repatriate it into the United States. You can carry it yourself in cash, or we can recommend a courier. It's a lot of money. It can also be transferred digitally from here to an entity of your choice, though we caution you to be very careful. Digital money flows are more traceable than you might guess. If you wanted to declare a bit of income, that would make it simpler. Suppose you did want to access that three percent interest rate for some portion of the …"

Yuri raised a meaty hand. He clicked his teeth at Mr. Johnson.

"Tut-tut-tut-tut-tuh."

Mr. Johnson stopped talking instantly.

Then he started right up again, only on a different path.

"I understand," he said. "It's quite a lot to process all at once. Please know that we treat our clients as we treat our own family. You are safe and in good hands with us. If you have any questions at all, I will always be happy to answer them."

Katherine was still looking at Mr. Johnson. He seemed quite a benign person. She found that she didn't doubt a word he said.

She felt a single tear slide down her cheek.

"Congratulations, Ms. Daniels," he said. "You're a wealthy woman."

CHAPTER THIRTY SEVEN

December 22
9:15 am Central European Time
A flat
La Latina
Madrid, Spain

"I love New York," Aliz Willems said.

Troy lay in bed, with the blinds drawn. The room was cool and dark. He was under a couple of heavy blankets. Cozy. The sun had just come up, maybe twenty minutes ago. The sun rose late in Spain. It was the shortest day of the year, and Troy just might spend it right where he was.

El Grupo Especial was back on the chopping block. Miquel had shown his superiors up again, and maybe it was one time too many. They were saying El Grupo had too much autonomy. They were saying maybe more people could have been saved if El Grupo hadn't gone rogue and had shared what they knew sooner. Troy didn't agree, of course, because nobody knew anything. They acted on a hunch. But the bigwigs at Interpol were hinting it might be better if El Grupo was folded back into the herd.

Troy didn't care that much about the politics of it. All he knew was Miquel had given everyone off until the new year. Of the three agents who boarded that train, Gallo was the most seriously damaged. He had gotten a brain scan and spent a night in the hospital for observation. Dubois had shaken off her injuries and seemed fine. Troy was stiff and sore, but all in all, not too bad this time around.

The thing was the cold. It was as if it had gotten into his bones, and it didn't want to get out again. The cold was like a spirit inhabiting an old house, and Troy's body was that house. He had known the feeling before. SEAL training in the cold water off Coronado could make you feel like this.

"Yeah?" he said. "What do you love about it?"

His mobile phone was on his chest, on top of the blankets, with the speaker phone feature on. He was chatting with Aliz. His upper body was propped up on fancy pillows that she had given him. He was perfectly relaxed.

Talking to Aliz was like wading in a gentle river. She could prattle on ceaselessly about things she enjoyed, things she didn't enjoy, places she had been, or items she had owned for years or had recently purchased. She purchased something new nearly every day. It made for very pleasant listening.

Also, it was almost Christmas. Here in Spain, the radio stations seemed to have replaced the normal wall-to-wall Christmas music with all Calment, all the time. Calment's trippy, dreamy dance music was okay, Troy supposed. And the man had died, so there was that. But after a while, enough was enough.

I like that old time rock and roll.

Troy was thinking about getting motivated and flying into New York for the holidays. It was nice here in Madrid, and it was nice in Luxembourg, but there really was no place like home.

He had asked Aliz to come with him. She hadn't met the family yet. Naturally, she had offered to fly them there on a private jet. The idea was enticing. It would save him the hassle of booking tickets or scheduling anything. But she was nervous about meeting his people. In fact, she hadn't actually committed to coming and was talking around the issue. Rather than make firm plans, she mused about visiting New York City in an abstract way.

"Here are some fun things about New York," instead of "What should WE do when WE go to New York?"

For example:

"Well, I love Broadway," she said. "I've seen about thirty shows, I suppose. And some of the best restaurants are in New York. Also, some of the best hotels. Have you ever stayed at the Waldorf? They have high tea there in the afternoon. The ladies wear long, white gloves and hats."

"Classy," he said. He let the river wash over him. Her New York was not his New York, and that was just fine.

"Do you know this very tall building on the West Side of Manhattan? There is a platform that juts out a hundred stories in the sky. It gives commanding views in every direction. I hear the place becomes crowded with tourists, but for a price, you can book your own private showing, with a champagne toast. That way, the whole city is yours."

He smiled. "That sounds nice."

He hadn't heard anything like a commitment yet.

A knock came at the front door to the flat. It wasn't a large flat, so he could hear it easily from here. It was the knock of a large, strong hand. The knocking went on for about ten seconds, then stopped.

Troy sighed to himself. There was always something. Maybe if he ignored it, whatever it was would go away.

No, there it came again.

KNOCK, KNOCK, KNOCK.

"SoHo galleries," Aliz said. "So many gems are hidden there. You know, one time I was in a basement gallery, a place you might walk right past without noticing, and they had a sheet of, I would call it newsprint, and it was ripped. Andy Warhol had drawn a charcoal sketch of a face on this piece of ripped newsprint. I mean, it was barely even a sketch. Practically just a circle with a suggestion of eyes and a mouth. But it was signed and verified. The real thing."

KNOCK. KNOCK.

Troy pushed the blankets aside and got out of bed. He was wearing long john pants and a t-shirt. His feet were bare, and the floorboards were cold. The flat was chilly. He shivered.

He moved through the apartment to the door. He opened the peephole and peered through it. On the other side were two men in long coats. They must have heard the peephole open. A hand appeared, holding an identity card. It revealed the holder to be an Agent Rudolph, of the US Marshalls.

"I just had to have it," Aliz said. "They wanted 250 for it, but I said I wouldn't go a penny over 220."

"Two hundred and fifty dollars?" Troy said. It seemed kind of cheap, even if the paper was ripped. It was Andy Warhol, after all.

"Oh my, no. You're so sweet. Two hundred and fifty thousand."

Troy nearly laughed. That sounded better. A quarter of a million dollars for a ripped piece of paper that somebody had scribbled on. What a world.

He opened the door.

"Can you hold on a second, hon? There's someone at the door here."

"Of course, darling."

Troy pressed the MUTE button and looked at the two men.

"Hi fellas. What can I do for you?"

"Troy Stark?" the lead man said.

Troy shrugged. "That depends on who's asking."

"I'm Agent Rudolph with the United States Marshalls Service. This is Agent Grossman."

It was nearly Christmas, and now Rudolph was here.

"Is that really your name?" Troy said. "Rudolph?"

The man nodded. He didn't seem to have a sense of humor. A lot of these guys didn't. That was one way to know they were for real.

"Yes. We're United States Marshalls, as I indicated."

He referred to a piece of paper he had in his hand.

"You've been subpoenaed to appear before a United States Senate select committee, investigating possible human rights violations committed by US military personnel in Latin America, in particular clandestine groups working under the Joint Special Operations Command. In your specific case, at issue is the behavior of Captain Enrico Morales and the men under his command. You haven't responded to multiple attempts at communication, so we were sent here to find you and speak with you."

"Am I under arrest?" Troy said.

"No," Rudolph said. "But as a witness, there are possible threats against your life. We can bring you safely back to the United States under our protection."

Troy smiled and shook his head. The last thing he needed right now was someone's protection.

"When's the hearing?" he said.

"January 5th."

"What are you guys planning to do, hide me in a motel for two weeks?"

Rudolph shrugged.

"Tell them I'll be there, okay? But if I'm not under arrest at this moment, I'm just gonna go back to bed, okay?"

"This is offered for your own safety," Rudolph said.

Troy nodded. "Yeah, I know. Thanks, but no thanks." He gently shut the door in their faces. And locked it.

He turned and padded back through the apartment. He undid the MUTE button.

"Where were we?" he said.

She continued on without missing a beat. "So, I bought the drawing. They packed it very precisely and shipped it to me. I have it here. I keep it in the climate-controlled room. I haven't hung it, but I can't believe I've never shown it to you."

He smiled and slid under the covers again.

237

"Next time I'm there."

"All right."

"Can I ask you a personal question, Aliz?"

"Of course, darling. What is it?"

He took a deep, calming breath, and mentally hit the reset button. He was having a nice day. US Marshalls and Senate select hearings weren't going to ruin it. The ghost of Enrico Morales wasn't going to be any part of it.

"Are you coming with me to New York or what?" he said.

NOW AVAILABLE!

ROGUE MISSION
(A Troy Stark Thriller—Book #4)

"Thriller writing at its best. Thriller enthusiasts who relish the precise execution of an international thriller, but who seek the psychological depth and believability of a protagonist who simultaneously fields professional and personal life challenges, will find this a gripping story that's hard to put down."
--Midwest Book Review, Diane Donovan (regarding Any Means Necessary)

"One of the best thrillers I have read this year. The plot is intelligent and will keep you hooked from the beginning. The author did a superb job creating a set of characters who are fully developed and very much enjoyable. I can hardly wait for the sequel."
--Books and Movie Reviews, Roberto Mattos (re Any Means Necessary)

From #1 bestselling and USA Today bestselling author Jack Mars, author of the critically-acclaimed *Luke Stone* and *Agent Zero* series (with over 5,000 five-star reviews), comes an explosive new, action-packed thriller series that takes readers on a wild-ride across Europe, America, and the world.

After elite Navy Seal Troy Stark is forced into retirement for his dubious respect for authority, his work in stopping a major terrorist threat to New York is noticed. Invited to join a secretive new international terrorist-fighting organization, Troy must hunt down all threats to the U.S. that originate from overseas—and pre-empt them by any means possible.

In ROGUE MISSION (Book #4), an isolated sex trafficking case leads Troy to a vast, underground network of organized crime in Europe. Hundreds of women, it seems, are being trafficked, and used to fund terrorist organizations. In this high octane action thriller, Troy must uncover a vast web of crime, protected at the highest levels, and take on his most complex enemy yet.

An unputdownable action thriller with heart-pounding suspense and unforeseen twists, ROGUE MISSION is the fourth novel in an exhilarating new series by a #1 bestselling author that will have you fall in love with a brand new action hero—and turn pages late into the night.

Future books in the series are also available.

Jack Mars

Jack Mars is the USA Today bestselling author of the LUKE STONE thriller series, which includes seven books. He is also the author of the new FORGING OF LUKE STONE prequel series, comprising six books; of the AGENT ZERO spy thriller series, comprising twelve books; of the TROY STARK thriller series, comprising five books; and of the SPY GAME thriller series, comprising six books.

Jack loves to hear from you, so please feel free to visit www.Jackmarsauthor.com to join the email list, receive a free book, receive free giveaways, connect on Facebook and Twitter, and stay in touch!

BOOKS BY JACK MARS

THE SPY GAME
TARGET ONE (Book #1)
TARGET TWO (Book #2)
TARGET THREE (Book #3)
TARGET FOUR (Book #4)
TARGET FIVE (Book #5)
TARGET SIX (Book #6)

TROY STARK THRILLER SERIES
ROGUE FORCE (Book #1)
ROGUE COMMAND (Book #2)
ROGUE TARGET (Book #3)
ROGUE MISSION (Book #4)
ROGUE SHOT (Book #5)

LUKE STONE THRILLER SERIES
ANY MEANS NECESSARY (Book #1)
OATH OF OFFICE (Book #2)
SITUATION ROOM (Book #3)
OPPOSE ANY FOE (Book #4)
PRESIDENT ELECT (Book #5)
OUR SACRED HONOR (Book #6)
HOUSE DIVIDED (Book #7)

FORGING OF LUKE STONE PREQUEL SERIES
PRIMARY TARGET (Book #1)
PRIMARY COMMAND (Book #2)
PRIMARY THREAT (Book #3)
PRIMARY GLORY (Book #4)
PRIMARY VALOR (Book #5)
PRIMARY DUTY (Book #6)

AN AGENT ZERO SPY THRILLER SERIES
AGENT ZERO (Book #1)
TARGET ZERO (Book #2)
HUNTING ZERO (Book #3)
TRAPPING ZERO (Book #4)